Mumtaz stopped wa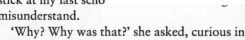
was facing Adam. Sh
this. 'I'm afraid you

'How do you kno
stick at my last scho
misunderstand.

'Why? Why was that?' she asked, curious in
spite of herself.

'I was at a public school with a load of upper-
class yobs. I got nothing but Jewish big nose jokes
for years.'

'So you left?'

'Just wanted to be somewhere real, with real
people.'

'And your grandfather, your family. Proud of
them, are you?' She couldn't contain her anger any
longer . . .

'Yes, actually, I am.'

'Well, so am I of mine,' Mumtaz said, and
stalked off. Bolshy workers and rude taxi drivers
indeed. No matter how polite this conceited young
man might try to be he had unwittingly shown her
that they not only belonged to different religions,
but also different sides of the fence.

# SHALOM SALAAM

an adaptation by
Alexandra Hine
based on the TV serial by
Gareth Jones

SPHERE BOOKS LIMITED

SPHERE BOOKS LTD

Published by the Penguin Group
27 Wrights Lane, London W8 5TZ, England
Viking Penguin Inc., 40 West 23rd Street, New York, New York 10010, USA
Penguin Books Australia Ltd, Ringwood, Victoria, Australia
Penguin Books Canada Ltd, 2801 John Street, Markham, Ontario, Canada L3R 1B4
Penguin Books (NZ) Ltd, 182–190 Wairau Road, Auckland 10, New Zealand

Penguin Books Ltd, Registered Offices: Harmondsworth, Middlesex, England

First published in Great Britain by Sphere Books Ltd 1988

Copyright © Sphere Books Limited, 1988

Printed and bound in Great Britain by
Richard Clay Ltd, Bungay, Suffolk
Filmset in Monophoto Sabon

Sadiq Sattar drove his taxi up to Southgates Sixth-form College near the business area of Leicester, and gave his daughter, who sat beside him in the front seat, an anxious glance. 'You're going to be fine,' he told her. 'Perfectly fine.'

'Yes,' Mumtaz replied, as she adjusted her veil, masking her own concern as he had done by turning his question into a positive statement. 'Of course I will.'

'Allah be with you,' he murmured, and watched, proud and worried, as she got out of the taxi and joined the young men and women crowding into the school on the first day of the new term.

Mumtaz, conscious of Sadiq's gaze following her, walked up the stairs to the college with a straight back and firm step. The squat and rambling building – a mixture of modern and Georgian architecture – was overwhelmingly different from the Muslim girls' school she had until now attended. Attached to the mosque in Highfield, it was like a remote cloister compared with this big noisy place, the jostling students, and the startling cacophony of deep male shouts.

A blond girl, wearing a green beret perched at a jaunty angle, came running up the steps and bumped into Mumtaz, startling her out of these thoughts.

'Oops,' the girl said, with an amused glance at Mumtaz's oddly spinsterish appearance: the old grey duffel coat, the black veil beneath the jacket's hood that obscured all but her incongruous long black plaits and large, intelligent brown eyes. 'Sorry, ducks.'

'It's all right,' Mumtaz said and turned to follow the new arrivals to the bulletin board where she worked her way to the front of the group, too intent on finding her name and classroom to feel self-conscious.

'Mind taking off your head – I mean your hood?' An arm reached over Mumtaz's shoulder. 'I can't see the lists,' a boy's voice, jovial and confident, said.

Embarrassed, Mumtaz quickly stepped aside and without

turning to see the speaker, continued searching for her name. It was this intensity, the determination and triumph that shone in her deep brown eyes, more than her oddly dowdy appearance, that made Mumtaz stand out from the other young people.

'Do you need any help?' the boy now asked her, but Mumtaz, pretending not to hear him, was already hurrying down the corridor.

Room 14 was an uninspiring grey rectangular box with two windows that faced north and overlooked the college's massive rear section of red brick.

'My name is Mrs Gordon,' a tall, stout woman with crinkly grey hair, said to the twenty students gathered there to prepare for their English A-levels.

'It's my custom to have students introduce themselves to the class and tell us a little bit about themselves before we get down to work and discuss this term's curriculum.' She gave an encouraging smile to her new flock of sixteen-year-olds. 'We'll start with you, young man, at the left in the back row.'

'I'm Adam Morris –'

Mumtaz, hearing the familiarly confident voice, turned around to see the stranger from the bulletin board. He was pleasing to look at with his wavy brown hair and blue eyes. The typical public schoolboy in his dark suit, she thought, were it not for the insouciant rainbow-coloured braces into which his thumbs were hooked.

'I'm not sure about long-term goals,' he was saying. 'I'm interested in art, but getting my A-levels is my only concern at the moment.' He smiled at Mrs Gordon and gave the class a mock bow, then winked as he saw Mumtaz staring at him.

Blushing, Mumtaz swung around, and was all the more embarrassed to see that the wink had been witnessed by the girl with the green beret, who now stood up to introduce herself.

'I'm Jackie. I come from London,' she said, tossing back her strawberry-blond hair. A pretty girl with a pert nose, and bold, sullen blue eyes, she was dressed in a mid-calf length black skirt and black leather bomber jacket. 'I thought I'd be better off going after my A-levels than working at the local fish 'n' chips.'

'I'm Candy,' a long, rangy black girl in a bright red jogging suit said, as she rose from her desk. Her shoulder-length hair was meticulously corn-rowed, and jangled with the wooden Caribbean beads at the end of each plait. 'I'm not so much interested in the A-levels as getting full use of the college's new gymnasium,' she said in a low drawl. 'But while I work out for the Olympics, I thought I'd dabble in the Arts.'

Mumtaz first stared, then lowered her eyes when she saw the next speaker. She was Asian, and yet her clothes defied her culture.

'My name is Meera,' the girl said in a pleasant and friendly voice as she smoothed down the skirt of her tight-fitting blue suit. She looked several years older than the other students in her high black stiletto heels and the heavy garish make-up that covered her broad, pretty face. 'For me it was either going after my A-levels or joining my mum at the mill.'

Mumtaz recognized Meera for the type of girl her Uncle Tariq thought she would become if she were allowed to attend Southgates. An Indian girl who had turned her back on her own culture as she tried to assimilate western ways. Tariq was against co-educational institutions and claimed they were in violation of the Koran. He had filled Sadiq with doubts, Mumtaz knew, but she also knew she had more influence with her father than the over-bearing Tariq. Though reduced in this country to driving a taxi, Sadiq was a scholar and a teacher who wanted a good education for his daughter. And, most important, he believed she could continue to be a good Muslim, while pursuing her studies.

'Next,' Mrs Gordon said, interrupting Mumtaz's thoughts.

'My name is Mumtaz Sattar,' she heard herself say in a surprisingly clear controlled voice. 'I'm here because I want to be a lawyer.' Her secret ambition was announced before she could stop herself; somehow being in this classroom made the dream seem within reach.

The college let out at four that afternoon, and, in the mass exodus, Adam found himself next to the pretty girl called Jackie.

'You're in two of my classes,' he said.

'Am I?' Her reply was nonchalant.

'So what made you leave London and come here?' he asked.

'My parents split up.' Though she remained cool, almost tough, Adam sensed her disturbance.

'And why did they expel you?' he asked, trying to lighten the moment.

'Set fire to the vestry,' Jackie gave him an unexpected pixie grin.

'You're joking.' He liked her spirit and unpredictability. Too bad he had to rush off, but today was his grandfather's birthday, and he was masterminding the surprise party.

'Look, I've got to run but I'll see you tomorrow, okay?' He gave her a warm smile and then made a dash for the main gate where Sadiq was standing by his taxi reading a newspaper as he waited for Mumtaz.

'Everything went well, then,' Sadiq said, smiling with relief as he saw how calm and collected Mumtaz looked.

'Have you been waiting long, Abagee?'

Sadiq shrugged. To him the important thing was that his daughter was safely escorted to and from school, not the time involved. 'It doesn't matter,' he said, just as Adam came rushing towards them.

'You're not going anywhere near Oadby, are you?' he asked Mumtaz.

'No.'

'It's my grandfather's birthday,' Adam explained. 'We're having a party. Which way are you going?'

'Highfields,' Mumtaz replied shortly, acutely conscious of her father listening to their exchange.

'Perfect,' Adam said to her amazement. 'I'll drop you on the way.'

Sadiq stepped up in front of the passenger door. 'But does the young lady wish to share her taxi?' he asked.

Adam turned to Mumtaz, and smiled. 'You don't mind, do you?'

Confused by his brashness, and the way Sadiq had assumed the anonymous role of taxi driver, Mumtaz said nothing, and ignoring the door Adam held open, she took her place in the front seat beside her father.

4

Sadiq manoeuvred the taxi through the afternoon traffic of Leicester's polytechnic area, and taking a detour on to the Stoughton Road, he drove through the leafy, wealthy suburbia, past a golf course, the Botanic Gardens and finally into Oadby. Neither Mumtaz nor Adam seemed to notice that he had bypassed Highfields in order to drop Adam off first. The former was intent on her thoughts, the latter on making pleasant small talk.

'I suppose it's all a big change for you?' Adam leaned forward, resting his arm on the front seat just behind Mumtaz.

'Not really,' she replied, staring out of the window. Should she say something to establish that Sadiq was her father; or that Adam was in her class?

'After a Muslim girls' school, I mean,' he said, unaware of his patronizing tone. 'Must seem a bit rough and noisy.'

'Only some people.'

'You're very ambitious, wanting to be a lawyer,' Adam continued, not at all discouraged. He was intrigued by this girl who had a woman's serious eyes and the long plaits of a child.

'Oh, that's just an idea,' Mumtaz said, her casual tone covering acute embarrassment. She had never confided her secret desire to Sadiq, afraid he might think her aspirations too lofty. Now for him to hear it from the mouth of a stranger . . . It was not right.

'On the left, over there.' Adam directed Sadiq to an imposing white house.

'Ah, Mr Astler's,' Sadiq murmured, reading the plaque.

'Yeah, he's my grandad,' Adam said.

Mumtaz's face was as expressionless as her father's though she knew they both were thinking of her mother Shehnaaz, an underpaid worker at Joe Astler's factory. Well, now she understood the boy's arrogance. He came from a family used to exploiting people.

'Look, I'm sorry for taking you out of your way,' Adam said. And then impulsively added, 'Why don't you come in for a sec, and have a drink? I'm sure the driver will wait.' He turned to Sadiq. 'You wouldn't mind, would you?'

'No, thanks,' Mumtaz said. If she hadn't been so embarrassed

sed she would have been amused. He must be very ignorant or full of himself to invite a Muslim for a drink. Still, she was touched that he had made the effort to be nice, even if it were only good manners that prompted him.

'Oh, well, maybe another time,' Adam said. 'How much is it?' he asked Sadiq as he got out of the taxi.

Sadiq switched off the meter. 'Three fifty.'

'And what about taking her back again?' Adam asked, only now wondering why the driver hadn't dropped Mumtaz off on the way.

'Four fifty.'

'Cheers.' Adam handed him a fiver, thanked Mumtaz once again and hurried into his grandfather's house.

Sadiq watched Mumtaz as he slowly pocketed the five-pound note, his thoughts on the stranger who had revealed something so new about his daughter.

'The law indeed.' His tone was teasing but subtly probing all the same.

'That was none of his business,' Mumtaz said. 'Our teacher asked us to introduce ourselves to the class and explain our aims in life. And why shouldn't I study law? It's a useful thing to know the laws of the country you live in.'

'As long as you are a good Muslim,' Sadiq replied, with mixed emotions. He knew his daughter could succeed on any chosen path, but he feared for the byways – anything from public violation to personal temptation that might distract or hurt her.

'And how did it all go?' he asked when they were heading in the direction of Highfields.

'Fine,' Mumtaz replied.

'Were there any people you already knew?'

'No.'

'Not even the Astler boy?' Sadiq persisted. 'He seemed very friendly.'

'I thought he was rude.'

Sadiq recognized the silvery glint in Mumtaz's dark eyes and the stubborn tilt of her chin.

'We'll forget about him, then,' he said, reassured, and turning into their street, drove past the small grocery, the DIY store and the local somoza chippie – all Asian businesses – to an end-of-terrace house.

Mumtaz went straight inside, ignoring the curious glances of the neighbours whom her father stopped to greet with a wary '*salaam*'. Sadiq was a respected member of the Asian community who spent a great deal of time at the Centre organizing events and giving lessons in English and the Koran. Most of the neighbours had come to him at one time or another for help or advice, yet now they were disapproving, shocked at his allowing Mumtaz to go to Southgates.

The Sattar house was homely, but faded and sadly in need of some structural repairs. The front door opened into a small, sparsely furnished sitting room for visitors. This led to the more comfortable and ever-crowded rear living-room where the family tended to congregate on the two couches. The wallpaper – cream with an insipid mustard-green motif of ferns – was standard council issue of the sixties. There was a telephone, but no television. Everything was well-ordered and clean, but surprisingly poor. Except, Mumtaz often reminded herself, for the series of ornately-framed family photographs which covered the walls recording the Sattars' life in Uganda before Idi Amin's reign of terror. Grandfather Sattar had left Lahore, Pakistan to expand his automobile parts business in Kampala, and the photographs showed Sadiq, then a teacher of some stature, and a petite and beautiful Shehnaaz with their three children, and a retinue of smiling African servants, in the lush garden of a white colonial house.

Hurrying across the room towards the stairs, Mumtaz's step faltered when she saw her Uncle Tariq emerging from the kitchen with a bowl of rice in his hand.

'Don't bother. I helped myself,' he said with meaning. But then, Tariq never wanted to hide the views he kept: in this case, that it was a Muslim woman's duty to serve the men.

'Uncle Tariq, what are you doing here?' Mumtaz asked, though she knew perfectly well he had come to see if Sadiq had let her go to college.

'Just a weary traveller seeking sustenance. Not much luck here though,' he said, indicating the bowl of plain rice.

'Ama's at work.'

'Of course.' Tariq nodded, then smiled at her. 'And you?' he asked pointedly.

'I'll be right down,' Mumtaz said, and made her escape upstairs as Sadiq came into the house with his youngest son, Rashid, a tall gangly fifteen-year-old, who had just returned from school.

'So, the ferryman returns,' Tariq said, but Sadiq was impervious to such taunts. It was awkward not to be as successful as his younger brother who owned a string of garages in Birmingham, but Sadiq did not miss material wealth as much as his teaching profession. In any case, there were all kinds of wealth and he often felt his three children made him more fortunate than Tariq.

Rashid threw down his books and ran to greet his favourite uncle. He knew that Mumtaz and his elder brother Hafiz sometimes found Tariq difficult, but he was genuinely interested in cars, and impressed by his uncle's flourishing business. He asked a few questions about a new engine the Porsche people were rumoured to be building, then went upstairs where he found Mumtaz and Hafiz in serious conversation.

'Tariq on the war path again?' Hafiz was asking sympathetically. He was a tall young man of eighteen with large dreamy brown eyes, a wide brow that seemed perpetually creased in a frown, and a sad, gentle mouth.

'He's not like Abagee. It's not easy for him to accept change,' Mumtaz replied.

'Oi, it's change you're after, is it, sister dear?' teased Rashid, who had come up behind Mumtaz and was undoing one of her plaits.

'Get away, little brat,' she said, but the slap she gave him on the shoulder was as loving as an embrace. Somehow Rashid's ebullient spirits infected everyone, no matter how idiotic his jokes, Mumtaz thought. He had only been four when the family left Uganda ten years ago, too young to remember it. For him, Leicester was home; he even had a broader accent than the rest of the family and somehow always seemed to fit right in.

Though Mumtaz was closer in age to Rashid, she was closer in spirit to Hafiz, who had spent his formative years in Kampala and had never quite got used to living in England. He was bright, and had easily acquired his science A-levels, but he'd begun to drift. Out of school for a year now, he was still unemployed and unsettled. He wanted to turn his life into something wonderful, yet couldn't quite decide where or how to commit himself. His latest interest had to do with computers and she hoped he would keep this new enthusiasm.

Mumtaz undressed and performed her religious ablutions. She rinsed her mouth, and washed her face, hands, arms and feet; her mind slowly unwinding as she repeated each motion three times. The events of the day – college, the Astler boy, Uncle Tariq – all fell away from her until she felt completely cleansed.

Downstairs in the family room, Tariq had set aside the bowl of rice untouched and was absorbed in his favourite conversation: objections to Mumtaz going to college. That it was too late to interfere, that the matter had been settled in spite of his advice and the school term begun, didn't stop him for a moment.

'I appreciate that your line of work is useful,' said Tariq, who never missed an opportunity to disparage his brother's taxi driving. 'Can you really afford the time to take and collect Mumtaz every day?'

'It's not too far to walk if necessary.' Sadiq had already talked to Hafiz about escorting his sister to or from school when the taxi was engaged.

'In the winter? In the dark?' Tariq raised his dark bushy brows in alarm and plumped out his lower lip.

'We'll take care of the necessary arrangements,' Sadiq said patiently.

'And can you take care of what happens inside the school?'

'The headmaster is very sympathetic. He's given Mumtaz permission to use one of the school rooms for her prayers.'

'A "he" –' Tariq interrupted, exploding. 'All of them "he's".'

'Brother, education is enjoined on every Muslim man, and woman.'

'Within their separate institutions,' Tariq shouted.

'Where available,' Sadiq finished quietly, his calm, steady gaze compelling Tariq to turn away. But only for a moment.

'What's the use of it all? That's what I want to know.'

'Mumtaz is bright: she has a good brain. I'm a teacher. I want my child to learn how to think!'

'For what? To drive taxis?'

Sadiq winced. 'For a better husband at least.'

Tariq gave a hoot of laughter. 'Oh, is it brains that men look for in a wife? My Hassan would run a mile in the opposite direction.'

Sadiq refrained from stating the obvious; that Mumtaz would never even consider her uncouth, foolish cousin as a candidate for a husband. A rustling of silk and satin drew his attention to the stairs where his daughter stood, exquisite in a yellow-and-white flowered *shalwar kameez*. A white silk veil trimmed in gold was drawn around her face, but it could not conceal the cold, sombre glance she cast her uncle.

'I shall start cooking,' she said, giving Sadiq a sympathetic look that told him she had heard more than he would have wished.

The kitchen was a narrow, cramped room with an old gas stove, a small wooden table on one side, and a sewing machine set up along its other wall. Mumtaz was untroubled by the shabbiness; this was her place of work and refuge in the house as it was her mother's. She put on a pot of water for rice, then started to peel vegetables, knowing her mother would get home from the factory in time to add the special final touch to the meal.

But Shehnaaz couldn't have been more distracted and less interested in food when she appeared ten minutes later. A small-boned fragile woman, she was dressed in a blue and green *shalwar kameez*, and her long black hair was drawn back in one long braid. Her mouth was turned downwards, and she avoided her daughter's eye as she juggled two pans and then began kneading dough.

'Amagee, school went really well.' Mumtaz was afraid that her mother, never as committed to her education as Sadiq, was already registering disapproval. 'I really can look after myself, you know.'

Shehnaaz loaded the main course on a tray. 'Take this through, will you, please?'

Had her mother joined Tariq's rank? Mumtaz wondered. 'I won't stop now,' she warned.

Shehnaaz covered her ears. 'Please. Serve the food to the men.'

Tariq began the moment Mumtaz came into the room.

'My niece, tell me, what's all this schooling about?'

'To serve Allah,' Mumtaz replied.

'Isn't this enough?' He gestured to the tray and the men seated on the sofas.

'I can manage both.'

Tariq stopped smiling. 'Don't be too sure, my dear.'

Mumtaz was quiet for a moment. 'Is the food all right?' she asked.

'Perfect,' Tariq replied with enthusiasm.

'Well, then, there you are.' Mumtaz caught her father's eye, and smiled.

'She's got no respect,' Rashid piped up, only half joking in Tariq's support.

'Give it and you'll get it,' Sadiq tersely advised his youngest.

Back in the kitchen Mumtaz sat watching as Shehnaaz served their food. Though she took care to give her daughter the choicest cuts of meat, she still did not speak to her.

'Please tell me what's wrong,' Mumtaz said, unable to bear the silence any longer. 'Why have you turned against the college?'

Shehnaaz looked at her and sighed. 'The college? No, it is not your college I am upset about.'

'What then?' Mumtaz asked, really worried now. She had never seen her mother with such an expression, such a queer look of fright and anger in her black eyes. 'Can't you tell me?'

'It does not really concern you.' Shehnaaz hesitated, and then finally blurted out her secret. 'I've left Astler's factory. I no longer have a job.'

'You left the factory,' Mumtaz echoed, the colour rushing to her cheeks as she recalled Adam commandeering the taxi to take him to the Astler house. 'But what happened? Why should you leave?'

Shehnaaz shook her head sadly and despite Mumtaz's anxious pleading refused to say anything more.

Later that night, after Tariq had gone, Mumtaz went upstairs to study the Koran. Her room was small and decorated in an unoriginal feminine pink: pink door, pink flowered wallpaper, and pink bedspread. But her Map of the Muslim World lent a serious touch to the room, as did the beautiful leather and gold-leaf embroidered Koran resting in its intricately sculpted *rehal*. Placing it in the centre of her bed, she covered her head in a praying scarf and kneeled. But she was unable to concentrate. Her parents' voices were raised in distress, and, she listened anxiously through the partition wall for the story behind her mother leaving Astler's.

'The foreman insulted me,' Shehnaaz was saying in a grieved voice.

'How? Did he touch you?'

'No.'

'Did he use racist language?'

'No.'

'What then?'

'The way he looked at me!' Shehnaaz said indignantly. 'You know!'

'Did you complain?' Sadiq's voice was low and worried.

'I went straight to Mr Astler. He said he didn't want me to leave. But he refused to do anything about the foreman.'

Sadiq was silent, trying to reckon, like Mumtaz in the next room, the consequences of Shehnaaz's impetuous action.

'I'll work at home. Mr Astler offered to help.'

Mumtaz strained to make out her father's murmurs. If only her parents would accept her as an adult and speak to her about these things.

'There are bills,' Sadiq said. 'The car, the family in Lahore.'

'Tariq has money. Let him send more.'

'I am the elder brother,' Sadiq raised his voice slightly. 'It is my duty.'

'Then earn more. Get a proper job,' Shehnaaz replied.

'Teachers are not needed here. I do what I can. At least I am of use.'

'To whom?' Shehnaaz asked, bitterly. 'Help us – your family – for once. I didn't come here to live like this. Look at the others from Kampala. We've been left behind.'

Mumtaz had forgotten her prayers as she knelt on her bed, absorbed in her parents' argument. It was the first time she'd ever known her mother to complain or speak to her father so disrespectfully. But then, she too was committing an act of disrespect in eavesdropping, she reminded herself. The thought drove her back to her devotions with a guilty start. By now both her mother and father were shouting, and she was too involved to ignore their voices.

'Give Hafiz a good kick. Make him do something useful for a change,' her mother was saying in despair.

'Perhaps when he finds work, he'll know how to keep it,' her father said bitterly.

'It wasn't my fault. Do you want me to go back?' she asked with resignation.

'I didn't want you there at all,' her father replied, in a sad voice. 'I shouldn't have let you –'

'It was our choice.'

'Always such difficult choices,' Sadiq sighed. 'Sometimes I worry that Tariq is right about Mumtaz. Maybe she shouldn't be going to the college.'

'She'll manage,' Shehnaaz reassured him. 'You've always said so.'

Their voices grew calmer, and though Mumtaz could hear no more, she continued to think about all that she had over-heard. She had only just begun her prayers when Sadiq came upstairs to listen to her recite. She lowered her eyes to the Koran as he shut the door, wondering if he realized she'd heard them downstairs. But he was calm and smiling as he listened to her recite the arabic verse from memory.

'Will you translate for me now?' he asked gently.

'The woman is,' she began haltingly. 'The woman is clothing for the man, and the man is clothing for the woman.'

Sadiq nodded. 'And what does that mean to you?'

But Mumtaz was thinking of her mother and she spoke out frankly. 'Abagee, is she all right?'

Sadiq did not reply for a moment, and when he finally did it was to answer far more than she had asked.

'It's an honour to be a Muslim. Never forget that.'

'I won't.'

There had been just as much tension at the Astler house in Oadby that evening. Joe had obstinately refused to put in an appearance at the surprise birthday party. Not even his beloved grandson could cajole him into leaving his room. Joe was troubled over an incident that had taken place that afternoon at the factory, though Adam couldn't tell what had really happened. According to Joe one of his workers had quit, and in doing so, accused him of being a racist. Aunt Alex, on the other hand, said that the Indian woman had only been upset by the foreman. But no matter how often she repeated this, it didn't seem to penetrate Joe's gloom.

It had been a really awkward affair, you couldn't call it a party, Adam thought, and most of the people left early. Sarah, his mother, and her elder sister, Alex, were seeing the last of the guests to the door, their voices syrupy with airs and graces. It was a role Sarah loathed, Adam knew, and he watched bemused as his social-worker, cause-conscious mother played up to the wealthy conservative couple she'd probably be picketing in a week's time.

'Shall we start clearing?' his father asked, and was then interrupted by his bleeper. Phil was a doctor who seemed to be 'on call' at every family occasion, as Sarah complained, and he handed Adam his stack of plates before disappearing into the study to use the phone.

'Everybody gone home?' Joe said, coming slowly into the large and somewhat ostentatious sitting-room of cream velvet sofas and gilded mirrors. 'It's about time. I thought they'd never go, the idiots.'

Joe managed to look both defensive and dignified in his flannel bathrobe. He assumed an exaggerated shambling walk as he passed his two daughters, and Adam wanted to sketch his grandfather all over again. His birthday portrait of Joe the Businessman standing in front of Astler's had been a great success. It was a sort of Citizen Astler – the Self-Made Man. But this man in the robe was definitely Joe the Old Patriarch.

'Feeling better, *Opa*?' he asked.

'I need a drink,' Joe said with a grimace.

'Well, I hope you're pleased with yourself.' Sarah laid right into her father, giving vent, Adam knew, to all her irritations of the evening.

'I didn't ask for a party.'

'How can you act this way? After all the trouble Adam went to.'

'Mum –' This was just what Adam didn't want. He had understood why Joe stayed away from the party. He only wished his mother would take the time to find out reasons, instead of just flying off the handle.

'I suppose he's not good enough for you now. You won't come to his party because he turned down your fancy school.'

Joe poured himself a tumbler of whisky, ignoring his youngest daughter. Sarah was always making problems. In her youth she'd fought against the family, now in adulthood, she fought against them from the inside.

Adam, fidgeting nervously in the background, wished his mother would stop. He and Joe had resolved their differences over the school business at least a week ago. When he'd first turned down his grandfather's offer to pay his tuition at a quality crammer, Joe had been insulted. But once Adam had been open with him, explaining that he was tired of boarding schools, and wanted to spend some time at home before university, his grandfather had understood. Adam was tired of the public school mentality, bored with being ribbed for being a Jew, yes, but more bored still by the small-minded, class-conscious boys he was forced to hang around with.

'Dad never wanted Adam to board,' Aunt Alex was saying, jumping right into the middle of the fray as usual.

'I certainly did not,' Joe said. 'Look how you two turned out.' Both girls had been sent away to boarding school until their mother, Leah, was struck with cancer. Then Alex came home – during her final year before college – to run the house and lend support to her devastated father. It was thought best to leave Sarah at school, where she was thriving, fast becoming a stalwart of the 60s causes.

'It's wonderful, Adam being in Leicester for a change. It's

great having him visit the factory,' Alex continued, trying to placate her sister.

'That's all very well,' Sarah replied. 'But he's got work to do if he wants to get his A-levels.'

'Darling, it's not our fault if he likes to come round to the mill for a chat. It's right down the road from his college. And besides,' Alex gave her nephew a fond smile, 'he likes the business.'

'First I've heard of it.'

'Yes, well, it would be, wouldn't it?' Alex replied, suddenly tired of mollifying her younger sister. Sarah was so busy with her causes, she was blind to the needs of her son.

'I don't want him selling clothes all his life.'

Adam gave his aunt a beseeching look, asking her not to pursue this, but now Alex too was angry. 'We're not good enough for him, then? Not papa, not me, not the mill that financed your fancy education so you could be a social worker for the working classes? You're too special to have a son interested in his family's clothes factory?'

'Enough!' Joe shouted, and went over to the sofa where Adam had taken refuge, his sketchbook in hand.

When people spoke about you as if you were not there, the best thing was to retreat into your own world. And this Adam had done, drawing outrageous caricatures of his mother and his aunt. Joe smiled for the first time that evening as he glimpsed Adam's work: Sarah with an angry aura of medusa snake curls, and little Alex, as rigid as a soldier, bearing a placard of the Astler crest – Joe's favourite snack of whole-wheat *matzah* and herring.

'Enough, you two,' Joe repeated. 'There are more serious things to be thinking about.'

'Not that factory worker again, Papa,' Alex said.

'I've been called many things, but never a racist,' Joe murmured, staring down at the amber liquor in his glass.

'She was talking about the foreman. She didn't mean us.'

'She did,' Joe insisted, and Adam felt a pang of fear as he saw how old and fragile his grandfather looked, sitting hunched over his drink. This was no humorous caricature, but a face lined with past hardships and present worries.

He was relieved when his father reappeared to say he'd drop Sarah and Adam at home on his way to the hospital. The day that had seemed to go so well – at college anyway – had ended on a sad and sour note.

The following afternoon Adam stopped in the factory after college. He'd hung around the school's emptying corridors looking for Jackie, but she hadn't shown up. Not surprising really. He'd noticed the interest she had stirred up among the other blokes in class. It was too early to go home. Sarah rarely got back before dinner-time, and Phil often didn't make it for dinner at all. And, anyway, Adam was anxious to reassure himself about his grandfather. He was still carrying around the image of an all too vulnerable old man and it made him uncomfortable.

As he walked through the production line of the factory, Adam slowed down to give the foreman a searching look. It didn't surprise him that there'd been a complaint against this tall man with his close-cropped, almost shaven head, steely blue eyes and thin cruel mouth.

'Afternoon,' but not a muscle moved in the man's face to acknowledge Adam's quick nod.

Joe was standing by his office window flipping through a material samples book while Alex sat at a small table with an adding machine. No reference was made to the fiasco of the night before. Adam told them about school, then settled down, propped his feet on the desk and began sketching. Joe's sighs of disgust or exclamations of pleasure, punctuated by Alex's adding machine, and underlined by the sound of his pencil moving about the page, gave Adam the sense of working in pleasant harmony. He was drawing the room – things not people – trying to concentrate on details. The arrival of an Indian woman obstructed his vision of the room, though he could clearly see the concern that registered on his grandfather's face.

'What can we do for you?' Joe asked.

'You said to ask if I needed help,' Shehnaaz said, pride masking the discomfort she felt at being back at Astler's so soon.

'The job's still yours,' Joe said, confirming Adam's suspicion that this was the worker who had caused yesterday's upset.

'And your foreman?' she asked.

'Now listen here. You made a number of allegations which I find disturbing.'

'If you read his eyes you would understand.'

'I can't sack a man for his eyes,' Joe replied, trying to keep the exasperation from his voice.

'It doesn't worry you, then?' Shehnaaz asked.

Joe sighed. 'I take the workforce I get. What do you want me to do, cross-examine them all? England is not a fascist state. We're supposed to be living in a democracy of sorts here.'

Alex stopped her calculations on the adding machine, and marched over to Joe's side. 'If you want to make a formal complaint there are legal channels available,' she said, but Shehnaaz ignored her, and continued to stare at Joe with penetrating black eyes.

'I'm working from home now. Will you take my stuff on commission?'

'I can't. It's against Astler's business policy,' Joe replied.

'I'd hire one of your machines,' she bargained. 'Give you the same quality goods.'

'I need my machines in use day and night.'

'Perhaps an old one then?' Shehnaaz asked, her eyes seeming to go blacker.

'If they're old, they're of no use,' Joe said, and nodding towards Alex, added, 'She says that about me.'

Shehnaaz did not smile. 'Could I start a new line – cheaper?'

'We make nothing cheap,' Joe admonished her.

'Then, perhaps you'd tell me what you had in mind when you offered your help?' Shehnaaz asked, her over-polite tone tinged with sarcasm.

Joe leaned back in his chair, gave the woman a steady glance and then handed her a card from his index file. 'Phone him. He'll give you a good deal in denim.'

'And who do I sell my clothes to?' Shehnaaz asked.

'Oh, you want me to sell for you, too?' Joe was exasperated now, and Adam didn't blame him. Here the man was, helping an ex-worker to find other work, at no profit to himself – in fact losing part of his own workday – all because she'd accused him of being racist. Blimey, it seemed as though the woman was trying to make his grandfather racist by being prejudiced on behalf of the Asians. None of it was good business as far as Adam could make out. In fact, this little interview didn't really seem to have anything to do with business at all.

'Everyone needs trousers,' Joe was saying.

'And everyone makes them.'

'Listen, my good woman, I started with hand-stitching in the East End back in 1945, and that was after five years in an internment camp.' He paused and composed himself. 'Have you got a machine?'

'Yes.'

'Then you're a damn sight better off than I was. You can show me your work,' he added. 'I might put our label on it.'

'That won't be necessary,' Shehnaaz replied tersely, and made a proud exit. Adam detected the slight trembling of her hand as she reached for the door knob and felt, though he did not understand, her fury. The woman was strung tight as a violin, yet Joe had certainly tried to be kind.

Adam stayed on at the factory to help Joe make an order from the new sample book, but neither of them had their mind on the task, and they decided to go to the pub instead. This evening visit to the pub was a custom Joe had never grown used to. He went to the local only with Adam, as if this 'English' grandson gave him a reason for being there. Then, he invariably ordered a schnapps. Tonight Adam had shown him how to work the newest slot machines, losing two quid in the process. Always the businessman, Joe insisted they stay on, and he continued to play the one-armed bandit until he'd won back Adam's investment and made a small profit of forty pence.

It was nearly eight o'clock before Adam got home. The Morrises lived in a comfortable spacious house midway between the hospital and the social services building. The equidistance from both Sarah's and Phil's work was an accident, but very much the equality basis on which their marriage was built. The house was designed for casual comfort, rather than display. The beige sitting-room was large and had a study alcove on one side. Sarah sat there now, still dressed in her workaday skirt and sweater.

'I went ahead with dinner when you didn't show up,' she said, without looking up from her papers. 'Phil's out on call.'

'Yeah, sorry I'm late,' Adam said. 'I got held up.' He sat down in an armchair near his mother, wondering why it was he always felt so much more comfortable in his grandfather's musky old office. Perhaps it was because none of the Morrises ever stopped in their own home long enough to give it a lived-in feeling. Adam certainly hadn't, with three years away at boarding school.

'So how'd your day go?' he asked, taking out his sketchbook and letting his hand do his thinking. It never occurred to him that he asked his mother the questions other mothers would be asking their sons.

'We're backing the miners,' Sarah said, giving him a victorious smile. She had to work hard to get the necessary support. 'I'm picketing on Saturday.' Sarah was so sure that his politics and sympathies concurred with her own that she never bothered to ask for his views.

'Great,' Adam said. 'Are you preparing a speech or something?'

'No, just some casework, an Asian girl,' his mother replied.

'Yeah?' Adam didn't look up from his drawing. He didn't know if it had been prompted by his mother's words, or the incident at Astler's that afternoon, but he'd drawn an Asian girl. The one from college, Mumtaz. He'd been trying to catch her eye in the hall today, but she always seemed to be looking the other way, as she was here in his caricature.

'What's the problem?'

'The usual stuff. Arranged marriage. She's run away. I've put her in the hostel.'

'Any chance at reconciliation?'

'No. It's pathetic. The family's disintegrated.'

Adam couldn't help but think of his own family last night, and wonder at his mother's strange, tunnel vision. He loved her dearly, but for an enlightened woman she was selective in what she chose to see.

'I'll just get myself something to eat,' he said, smiling as he closed his sketchbook on Mumtaz's profile and promised himself he'd get her to talk to him tomorrow.

For the first week of the new term the Great Hall of the college was given over to the Liberal Studies Fair. There was a holiday atmosphere to the school as hundreds of students milled around the different stands, wondering, with varying degrees of enthusiasm, what extra-curricular courses to take. There was the usual plethora of sporting activities, a music society, a theatrical club, a Leicester historical society, a break-dance club, as well as a book club, a cooking class and a self-awareness course. Mumtaz had never seen such a spectacle, and had to keep reminding herself that she was at college and a part of it all. She wasn't worried about making a choice, because she had received a note from Mrs Gordon, asking her to work on the college newspaper. It was the very thing she would have chosen had it not been dropped right into her lap. She was immensely pleased and when she saw her classmates, she decided to ask for their contributions.

'Right, who's signing up for netball?' Candy was saying as she dribbled a ball around the stand. 'It's only once a week, for God's sake. Meera? What about you?'

'I'm hopeless. Really. No co-ordination at all.'

'Put her name down,' Candy told the girl who stood behind the stand.

'What about you, Jackie?' Candy asked, collaring her as she passed by with Adam.

Jackie smiled. 'Ruin my social life, it will. Yeah, go on then.'

'Adam?'

'Sure,' he replied, his eyes on Jackie, thinking she'd look fetching in a jogging suit.

'We'll see how sure,' Candy quipped. 'Hey, Mumtaz? What about you?' she asked, throwing the ball to the startled girl.

Mumtaz missed and blushed. 'I'm sorry?' She couldn't accustom herself to Candy's loud, exuberant manner.

'I think you just answered my question,' Candy said, laughing.

Mumtaz joined in, relieved at not having to explain that she couldn't play in a team whose members were boys as well as girls.

'By the way, would any of you like to write for the college magazine?' she asked, perplexed at the stifled giggles her question received. 'Mrs Gordon asked me if I'd like to edit it,' she explained.

'Far out,' Candy said, grinning widely at the ball twirling on her fingertips.

'You can have my poetry,' Jackie said off-handedly. 'I won first prize at Butlins.'

'Good,' Mumtaz said, not realizing the other was teasing her.

'And print Meera's diary, why don't you?' Candy threw in. 'It's pornographic.'

'Get lost,' Meera told Candy, whacking the ball out of her hand. 'I'll do the astrology,' she told Mumtaz.

'Fine. Well, I'll ask around a bit more,' Mumtaz said, and backed away from her classmates, alarmed and confused by the continuing giggles. Only Adam didn't laugh. In fact he was frowning. She had noticed that he always carried a sketchbook and had wanted to ask him, too, if he'd like to contribute to the mag. Well, if he wanted to help, he could offer.

'Er, listen –' Adam had followed her.

'Yes?' Perhaps he did want to submit his work.

'Have you spoken to Mrs Gordon?' he asked, his blue eyes gazing directly into her own. There was something about his mouth – even when he was serious he seemed to be smiling.

'No, not yet,' she said. 'I thought I'd get staff for the magazine first.'

'Look, I don't think she wrote that letter to you,' he blurted out.

'What do you mean?' Mumtaz asked weakly.

'The college mag's a big hassle no one wants. A few of the kids probably thought they'd have a laugh with it. You know how they are, anything for fun –' he finished lamely.

Mumtaz stared at him speechless, then pulled out the letter.

'That's not her writing,' he said. And when she didn't reply, he added, 'Maybe I shouldn't have told you.'

'Why did they do it?' Mumtaz asked, looking to the other end of the hall where Candy and Jackie were still laughing.

'It's just a practical joke. They're a boisterous lot.'

But Mumtaz wasn't listening. She had suddenly had a horrendous perception.

'They think I'm funny.'

'No, of course not,' Adam said quickly. 'They sent me a letter too. That's how I knew.'

Mumtaz guessed that he was lying to protect her feelings. For a second she was touched that he should try to spare her feelings, yet she couldn't understand why he was doing it.

'Oh, well,' she murmured, dropping the letter in a nearby rubbish bin. 'Maybe you should do it.' She headed for the exit, trying to damp down her rising anger and hurt, but Adam came chasing after her.

'Yes?' She wished he'd go back to his crowd, to Jackie who was watching them from the other side of the room.

'I just wanted to say thanks for the lift the other day. I never got a chance before,' he said.

Mumtaz gave him a small polite smile though her mind was reeling with unhappy thoughts.

'I must've seemed crazy,' he continued. 'It's just that my grandad keeps bugging me about the family business, and so I try to be good at parties instead. Turned out I needn't have bothered. He never showed up. Some bolshy worker had made trouble at the mill,' he rambled on, unaware that Mumtaz had slowed her step and was staring at the floor, her eyes widening with outrage.

'It's a shame you couldn't stay. I'm sorry the driver was so rude.'

Mumtaz stopped walking, and turned so that she was facing Adam. She couldn't let him go on like this. 'I'm afraid you really don't understand.'

'How do you know?' he asked. 'I got a lot of stick at my last school,' he said, continuing to misunderstand.

'Why? Why was that?' she asked, curious in spite of herself.

'I was at a public school with a load of upper-class yobs. I got nothing but Jewish big nose jokes for years.'

'So you left?'

'Just wanted to be somewhere real, with real people.'

'Like them?' Mumtaz asked, with a shade of sarcasm as she nodded towards Candy and the others.

'If you like, yes. They're not a bad lot.'

'And your grandfather, your family. Proud of them, are you?' She couldn't contain her anger any longer, though it was obvious from Adam's perplexed frown that he didn't understand where the conversation was leading.

'Yes, actually, I am.'

'Well, so am I of mine,' Mumtaz said, and stalked off. Bolshy workers and rude taxi drivers indeed. No matter how polite this conceited young man might try to be he had unwittingly shown her that they not only belonged to different religions, but also different sides of the fence. She could hear Jackie yelling for him as she went through the door and wondered why he had bothered to leave the side of that sultry blond in the first place. Though she found the London girl rather intimidating, she had noticed the softness that came over her when Adam was near. Yes, they were a good match. He so insensitive, and she with her insouciance.

Adam hadn't been able to forget the vulnerability he'd seen in Mumtaz's face when she learned that she'd been the butt of a joke. For the briefest moment, her proud 'lawyer' demeanour had given way, and she seemed like some exotic plant or reed, blown over by a sudden wind. His own experiences at school, and the incident at Astler's mill, made him aware of the racism that could be read into the joke. This had been his main reason for wanting to set things right, and he couldn't understand where his good intentions had gone astray. He thought he'd been offering Mumtaz sympathy and friendship, yet she had been even more upset when she left him.

At the end of the day he met her at the school entrance.

'Here, from all of us,' he said, and handed her an envelope.

Mumtaz cautiously opened the card and it was a sketch of Adam, Meera, Candy and Jackie, all four looking unusually shy and apologetic – even in caricature – with 'sorry' bubbles over each head. She smiled in spite of herself, handed the sketch back to Adam, and nodded her acceptance of the tender, though she seriously doubted the others had played any part in this gesture.

'It's for you,' he insisted.

'I can't take that home.'

'Oh, I see,' Adam said, though he did not. And Mumtaz's subsequent, 'Do you?' made him wonder why he did not. But before he could pursue the matter Jackie came up behind them, throwing an arm around them both.

'Hiya, Taz,' she said. And smothering a fit of giggles, asked, 'How's the mag coming?'

Mumtaz made no reply, but shook herself free and hurried away, while Adam awkwardly pocketed his card, for some reason not wanting Jackie to see it.

'What did I say?' Jackie asked, with exaggerated innocence, but Adam was gazing after Mumtaz and didn't reply. He recognized Sadiq by his taxi, down at the main gate, and now his mind was spinning. It wasn't just the college mag jibe Mumtaz had been reacting to. It was what he had said about the taxi driver being rude. He'd managed to insult her father, for of course that's who the driver was. Why hadn't he realized it? No wonder she had said that bit about how she was proud of her family.

'What is it?' Jackie asked, watching him closely.

'Nothing.' He'd certainly started off on the wrong foot with Mumtaz; it had been stuck in his mouth, for God's sake.

'Are you going home?' Adam asked Jackie, as they followed the pedestrian path through the centre of Leicester; ambling past Astler's, the fish and chip shop, and an off-licence.

'Not before ten. Can't stand it in the house.'

'Really?' Adam asked, giving her a curious glance.

'Well, I don't notice that you're in such a rush to get home yourself,' she said defensively, throwing her slender shoulders back.

'My parents don't usually come in till late.'

'Middle-age ravers, are they?'

'Actually, my dad's a doctor at the General and my mother's a social worker.'

'Crikey,' Jackie pulled a face. 'Remind me not to blab.'

'Why?' Adam asked. He wasn't sure how to take Jackie. So much of what she said, or implied, seemed to be bravado and yet she did seem to know a lot about life.

'My dad thought I was bringing blokes back to the flat. Reported me under age.' She paused, took a breath, then continued nonchalantly, speaking of her parents as if they were strangers on the tube – an Eastenders episode – 'Course, it was me mum who was doing it. She was looking to earn a bit of cash on the side. But she wasn't about to stick her neck in the noose to help me.'

'No, I suppose it must've been a bit awkward,' Adam said, feeling out of his depth. 'So what happened?'

'Oh, my dad found out about her anyway. He went berserk and chucked her out.'

'So you stayed with your old man?'

'No, I came here with me mum and her boyfriend. He's a British Rail executive.' She kicked a pebble off to the side of the path. 'He's getting too close to there.'

'Where?' Adam asked.

Jackie stopped and shook her head at Adam's obtuseness. 'Into my knickers if I let him, the bloody pervert.'

Adam blushed, unused to such a blunt conversation with a girl. But Jackie didn't seem to notice his embarrassment. The family situation she chronicled in so off-hand a manner was very much on her mind. 'What he doesn't know is me mum's still doing it.'

'Really?'

'Whenever he's away, even just out for a pint.'

'You're having me on,' Adam said, disbelieving.

Jackie gave him a cold glare, her blue eyes narrowing slightly as she looked up at him. 'Look, I don't need your company,' she said, as if she resented him for having heard too much.

'I didn't mean it like that,' Adam replied. He didn't seem able to keep from hurting people's feelings today.

The Asian Community Centre was in an old, decaying red-brick Victorian school on Highfields Road where well-executed murals recording the life of the prophet Muhammed and fresh paint did the best they could to disguise the huge cracks that climbed up the walls and spread to the ceilings. Sadiq, one of the centre's organizers, strolled past various groups of Asians busy with art exhibitions, craftwork and sport, then paused at a classroom where a group of Asian women worked and chatted. Mumtaz was sitting at the teacher's desk, speaking in Punjabi to a wizened old man, trying to explain the official letter he'd received from the Home Office.

'It says your visa has run out and that you must re-apply if you want to stay on in England. You'd best speak to the people at the law centre,' she advised the old man. He bowed, offering her many blessings with his thanks, and backed out of the open door.

'Getting in practice for your legal career?' Sadiq asked, coming into the room.

Mumtaz looked up from the papers she was studying for another non-English-speaking Asian who was trying to qualify for a council flat.

'Don't tease me,' she said, smiling. 'One can never get enough practice when it concerns one's chosen path in life.'

Sadiq nodded with approval, but before he could speak there was a light tapping on the door.

'Am I interrupting?' the Imam said. He was a tall formidable man with penetrating black eyes under dark bushy brows, and was most apt to enter when there was something to interrupt.

'Imam. An honour to see you here,' Sadiq hastened to greet him with a double handclasp. '*Salaam-aleikum.*'

'May I introduce my daughter?' Mumtaz stood up, keeping her eyes cast down as she bowed before the man. A slight chill seemed to descend over the room as he looked not at her, but the papers on her desk.

'Mumtaz is helping those who have no English but many English problems,' Sadiq said proudly, giving his daughter his full support.

But the Imam's attention was now on the Asian women who were filing out of the room, and he shook his head.

'We're short of space,' Sadiq explained. 'The women will have separate facilities soon.'

'And this college place –' the Imam said, lowering his voice, but not enough to keep Mumtaz from hearing both his words and his discontent. 'Does she have separate facilities there?'

'Ah, you've heard, then.'

'Who hasn't? People look up to you, Sadiq. You should be setting an example.'

'Yes, Imam,' Sadiq replied. It was one thing to argue with Tariq, another to quibble with the Imam; this much Mumtaz knew. One always showed the Imam respect.

'And why are there all these Hindus around?' the Imam asked, in a voice so loud that Mumtaz blushed. 'We Muslims must keep to our own.'

'Yes, Imam,' Sadiq repeated. Though Mumtaz knew her father's code of behaviour was strictly according to the practice of Islam, it humiliated her to watch him placating the Imam. How not, when she knew her father was the more learned and serious scholar of the Koran?

'Islam is under threat in this country,' the Imam continued.

'I got it!' Hafiz cried, bursting into the room, excited and out of breath. He stopped short when he saw the Imam, and gave a bow.

'*Salaam-aleikum.*'

Delighted for her brother, Mumtaz gave him a thumbs-up sign, then quickly reassumed the prescribed feminine aloofness.

'Got what?' asked the Imam.

'A computer training course. Computers are big business these days.'

'Excellent,' the Imam said with approval. 'I expect your father will tell me more about it as we make the rounds.'

'We'll talk later,' Sadiq told Hafiz, giving him a congratulatory pat on the back as he left with the Imam.

Mumtaz couldn't remember the last time she'd seen her brother so excited and happy. His face glowed with his smile and even his dreamy eyes were alive and dancing. He was talking a mile a minute, elaborating on his afternoon at the computer training centre with each telling.

'I thought they'd never stop. Three quarters of an hour and then –' Hafiz broke off suddenly and Mumtaz, following his gaze, saw a young girl in traditional Hindu dress standing in the doorway.

'Hello,' the girl said, and it took Mumtaz a moment to recognize her.

'Why, Meera – I didn't know you came here,' Mumtaz said, thinking how much prettier she looked in her pale pink silk sari, her broad face clear of make-up except for the kohl lining her sloe eyes and the red dot on her forehead.

'My mother gives a cookery class.'

'This is my brother, Hafiz.' Mumtaz indicated her brother who was still staring at Meera, transfixed. 'We go to college together,' she explained to him.

'Nice to meet you –'

'Meera.'

'That's a beautiful name,' Hafiz said, computers evidently gone from his mind.

'A Hindu name, isn't it?' Mumtaz asked, thankful the Imam and her father were gone. It didn't matter to her, but Muslims were not Hindus and the one did not consort with the other. Muslims had one god, while the Hindus worshipped many.

'Yes, it is,' Meera replied, amused.

'Mumtaz likes to keep school a secret,' Hafiz said, 'though now I really can't see why.'

It wasn't so much that Mumtaz kept school secret from her family as separate. Each day she experienced embarrassments or awkwardnesses which left her feeling an outsider, small things that she'd never want to worry her parents or brothers with. After several weeks she was learning how to maintain her personal and religious standards within an institution that was a microcosm of the western world. She performed her ablutions in the girls' lavatory three times a day, before retreating to the 'religious studies' room where she'd been given permission to pray. She was quiet and unobtrusive, and when there were other girls in the loo they didn't pay her much attention. She thought she was managing well enough, but often she felt lonely when she heard the camaraderie of the others.

One Friday afternoon as Mumtaz stood washing at the

farthest basin, Candy stormed in with her netball team. Mumtaz kept her back to her classmates, and tried to concentrate on the water pouring from the tap.

'Told you he'd ask,' Candy was saying, chuffing a very pleased looking Jackie under the chin.

'Ah, so you're going out with Adam, then?' Meera hooted.

'Couldn't think up an excuse,' Jackie said.

Though she tried not to listen, Mumtaz was riveted to their reflections in the mirror, and continued to follow the conversation in spite of herself. She was surprised by the disappointment she felt at the idea of Adam and Jackie really going out together. She knew they liked each other, yet she had begun to see that there was something special about Adam; whereas Jackie's behaviour was often loud and common.

'He is sweet,' Meera commented.

'Sweet,' Jackie echoed, salaciously licking her lips.

'As well as loaded. He's Jewish, you know. His grandfather runs the mill.'

'Adam's Jewish?' Jackie asked.

'Yeah, my mum works for them. So does hers,' Meera said, gesturing towards Mumtaz.

'Used to,' Mumtaz had spoken before she realized it.

'Eh, speak up!' Candy cried, but Mumtaz ignored her.

'Does that mean he's circumcised?' Jackie asked.

'One way to find out,' Meera said, grinning.

'Doesn't half fancy himself though,' Candy said, still watching Mumtaz. 'Bloody hell, Taz. Just how dirty can one person get?'

'I'm not dirty.'

'Then why are you always washing?' Jackie asked.

'It's my prayer time.' Mumtaz ignored the hilarity this remark was met with and slipped off her shoes to splash water over her feet.

'Oh, disgusting, man! Look at the mess,' Candy cried, nudging Jackie.

'Hey, leave her alone,' Meera told Candy, but by now Jackie had joined in, giving vent to a deep-seated bitterness that shocked Mumtaz.

'You think you're so special, don't you? Too good for the team or the likes of us.'

Meera raised her voice. 'I said leave her alone, Jackie. You don't know anything.'

Mumtaz kept her back to the commotion, and crouched down on the floor, carefully wiping up the water with her towel in slow circular motions until most of the girls had gone. What had started out as the usual ribbing session had somehow got out of control. She wondered if she were to blame. Did her classmates really think she was stuck up? Would being a good Muslim mean that she wouldn't have any friends?

'You know, I could lend you a track-suit,' Meera said, taking the towel from her hands.

'Thanks,' Mumtaz said, not for the offer of the track-suit but for the support. 'I really wouldn't be any good in the team.'

'It's because it's mixed, right? Boys and girls, together.'

Mumtaz shrugged. There was no reason for her to explain to Meera.

'Is your family really that strict?'

'No,' Mumtaz replied.

'Then, why bother with all the laws?'

Mumtaz replied with her own question. 'Do they let you wear those clothes at home?'

Meera grinned. 'I change in the public toilet on the way in.'

'Why bother?' Mumtaz asked, making her point succinctly.

'I'd die if I went around looking like you,' Meera burst out.

'Why?' Mumtaz knew that Meera wasn't trying to be unkind; in fact, that she was trying to be friendly. What she didn't understand was that Mumtaz felt exactly the same way about her.

Meera held up the old grey coat that Mumtaz had left on the chair, then pointed at her baggy grey trousers. 'No form, no colour, nothing. What does your brother think?'

'I've no idea,' Mumtaz said, though she was sure Hafiz didn't see anything odd in her appearance.

'Look,' Meera went on, determined to help her. 'You can trust me!'

'I know,' Mumtaz smiled. 'But you don't really understand. This is how I am.' Both girls stood staring at each other in the mirror over the basins and laughed, puzzled by their differences, but united in friendship because of them and an ancient eastern background.

As she went up to the 'religious studies' room on the second floor to say her prayers, Mumtaz realized she felt better for having spoken to someone about who and what she was. While she clothed herself to cover her body, Meera dressed in the western fashion for display. But different ways did not mean there were irreconcilable differences between them. Sometimes it might mean there was all that much more to share. She covered her head with a prayer shawl, faced east to Mecca, and with a sense of peace listened with her heart to the Prophet's words.

'Oh, I'm sorry.' Adam had opened the door, and was now hastily closing it again.

'It's all right,' Mumtaz said, removing the cowl from her head. 'The headmaster said I could use this room. Did you need something in here?'

'Actually I saw you come in. I mean I was looking for you. I was wondering if you'd edit the magazine with me.'

Mumtaz looked at him with a steady gaze, and waited to hear more. For some reason now that she knew he was dating Jackie, she didn't feel so self-conscious near him.

'It's not a joke this time, Mumtaz,' Adam was saying earnestly. 'Mrs Gordon talked me round.'

'Well, I'm sure you're right for it.' Mumtaz began to pack up her prayer things.

'Yeah, well – it's just that I'd really like to work with you. We could make it a joint venture.' He paused, waiting for her reply, and somehow Mumtaz could neither meet nor look away from his eyes, now light blue.

'Can I think about it?' she asked, reluctant to commit herself, though she wanted to say yes.

'Sure. That would be great,' Adam said, bumping into Jackie who was waiting in the hall.

'You coming or what?' she asked with a wary glance at Mumtaz as she took Adam's arm.

'Yeah, okay,' he said complacently. 'See you then, Taz.' He smiled and held up crossed fingers.

*

A week later, Shehnaaz and Mumtaz sat working together in the kitchen, each woman absorbed in her task. The narrow room was filled with huge bolts of denim, and a second sewing machine stood next to the stove where they'd once kept a small cupboard. Shehnaaz was working at a furious pace, stitching up trousers, first at one machine and then the next. Mumtaz sat at the one free corner of the kitchen table writing in a notebook, oblivious of the noise and clutter around her.

'What are you writing? That Hamlet essay?' Shehnaaz asked, as she started on the last pair of jeans.

'No, it's a short story.'

'What about?'

'A woman who leaves a clothes factory and sets up in business for herself,' Mumtaz explained, smiling. She was writing the story as much for her mother as Adam.

'What are you writing this for?' Shehnaaz stopped working to stare at her daughter in disbelief.

'The college mag. Don't worry. I've changed all the names.'

'How can you? After those people played that joke on you.'

Mumtaz had anticipated this reaction, though she hardly thought it was fair. Her mother always seemed to be saying do what I say, not what I do. Double standards were odious. In fact, that was why she was writing the short story; to show Shehnaaz's side of the Astler labour dispute. 'Well, how could you go back to the Astlers?' she asked reasonably.

Her mother did not reply for a moment, but returned to her sewing, wrestling with the stiff, unyielding denim as she stitched the inside seam. 'Do you see the Astler boy?'

'He's on the magazine committee.'

'Does your father know?'

Mumtaz stepped over the finished trousers piled on the floor between them, and knelt down at her mother's side, putting an arm round her. 'Ama, it was Abagee who sent me there. I won't run away from any opportunity to learn more.'

'Just don't make him regret it.' Shehnaaz pulled the second leg through the machine so vigorously that the thread snarled out of control.

'I'll finish,' Mumtaz said.

'You don't know how,' her mother said wearily.

'I've been watching.'

'Then maybe you could give it some of your time,' Shehnaaz said, letting Mumtaz take her place while she began to prepare the evening meal.

Sadiq arrived home an hour later, after putting in a full day between his taxi and the community centre. Hungry, tired and disturbed by another chat with the Imam, who was now asking very pointed questions about Mumtaz, Sadiq felt unequal to the chaos he found in the kitchen.

'Shehnaaz, who are you working for?' he asked, his voice low, as he picked up a pair of trousers from the top of the pile.

'Myself,' she replied briefly and continued to gather up scraps of material that littered the floor.

'What did you buy this material with?' Sadiq asked, wondering when and how he had become the silent partner of their marriage.

'I sold some jewellery,' Shehnaaz said, and cut him off before he could protest. 'It was nothing important, only some trinkets.'

'And who did you buy all this from?' He was trying to keep calm, but he felt betrayed that his wife had taken these decisions without consulting him.

'A tradesman Mr Astler recommended.' Shehnaaz's black eyes were defiant.

'You went back to Astler's?' Sadiq asked, no longer able to keep his voice down.

'We need the money! And don't look at me like that. I've done nothing to shame you. Many men would be proud of such industry and integrity.'

'As if I didn't have trouble enough with Mumtaz in the college,' Sadiq said, his ears still ringing with the Imam's disapproval.

'If she can attend school, I can run my own business,' his wife said. 'You don't forget that the Prophet married his boss, peace be upon him.'

Sadiq bit back a retort. It was really too much to have Shehnaaz more or less defy the Muslim customs of marriage in starting her own business without consulting him, and now to cite the Prophet in her defence.

'Well, who was it this time?' Shehnaaz asked, knowing she alone was not to blame for Sadiq's mood.

'The Imam –'

'You're a fool, Sadiq. Get rich and they'll stop pushing you around.'

'Oh, rich. So that's it.'

'Yes, you'll see,' Shehnaaz picked up the box of finished trousers and went to the sitting-room where Hafiz and Rashid were playing with a mini-computer. Neither heard their mother come in, so absorbed were they in their game.

'Where did you get that from?' Shehnaaz asked curtly.

'I got it on a fortnight's trial,' Hafiz replied, without taking his eyes off the screen.

'We can't afford it.'

'In a fortnight, I'll take it back,' Hafiz explained. 'But I need it for my course.'

Shehnaaz wasn't interested in Hafiz's computer dreams. Her son had been out of work for a year, and now she needed his help. 'I have a job for you.'

'What?' Hafiz asked, still smiling at the screen, where he and the giggling Rashid were fighting a galactic battle.

Shehnaaz pulled the machine's plug from the outlet, then stood facing her two sons. 'I want you to take this box of jeans to the market on Saturday and hire a stall.'

'How?' Hafiz asked, removing his wire-rimmed glasses.

'Find out,' was all that Shehnaaz replied.


On Saturday Adam went to the synagogue with his grandfather and Alex. He didn't often attend the orthodox service, the Morrises being members of the 'progressive' congregation. Not that he often attended those services either. In fact he had forgotten how peaceful the synagogue was with its high sculpted ceilings, and the old rabbi who read from the ancient scroll, handling the *Torah* as if it were a new-born babe. He didn't really understand the verse, but Joe's running commentary and the rabbi's melodious voice helped him to grasp its intent. Something the rabbi said had triggered Joe's memory and after the service, as they waited outside the synagogue for a taxi, he began talking about his youth in Germany.

'My father would bring out his bassoon and there in the dining-room we would dance. The whole family, and all our friends too. We knew everyone in Frankfurt.' Joe hailed a passing cab, his smile already fading, for his happy memories were transitory, always obliterated by the Holocaust. 'It's all gone now. We don't dance any more,' Joe murmured as they walked to the cab.

Adam didn't recognize the driver; indeed, did not even look at him, until Alex and his grandfather got in the back seat and then he found himself seated next to the slender dark Indian who was Mumtaz's father. He tried to smile, but felt so awkward about their last meeting that he didn't quite know what to do. And it was unnerving the way Sadiq seemed to be watching him with the same curiosity.

'So . . . made any friends yet?' Joe asked some time later, as they drove past the college. 'Any nice Jewish girls?'

'Dad, give him a chance,' Alex intervened.

'Don't tell me there aren't any?'

'One or two,' Adam said vaguely. He was still thinking about the driver, and wondered how he could have been so unobservant the last time he'd been in the cab. He bore a striking resemblance to Mumtaz, the large dark eyes, and most of all the same quiet dignified bearing.

'You should come to Maccabi,' Alex said, naming the Jewish youth club. 'They always need more boys.'

'Yeah, I'll try,' Adam replied absently, and then impulsively asked, 'How's Mumtaz?'

'Very well,' Sadiq replied, giving Adam a startled sideways glance.

'She's very bright,' Adam went on, happy just to be talking about her for some reason, but Sadiq merely nodded.

'Who's this?' Alex asked.

'Just a classmate from college,' Adam explained, his eyes on the rear view mirror.

That evening Adam took Jackie to the movies where they bumped into Candy, Meera and a few others from their class. Egged on by each other, they took turns rewriting the dialogue of the latest James Bond thriller. In other words, they committed a public nuisance, as his aunt Alex would say. All the same Adam couldn't remember when he had laughed so much. Predictably, it was Jackie who came up with the real side-splitters. That was the wonderful thing about Jackie, her quirky, bizarre sense of humour. Sure, she acted tough and streetwise, but he was beginning to suspect this role was only to pursue the laughter which kept her from acknowledging pain. She was rather like his grandfather in an odd way. Joe was always cracking jokes to ease the anguish he felt about losing his family in the Holocaust. But then, he shared his grief as well. Adam wondered if Jackie would share hers, or perhaps she hadn't even recognized it yet.

They went off on their own after the film and strolled along the Grand Union Canal, at first not speaking, just clinging to each other, walking like some four-legged, two-armed set of Siamese twins. Until Jackie spotted a falling star, then she wouldn't let him near her while she made a wish that ran on long after the star had disappeared. Adam was touched by the sight of her, eyes squeezed shut, graceful chin tilted upwards, and her lips mouthing a silent litany. For some reason he thought of Mumtaz, that day when he had walked in on her saying her prayers; it was not the similarity of their poses that struck him, but the differences. Jackie looked like a young child, sitting there before him in her pagan ritual, while he'd been struck by Mumtaz's adult composure beneath that voluminous prayer shawl, her calm and serenity.

'What did you wish?' Adam asked guiltily, realizing that Jackie was watching him. Why on earth was he thinking of Mumtaz when he was sitting here with this beautiful girl?

'I'm not telling,' Jackie said, snuggling close to him once again, and they embraced in a long, intoxicating kiss that made Adam yearn for more. He reached for her breasts involuntarily, then winced as she removed his hand.

'I just don't want to get hurt again,' she said, very quietly.

'Who's hurt you?' he asked.

'Dozens of blokes. No one. Well, there's always a first time,' she finished, contradictory as ever. Adam studied her face wondering which was the truth.

'Well, I won't hurt you.'

'Yes, you will.' Jackie paused, and then startled Adam by saying, 'You like Mumtaz, don't you?'

'Mumtaz is a nice kid,' he said, confused and defensive. 'Why shouldn't I like her?'

'I can't bear people who believe in things. It reminds me of the convent and those bloody nuns.'

'Well, I don't believe in things, if that helps any,' Adam said, putting his arm round her once again. But Jackie was on another tack.

'Really? I thought –'

'What?'

'Well, why didn't you tell me you were Jewish?'

Adam was momentarily thrown by the question. 'Does it matter?'

'Course not,' Jackie assured him. 'It's just that Taz never stops being a bloody Muslim . . .'

'So what does that have to do with anything?' Adam asked, though he was thinking that no matter what his religious practices were, reformed or orthodox worshipper, he would never stop being a Jew.

'You never asked *me* to work on the college mag, did you?' Jackie blurted out.

'But I didn't know you wanted to,' Adam said, remembering how mad she had been earlier in the week when he'd been working late with Mumtaz. Had her anger been over Mumtaz or being left out of the magazine?

'I don't want to!' Jackie said, defiantly, her blue eyes as sullen as her pouting mouth.

Adam stared at her and laughed. 'You're crazy!'

'Yeah, that might be true,' Jackie said, suddenly smiling like her old self. 'My dad tried to lock me up once, then he said he loved me too much and sent me to the convent instead.' She sighed. 'Do your parents love you?'

Adam was startled to find he could not answer her. If she'd asked about his grandfather or Alex, he wouldn't have hesitated. But he really saw so little of his parents. Of course one knew they cared, but love was something they never talked about. In fact, he couldn't remember either Sarah or Phil ever using the word to each other or him. He was certain they must have loved each other when they met at university. But now they were entrenched in their separate lives – all three of them – and only met in passing.

'They don't, do they?' Jackie asked, curling up closer under his arm and hugging him with all her strength. 'It's not the end of the world. If *you* know how to love.'

Adam was silent, wondering if he loved Jackie. They'd been going out together for over a month, and he thought about her a great deal. But then he thought of Mumtaz too.

'You don't have to be with me, you know,' Jackie said, breaking the silence.

'I know that, but I want to be with you,' he said, and hugged her. Jackie embraced him more tightly.

'I want you to make love to me,' she said.

Adam looked around at the damp, cold riverbank. 'Bloody hell,' he murmured, his mind and heart racing, but on different courses. He had never made love to anyone before, and this wasn't exactly the way he had imagined it. The fact was he longed for Jackie, but he was scared.

'Well, if you want it so much,' Jackie said, trying to laugh at herself.

'I do,' Adam protested, awkward. 'It's just . . . I never – Well, have you?'

'Oh, blimey!' Jackie moved away.

'No, wait.' Adam drew her back and began making love to her in earnest, thinking how sweet her mouth was, how soft her body. 'Look, are you sure?' he whispered breathlessly.

'Just tell me you love me,' she replied, arching her body to meet his.

'I do –'

'And don't stop loving me,' Jackie moaned.

'I won't, but –'

'No more words,' she interrupted him. 'It's bloody cold and I want you now.'

What pleased Adam the most was the discovery that Jackie, despite her knowing manner and innuendoes, was, like himself, a virgin. He felt that they were irrevocably bound to each other now, and her new dependency, the soft, uncertain side of herself that she revealed to him, thrilled him as much as the act of making love; in fact, he considered it proof of their intimacy.

And yet in the following days he continued to look forward with an inexplicable eagerness to the afternoons he worked on the magazine with Mumtaz. In fact he always seemed to arrive early, even if it meant leaving Jackie angry, as he had done today.

'I thought we could do a survey of people's attitudes on education, religion, and politics,' Mumtaz was saying, as they discussed the Christmas issue. She looked so serious Adam felt he had to make her smile.

'That'll be easy. Most of the kids here don't have any,' he said, and was rewarded by a brief mischievous grin.

'Maybe they've never been asked.'

'Possibly. We'll give it a try,' Adam said. 'I thought I'd ask Roger, the drummer, to do a music review. There will be lots of new releases coming out in December and he'll have heard them all well in advance.'

'Fine,' Mumtaz murmured, thinking how surprisingly well-organized Adam was. She was pleased to be sharing the magazine work with him, and glad, too, for his friendship.

It used to irk her in the beginning of the term to hear Candy and Jackie call her Taz, but when Adam used the strange nickname, it simply sounded warm and friendly.

'Then, of course, we'll have to do something on sport. Candy would never forgive us if we didn't list our team's fantastic scores,' Adam said, wishing this were something he could get Jackie to do. She wouldn't feel left out then, and he wouldn't feel so guilty.

'What about you doing a Scrooge in School strip?' Mumtaz suggested. 'Your drawings are very good. I saw the one you did of me, you know.' She was smiling now, but when Jackie had first shown the caricature to her she had been hurt. The exaggerated nose, the dour mouth and long braids, that sketch had seemed worse than the college mag joke. But that was before she knew Adam, and before she'd learned to laugh at herself.

Adam's face had turned red and worried. 'It was just a silly caricature,' he explained. 'It's nothing like the way you really look.' As he said this, he realized that she had changed somehow during the last month or so. Perhaps it was simply that she smiled more.

'What about photographs? We'll need a camera.' Mumtaz consulted the notebook on her lap in order to escape Adam's intrusive gaze. 'Of course, I've never used one. My father only takes his out for weddings.'

'Actually, I've got a decent Nikkon. I'll teach you how to use it, if you like.'

Mumtaz hesitated before she gave her reply. Learning to use a camera was all in the line of her school work. There really wouldn't be any reason to discuss it at home, she thought. Not that there was anything wrong with accepting Adam's offer. 'Yes, I'd like that,' she said, raising her eyes to his.

For a moment Adam was lost in the discovery of the long, dark eyelashes that shadowed Mumtaz's eyes. How was it possible that he hadn't noticed them before?

'There's really not all that much to learn,' he told her. 'How about tomorrow after school?'

Again she hesitated. 'Yes, that will be fine. But now I'd really better be going. I'm already late.'

'I'll walk out with you,' Adam said, helping Mumtaz on with her coat, a gallantry that both pleased and flustered her.

'By the way, I've been working on a short story. I don't know if it's any good. You'll have to decide if it's worthy of our rag,' she told him as they went downstairs, too intent on each other to notice Jackie at the end of the hall, watching them.

'What's it about?' Adam asked, wondering what kind of stories would run through her mind. He'd be afraid to trust his own imagination in these confusing times.

'A clothes factory. In Leicester.' She was vague, and relieved when he didn't catch on. 'You'll see when it's done.' For a moment she wished her mother had never worked for Astler's and that she and Adam could just be ordinary friends.

'Taz –'

They were outside now and Adam, seeing Sadiq's taxi waiting, plucked up his courage to settle the misunderstanding that still nagged him.

'The taxi driver, he's your father, isn't he?'

'Yes.' She cast her eyes down again and he didn't know what she was thinking.

'I didn't get you into any trouble that day when I hi-jacked the car, did I?'

'Not really,' she murmured, as pleased as Adam to have the issue of her father's mistaken identity sorted out.

'I kind of apologized to him when he drove me and my grandfather home from the synagogue once.'

Mumtaz was surprised by this, and embarrassed. Why hadn't Sadiq mentioned it to her? She wondered what he thought of Adam's behaviour, and hers.

'Well, he's waiting,' Mumtaz said. 'I must run. Goodnight.'

''Night.' Adam watched her until the taxi was out of sight, and only then did he realize he was standing there empty-handed. 'You clown,' he told himself as he went back into the building to collect the books he had forgotten. 'Where's your head?'

Apparently he wasn't the only one to wonder. As he went back to the classroom to get his books, he met Candy in the hall.

'You still here?' Adam asked with a friendly smile.

'Yeah. I had practice. What's your excuse?' Candy said without returning his smile. 'You know you ought to be more careful.'

'Careful? Of what?'

'Of Taz,' Candy said, giving him a hard look as she stood in front of him, hands on hips. 'You can't do that with her.'

'Do what?' Adam protested. 'We're friends.'

'Muslims –' She shook a finger at Adam. 'They don't understand that.'

Startled by her unexpected attack, Adam gave her a shaky grin. 'Thanks for the advice. It's always nice to get something free, hey?'

He turned to leave, but Candy hadn't finished with him yet.

'Look after Jackie, that's a big enough job. She was already screwed up before she met you. But I guess you could make it worse, without half trying.'

Adam knew Candy was right. And it wasn't as though it were any kind of hardship to 'look after' a girl who was beautiful and funny, and whom he loved anyway. Yet the next day when he and Mumtaz had their photography session, he found unaccountable pleasure in her enjoyment as she played photographer.

'Get farther to the left, Adam,' Mumtaz called, focusing the camera lens on him. 'Sorry, I mean my left.'

'Hurry up, my smile's going.'

'Don't worry, I've caught it.' She laughed. 'Adam Morris's smile preserved for ever more in Southgates' archives.'

Adam watched as she packed the camera back into its leather case. 'Why don't we go somewhere else, Taz?' he said impulsively.

'No. Thanks all the same.' Mumtaz's eyes were downcast now, suddenly Eastern and mysterious.

Adam was silent for a moment. 'It's all right,' he said. 'I understand. You're not allowed.'

'I choose not to!' Mumtaz replied with a flash of temper. She read the incomprehension on his face. 'You really don't understand, do you?'

'Explain then, for God's sake!' Adam raised his voice in frustration. What was she on about, anyway? 'I'm only trying to be a friend.'

Mumtaz handed him the camera. 'Right, let's go.' When he remained standing where he was, she tossed her plaits back impatiently and said, 'You wanted to go somewhere. Let's start.'

She didn't speak to him again until they had caught the first bus that passed and were sitting down on opposite sides of the aisle.

'Happy?' she asked. 'This is what you wanted?'

Adam sighed and looked away. Why was she making it so hard?

'Getting to know me, are you?' she continued doggedly.

Adam had seen her get upset before, but what exactly was bothering her now, he didn't know. She could be really baffling sometimes.

'No, not yet,' he replied, meeting her eye. 'I think you're difficult.'

'If you believe in something, it makes you different,' she said, calming herself with her words. 'Don't you believe in God?'

'No, not really. I mean, how can you believe in God with everything that's going on in the world?' He shrugged, tossing back a dark curl from his forehead. And yet he did believe there was something. Maybe simple humanity.

'I thought you knew,' Mumtaz said, even more dismayed now. 'I thought you were different.'

'No. I'm just the same as everyone else.' Adam sighed, and then, noticing they had come to Abbey Park, he jumped up. 'Let's get off here.'

They walked in silence for a while, past joggers and mothers with babies in prams, and then cut across the lush green lawns, slowing down as they came to a bower of trees.

'You mean you don't care what you are?' Mumtaz spoke first, resuming their conversation as if there had been no interruption.

'Let's say I don't know what I am.' Adam searched her dark eyes for understanding, but saw only disbelief.

'You've got a family, a history!'

'Yes, that's fine. But it's also the past. We're here now in the present. You can't hide from it.'

'I'm not hiding,' Mumtaz said so quickly and defensively that he realized he had touched a nerve.

'You're only useful if you belong,' she said. 'If you're a part of something.'

'You belong to the human race. Go for the melting pot. The sooner, the better.'

Mumtaz shook her head, her plaits swinging with fierce denial. 'That is not the answer.'

'It would certainly do away with racism.'

'It wouldn't,' Mumtaz said, in a quieter, resigned voice. 'Maybe you'll understand after you read my story.' She stopped. 'I can't stay any longer. I really shouldn't be here at all. I'll see you tomorrow.' Without waiting for an answer, she hurried back towards the road.

'Wait, Taz.' Adam ran after her, and threw an arm over her shoulder. 'Don't be cross.'

Mumtaz swung round, shaking off his arm and glaring at him as if he had assaulted her.

'What? What is it?' he asked.

'Friends don't do that,' she replied coldly, and left him staring after her.

Mumtaz found it difficult to concentrate on Mrs Gordon's Shakespeare lecture the next day when Adam didn't show up for the class. She kept thinking of their argument, if that's what it had been. It bothered her that they always seemed to be talking at cross purposes. Especially as a part of her seemed to respond to him no matter how she disagreed with him. But it wasn't a part of herself that she knew or trusted. She wrote down the words Mrs Gordon spoke, but continued to listen for the sound of the door opening until the bell rang. She rose with the rest of the students and was following them out of the classroom when Jackie called to her.

'Mumtaz! Could I have a word with you, please?' She was still sitting at her desk in the back row and as Mumtaz approached she stood up to face her.

'Lay off Adam, will you?' Jackie's voice was low and menacing, but Mumtaz was even more shocked by the entreaty in her eyes.

'Sorry?' she said, unable to take it all in.

'He's chasing you and he's sleeping with me.'

'No, you are really quite wrong.' Mumtaz spoke haltingly, above the tumult of feelings within her. Guilt, shock, horror, jealousy. She hardly knew what she felt. But no, not jealousy. She knew Adam and Jackie belonged together. She had known it from the first day.

'Adam and I work together on the magazine. That's all.'

'Do you have to?' Jackie asked, frowning.

Mumtaz regarded her silently for a moment. 'Yes,' she said, her voice steady and assured.

'Oh! Well, then, I see. You're determined to keep your claws in him.'

'But we are only friends.' Mumtaz stood her ground firmly.

'Hardly that. Nothing has happened.'

'Yes, it has,' Jackie insisted. 'He can't see it, he's just a kid. But it has definitely started.'

'Honestly, you have it all wrong. But perhaps if I talk to him –' Mumtaz said, wanting to placate the other girl and clarify the situation for herself.

'No! Thank you very much. Just keep your sodding hands off him. And keep away from me as well,' Jackie said, and swept out of the room.

'Taz?' Meera poked her head in the door, and from her startled and concerned expression, Mumtaz knew she had heard the whole thing.

'Are you okay?'

Mumtaz nodded, though now that the confrontation with Jackie had ended, she found herself trembling.

'She'll get over it,' Meera said reassuringly.

Mumtaz managed a smile. 'Maybe,' she said. 'But will I?'

On Saturday Mumtaz met Meera at the market at Cheapside. The Hindu girl had persuaded her to come if only to show Jackie that Adam wasn't her only friend from college. As it turned out, it was pleasure mixed with business, for Shehnaaz gave her a box lunch to take to her brothers who had hired a stall.

'Let's stroll and – you know – window shop,' Meera said, leading the way around the clothes stalls, while Mumtaz, distracted by the crowds, worried about finding Hafiz and Rashid.

'We must keep an eye out for my brothers,' she said more than once, but to her surprise and relief, it was Hafiz who found them. He wasn't at all interested in the lunch Shehnaaz had packed, however.

'I've got a better idea,' he said. 'Why don't both you girls come and have a proper hot meal with me?'

'And Rashid? What about him?' Mumtaz asked. 'Should you leave him alone at the stall? You forget he's only fifteen.'

'He's doing great. If anybody forgets he's only fifteen, it's Rashid,' Hafiz said, but although he was replying to Mumtaz, his eyes never left Meera's face.

The smile that Meera gave him convinced Mumtaz that this was not the first time her brother and friend had bumped into each other like this. She was disturbed at the Hindu–Muslim complication and, yet, why shouldn't two people be free to fall in love? Meera had proved herself to be a good friend already, and Hafiz was a kind, loving man.

'This is a wild idea of Mum's, you know,' Hafiz was saying. 'We're spending more money on that stall than we make.'

'You can't tell yet. She's only just started,' Mumtaz told him, worried for Shehnaaz and feeling she needed all their support. 'Give it a chance.'

'That's what we're doing.' Hafiz turned to Meera. 'Computers, that's where I'm going to make my money.'

'Good luck to you,' Meera said, smiling at him again.

'Let me show you the computer I'm working with,' Hafiz said, stopping as they came to an electronics shop.

'I've been through this before,' Mumtaz told Meera. 'I'm going to take Rashid his lunch.' She left them alone together, feeling slightly apprehensive at the thought of making herself an accomplice to a forbidden relationship. If only there were a way to reconcile loyalty to one's family and heritage with fulfilment of oneself.

Half an hour later, Hafiz was still sitting at a display unit, playing with a word processor, while Meera, bored but indulgent, looked on.

'Is this your idea of buying me lunch?' she teased.

'What would you like to know?' Hafiz asked. 'Ask anything.'

'What about me and you?'

Hafiz typed a code into the machine. HAFIZ LOVES MEERA flashed across the screen.

She smiled and let herself fall into his embrace. 'And does it know when you'll tell your parents about us?'

Hafiz made no reply.

Meanwhile, Rashid was so intent on his sales patter that he didn't see Mumtaz approach the stall, and she listened to him, surprised at his easy, faintly lurid, patter.

'Try them on, go ahead. I won't look,' he told a young woman who was passing. 'You don't trust me? You want me to look? Okay, don't buy them,' he called, as the prospective customer wandered off.

'Is Hafiz often away?' Mumtaz asked, noticing Rashid's guilty reaction to her unexpected arrival.

'What are you doing here? Checking up? Well, everything is fine and everyone's happy.'

'I brought you some lunch,' Mumtaz said absently, thinking of the lies, the subterfuge in store for them all if there really were something going on between Hafiz and Meera.

'Hiya, Taz.'

She started at the sound of Adam's voice, and turned to see him approaching the stall, his arm entwined with Jackie's.

'Hello,' she murmured, stepping round to the other side of the stall.

'How are things?' Adam asked casually.

'Fine.' Her tone matched his, and she avoided his eyes, restraining herself from seeking the special look she always found there.

'Mind if I browse?' Jackie asked.

'Go right ahead.' Mumtaz spoke quickly, noticing Rashid's wary expression as he eyed the couple.

'Hey, I read the story you left in the mag file,' Adam told her. 'Was it based on fact? I mean did something like that really happen?'

Mumtaz was stunned, and offended. 'Well, yes, it did, actually.'

'I thought so,' Adam said, shaking his head.

'But you don't understand, do you?' Mumtaz said, unable to suppress her disappointment.

'Hey, who is this guy?' Rashid asked.

Adam put out his hand. 'Adam Morris. I'm a friend of Mumtaz.'

'This is the bloke you've been seen with?' Rashid asked her, still gazing at Adam with a malevolent eye.

Jackie glanced up from the counter. 'Night and day, kid,' she told Rashid. 'But I'm working on it.'

'Jackie!' Adam cried, shocked. 'Be quiet. You don't know what you're saying.'

'Rashid, he's the magazine editor.' Mumtaz was speaking at the same time to her brother, appalled at the mounting tension.

'Sounds like a good excuse.'

'Is he always this pleasant?' Adam asked Mumtaz.

'You just leave her alone,' Rashid said.

'What's going on here?' Hafiz had returned to the stall and was taking in the scene. He gave Adam a long look, then turned to Mumtaz with a stern expression as if, she thought, he'd not just spent several hours with the forbidden Hindu Meera.

'They're friends from college. They were just passing,' she told him, hoping Adam and Jackie would just leave.

'I need a pair of jeans actually,' Adam said, trying to ease the situation.

'You trying to be funny or something?' Rashid asked.

'No, why should I?'

'You're Astler's boy, aren't you? What do you want with our jeans?'

'They look different,' Adam said, meaning original. It was a poor choice of words, and he regretted it.

'Yeah, crappy,' Jackie threw in.

'Shut up, okay?' Adam warned her, casting an oddly pleading look at Mumtaz, but the situation was already out of hand.

'Serve the gentleman his jeans,' Hafiz instructed his younger brother.

'Size, sir?' Rashid spat out the words.

'Medium, but with long legs,' Adam replied. 'Sorry about all this,' he told Mumtaz as he handed Rashid a tenner. 'Keep the change. I'm sure they're worth it,' he said awkwardly as he took the package.

'Christ, you've got to be joking,' Jackie said. 'You're going to let them behave like that to us?' She turned to Mumtaz. 'You keep that ape on a lead,' she said, pointing to Rashid.

'What did you say?' Rashid flinched at her jibe.

'That's it! We're going,' Adam said, grabbing hold of Jackie.

'You call me an ape? You cow – you filthy tart!' Rashid screamed.

'Hey, lay off her, okay?' Adam warned.

'Piss off, Jewboy!'

Adam went white, seized with rage and a strength to match. 'Don't you ever say that again,' he said, lifting Rashid off his

feet and throwing him across the stall. When Hafiz stepped
forward, he laid into him with the same ferocity, but got as
good as he gave.

'Adam! Christ, Adam, that's enough!' Jackie cried.

'Stop it! Both of you stop it!' Mumtaz pleaded, appalled
and ashamed in front of the gathering crowd.

'Just stay away from us, all right?' Hafiz told Adam.

'No problem,' said the panting Adam, and turned to
Mumtaz. 'Sorry, really I am.' He started to go; then turned
back. 'By the way, you got it wrong in the story. We're not
the racists.'

Mumtaz was stung by the truth of his words, ashamed, and
still angry.

'What did that mean?' Rashid asked, watching Adam and
Jackie disappear in the crowd.

'You behaved like a pig,' Mumtaz replied, and turned to
leave. But Hafiz stopped her, his face stern and cold with
anger.

'You'll never see him again. Understand?'

'How dare you try to bully me? You hypocrite, sneaking
away for your afternoons with Meera! She's a nice girl and
you better not hurt her.'

Adam and Jackie wandered through the Christmas crowds, as
the Salvation Army band played 'In the Bleak Midwinter'.
Once on the other side of the market, Adam stuffed the
Sattars' jeans into a rubbish bin.

'Bastards,' Jackie muttered righteously, squeezing Adam's
arm. But he remained stiff and aloof, and pulled away from
her.

'You all right, love?' she asked.

'Yeah. I just need to be by myself for a while.'

'Adam, wait.'

He turned round, sighing. 'It's done now. Just let it go. I'll see
you, okay?' and he hurried away before she could stop him again.

That night Mumtaz spent a long time at her prayers, reciting
the Arabic verse under her breath again and again, but her
mind was elsewhere. Try as she would to erase her memory

and regain her serenity, she found herself reliving that afternoon at the market; the ugly fight, the staring crowds, and Adam's part in it all. She had never seen him lose his temper before, and his violent reaction to Rashid's racist taunt showed her that he did believe in his heritage, even if he was uncertain about God. They were not so different as he pretended. She renewed her efforts at concentrating on the Koran as she heard her father coming up to her room. She dreaded this confrontation, sure he'd have heard about the incident in the market place.

'Verse 251.' Mumtaz quickly handed him the Koran.

'Who is the boy?' Sadiq asked.

'What boy?' she said, with feigned indifference.

'You've been seen!'

'By whom?' Mumtaz asked, indignant.

'Never mind by whom! Who is he?'

She knew that her father was perfectly aware of Adam's identity. Why must she 'confess'? And what?

'We've been working together on the college magazine.'

'And the walks in the park? The brawling in the public market-place? Who is he?'

'His name is Adam. You've met him. He's Astler's grandson.' Mumtaz had to keep reminding herself she'd done nothing wrong.

'Allah –' Sadiq murmured, and then stared out of the window, shaking his head.

'I don't know what they told you and I don't care,' Mumtaz suddenly burst out, unable to stifle her feelings any longer. 'If you don't trust me, then keep me at home or marry me off!' She hadn't known how much she longed to cry.

'Just tell me what's been going on.'

'There's nothing to tell. Either believe me or throw me out.'

'Why him?'

Mumtaz got up and went to her closet. 'I don't deserve this. If you cannot trust me then I'll go.'

Sadiq put a restraining hand on her shoulder. 'It's my fault. Maybe this school is too much for you.'

'What? Oh, no. Now you want to take me out of college?' she asked, her heart sinking at the possibility.

'Your mother needs help.'

'I'm sorry,' Mumtaz murmured, unwilling to discuss the idea of leaving school. 'I do try and help every evening. I'll find time to do more.'

'Go to your mother now. She's waiting in the kitchen.'

Mumtaz dreaded talking to her mother, knowing the bitterness Shehnaaz already felt for the Astlers. She went downstairs slowly, pausing to cast a reproachful glance at her brothers who were packing up jeans and sweeping scraps of material from the floor.

'It wasn't us,' Hafiz called after her, but Mumtaz did not turn.

'Mum?'

Shehnaaz was sitting at the sewing machine that faced the kitchen door, and looked up with an accusatory glance, her black eyes wide and disbelieving.

'Why? Why an Astler?' she asked.

But Mumtaz could take no more. 'Nobody listens to me!' she cried. 'I don't know him! I don't like him! He's nothing!'

Adam had been surprised by the fury of his reaction to Rashid's taunt, and kept to himself over the next few days, trying to puzzle out his feelings. He went down to the Maccabi Jewish Youth Club, simply to wander around on his own and talk to a few friends from his early childhood. He thought a lot about Mumtaz and Jackie, in that order. He worried that he had inadvertently got Mumtaz into more trouble. Her life was so much more rigid than his; a street fight would certainly have repercussions. Adam's own family had believed his story about walking into a door. They had no idea of the incident that had taken place between the 'Sattar Sons' and the 'Astler Boy'.

'Are you joining us for Chanuka? How lovely, darling,' Alex said when she came into the lobby and saw him there.

Adam felt a twinge of remorse at his aunt's warm welcome. He had arranged to meet Jackie outside the synagogue, and he couldn't let her down. He had spent little enough time with her since the market fight, as it was.

'I can't. I'm sorry.'

'Any special reason?'

'Yes, there is,' Adam said, but offered no more.

'You'd better go then,' his aunt told him with an understanding hug, though what she understood he couldn't imagine.

Adam got to the synagogue just as Jackie was coming out of the building.

'What were you doing in there?' he asked, puzzled.

'Just looking around. Nothing secret, is it?' Her blue eyes had taken on that suspicious look.

'Course not.'

'Good. 'Cause it's a bloody funny place to meet.'

Adam sensed they were either on the brink of laughter or a beastly row.

'Sorry. It hasn't been easy to get away,' he lied, and was relieved to see the tension lift from her pretty face. 'Now, what do you want in your stocking?' he asked.

'Not you, mate,' she said, and Adam laughed with her. But he wondered at how hollow his laugh sounded – hollow and meaningless.

Like his life, he found himself thinking some nights later, as he sat staring down at his homework and filling the margins of the paper with minute designs. He knew that sounded like a dramatic, and worse, middle-aged pronouncement, and he supposed he didn't mean it entirely. It was just that when he first started college, he had a fairly sound sense of who he was. Now there was so much he felt uncertain about. What did he, in fact, believe in? And in which direction was his future? He had assumed he would continue his studies, but perhaps he should join his grandfather's business. Then there was Jackie who was lovely to look at and, for the most part, fun to be with. So why wasn't he more certain about his feelings for her? He couldn't imagine being without her, yet he couldn't really imagine their being together for ever.

'What is it? The girl?' Sarah asked, regarding him from her study alcove, and Adam sat up straight, startled at how close his mother had come to reading his mind.

Adam shrugged, thinking how strange it was that his mother's question should make Mumtaz pop into his head, along with Jackie.

'I want to talk to you, Adam,' she was saying. 'There's a school near Loughborough that does special A-level work.'

'A private school?'

Sarah nodded, not bothering to explain why she was changing sides on the issue she'd fought over with Joe.

'You'd sell out, then?' he asked, surprised and touched.

'You're worth it.'

'Well, thanks, but I'm staying here,' Adam said, at least feeling sure about this one factor of his life – for the moment.

A week or so after the market fight, Adam saw Mumtaz working alone at a table in the library and decided to use the magazine as an excuse to interrupt her. There had been so many editorial chores to ensure its publication before the end of term that they'd written a list and divided it between them. They had hardly seen each other since, and Adam suspected that Mumtaz had meant it to be that way.

'I've collected all the material,' he said. 'There's only some editing left to do now.' Mumtaz nodded and continued writing in her notebook. She planned to give him her resignation as soon as the magazine was ready for publication. But she mustn't get into a conversation about it. Or anything else.

'How's your brother?'

'He's fine,' Mumtaz said, glancing up from her notes briefly. She felt sorry for Adam. She knew he meant no harm, and she would miss his friendship. But it was the only way.

'I'm so sorry –'

'Rashid was foul to you.' She had to tell him that much.

Encouraged, Adam gave her a smile. 'I've written a sequel to your factory story. Well, an explanation of the other side.'

'Adam, I can't get any more involved,' Mumtaz said, meaning in the Astler–Sattar story, but the sound of her words brought the colour to her cheeks.

'That's okay.' He paused for a moment with a vague, somewhat lost expression in his blue eyes. 'As long as it's your choice,' he added, and then wandered along the halls to the college canteen for a cup of tea.

He'd only been sitting there a few minutes when Candy came and sat down opposite him with a stern look.

'God, man, what is it with you? I've got Jackie cracking up on me and Taz won't even speak. What's going on?'

Adam was silent.

'Are you some kind of idiot, or what?' she asked, and got up, still with that cold, unsympathetic look that Adam supposed he deserved. But she was right. He probably was an idiot because he didn't honestly know what he had done wrong.

The college was open to parents on the last day of the term and the Great Hall was lined with trestle tables, a group tutor behind each to speak to the parents. Mumtaz proudly watched as ushers handed out the college magazine to visitors at the doors, knowing she and Adam had succeeded. Sadiq and Shehnaaz were talking to her tutor, Mrs Gordon, while she stood off to the side, trying not to hear, and she didn't notice that Adam had arrived with Sarah and Joe. Adam for his part, was too busy listening to Joe to realize they had drifted right up to Mumtaz.

'Hello,' he said, embarrassed and appalled to see her almost wince as she became aware of their presence. 'May I introduce my grandfather, Joseph Astler, and my mother, Sarah? This is Mumtaz.'

Joe and Sarah smiled, but before they could speak he had burst out, 'The magazine turned out great, thanks to you.' He felt for all the world as if they were parting for ever.

'You, too.' Mumtaz gave him an unexpectedly gentle smile, and then her face went blank as she saw her mother and father approaching.

'Well, hello again,' Joe smiled at Shehnaaz. 'Mrs Sattar, isn't it? So, this must be your daughter,' he said while her mother simply stood there and stared at him.

'And this is Mrs Morris and Adam,' Mumtaz quickly said, but Shehnaaz and Sadiq scarcely acknowledged the introduction.

That, at least, was how it felt to Adam, who nonetheless tried to break the ice. 'Nice to meet you,' he said. 'It's quite an occasion, isn't it? Well, I'd better introduce my family to Mrs Gordon.' He turned to Mumtaz. 'See you next term.'

'I doubt it,' Sadiq said and Mumtaz felt her heart catch.

'Mumtaz may be changing schools,' Shehnaaz explained, avoiding her daughter's startled face.

'Why?' Adam asked Mumtaz.

But she was walking away with her parents, and her farewell was casually thrown over her shoulder.

'Wait, Taz,' Adam called after her, but his voice was lost in the noise of the crowd, and, seeing Jackie come into the room, he resisted the urge to follow the Sattars and crossed the room to greet her.

The fight in the market between Rashid and Adam had marked a definite turning point in Mumtaz's life. True to her promise, she broke off contact with Adam. She quit the magazine and concentrated on her dual role of scholar and Muslim. Her single-mindedness and singleness, for she saw no one from college and her social life consisted only of volunteer work at the Asian community centre, so impressed Sadiq that he allowed her to continue at Southgates. He could not lay down laws which would prohibit or restrict his daughter's education; he had far too much respect for her mind.

Mumtaz's life followed a careful routine over the next eighteen months. She continued to keep college separate from home, but she brought her role of dutiful daughter into the school gates, and tried to make sure she was following all the rules. She needed this rigidity both for herself and for her father. Curiously, she was striving to be his good Muslim daughter in direct proportion to Shehnaaz's lapses as a dutiful Muslim wife.

Shehnaaz's business had grown over the past year and a half, and with it, her reputation. She had become something of a heroine to the women still working at Astler's. Her name inspired them to voice their growing discontent over working conditions and wages, much to old Joe's annoyance. He couldn't really understand their complaints. All he knew was that ever since Shehnaaz quit, his troubles had multiplied. Now his workers were holding meetings in the factory. There was a tangible feeling of mutiny in the air; and Shehnaaz watched and encouraged her downtrodden sisters to fight for better working conditions.

Mumtaz tried to stay clear of any Astler-related conversation because she still reacted to the mention of Adam's family. Unlike Shehnaaz, she tried to keep her feelings to herself, even if she couldn't manage to keep them *from* herself. There was nobody at school or the community centre who interested her as Adam had, and she concentrated wholly on the dreams of her future as a lawyer. Yet as the A-levels drew nearer, she couldn't quite accept the fact that college would be over and she'd probably never see any of these people again.

She found it hard, at times, not to be envious of Hafiz and Meera, who'd fallen deeply in love and continued to meet secretly. But she was too fond of Meera to begrudge her the happiness she found with Hafiz. And she was too sympathetic to her brother's plight as he tried to work up enough courage – and perhaps commitment – to tell his parents about Meera. She didn't like being put in the position of condoning, and sometimes abetting, Hafiz's secret trysts, but she couldn't bear the idea of the lovers being separated.

The pangs of envy Mumtaz felt when she saw Jackie and Adam were far more acute. They were still together, closer than ever, with Adam now dressing as punkishly as Jackie, earring and all. Mumtaz hadn't been able to avoid them completely; not the teasing, puzzling Jackie with her odd jibes, nor Adam's glances that always had the threat of something more, and made her rush away.

Her head was so filled with revisions, notes, facts and figures that she wandered about the college in a scholastic daze. Late one afternoon she made her way to the 'religious studies' room, and though the door was closed, charged right in. After two years she considered it her private office. And there to her astonishment was Jackie, naked to the waist, her blond curls falling softly round her face as she sat jotting notes in the margin of a textbook. Mumtaz stared at the naked girl, then at Adam who was painting her, struggling with the unexpectedness, the unreality, of the scene.

'Hi,' Jackie said, turning round, unperturbed.

'Sorry,' Mumtaz murmured. She had never known anyone could be so comfortable in their nakedness.

Adam looked up from his painting, lost in his work, his blue eyes vague and dreamy.

'We thought you'd be locked up at home by now,' Jackie said, explaining their presence.

'I'm trying to revise.'

'You're the only one who ever comes here, right?' Adam gave her a small, guilty smile.

'I always thought so,' she replied, stiffly.

'Oh, my bum's gone all numb. Adam has to get this done for the exhibition,' Jackie moaned, stretching languorously. 'Wouldn't take over for me, would you?'

Mumtaz didn't even try to smile at her joke.

'Good luck for your exhibition,' she said, and ran downstairs to her locker, still clutching the library books she had been planning to study in the solitude of the 'religious studies' room. The books were on special reserve and students weren't allowed to take them home. But suddenly Mumtaz didn't care about rules. The scene with Jackie and Adam had upset her more than she would have thought possible. They were like a married couple, so intimate with each other that they could sit talking to a third person while Jackie exposed her round, full breasts. In Mumtaz's prayer room! It was impossible to understand why they had gone there to – to violate her place.

'Finished your swotting?' Jackie's voice startled Mumtaz out of her thoughts, and she glanced up guiltily from her locker.

'Look, Taz,' Jackie began, herself startled – and hurt – by the look of alarm on the other girl's face. 'No need to die of fright.'

'Really – I was just – I thought I was alone.'

'I know I've been shitty,' Jackie continued. 'Two years and I've done nothing but pull your leg.'

'It doesn't matter,' Mumtaz interrupted before she could say any more.

'I thought you were after Adam. And you were in the beginning, weren't you?' Jackie asked with a searching look.

'No.'

'Oh, well.' Jackie offered her her hand. 'It only hits you when it's too late. I'm sorry I wasn't nicer.'

Oddly moved and embarrassed, Mumtaz finished packing the reference books into her bag. 'I'm taking these home. I can't stay here any longer.'

'Why, you devil.' Jackie smiled delightedly. 'Still waters run deep, eh?'

'I'll return them first thing in the morning.'

'Nervous about the exams?'

'Very,' Mumtaz confessed. 'I mean, for two years this is all I've been working for.'

'You'll do fine, an old swot like you.'

'Are you worried?' Mumtaz asked, unused to this gentle side to Jackie. She couldn't help but wonder if she'd been sent by Adam. Or was she really being a friend on her own?

'Just worried about afterwards, really,' Jackie said, a far-away look in her eyes.

Clearly she wasn't referring to any academic future. 'I think you'll be very happy,' Mumtaz said awkwardly, remembering, with a pang, how comfortable Adam and Jackie had looked together in the intimacy of the small prayer room upstairs, the way Adam had studied his lover as he painted her, like one absorbed in a magnificent dream.

'Don't fancy a drink, do you?' Jackie was saying. 'We're just having a quick one.'

'Another time.' Not that Mumtaz would ever consider breaking the Muslim code, but this close to the end of the term she felt she could make that little gesture.

'Yeah, I bet,' Jackie said dubiously.

'Well, 'night.'

'Ta-ra, love. Look after yourself and don't study too hard.'

That's that, Mumtaz thought, still puzzled by Jackie's sudden warmth. Perhaps that's just what happened to people as school came to an end. Fears for the unknown future – in the world out there – made them suddenly feel close to what was familiar. She even felt a kind of affection for Jackie too, now. Whether Jackie had come of her own accord, or was sent by Adam, did not much matter at this point; it was all over now.

Or so she thought until Adam himself approached her the next afternoon, as she was leaving school.

'Taz –'

The familiar nickname, the warm deep voice, made Mumtaz catch her breath with dismay and pleasure. She had just come out of the door, and Adam was running down the steps after her, while her father looked on from the main gate.

'Go inside, I'll be right there,' she said, without turning. She stood for a moment rummaging in her bag, signalled to Sadiq that she'd be five more minutes, then hurried back inside, very edgy from her performance.

'What is it?' she asked.

'Taz,' Adam began, and then broke off, regarding her with a sad smile. 'You can't be seen with me, even like that?'

'I promised. That's why I'm still here,' she said, her dark eyes downcast.

'I thought it was you avoiding me.'

'It is me!'

'We could have been friends.'

'We are,' she said and meant it, but there was an awkward pause. 'My mum's still very bitter, you know. About Astler's.'

'She's got it all wrong. And things are getting worse.'

'I don't think so,' Mumtaz said, loyal to her mother. 'Anyway, it's nothing to do with you.'

'But we're responsible. Isn't that what your short story meant?'

Mumtaz didn't reply. She was no longer so sure of her answers.

'Well, good luck for next week. And good luck with the law.'

'Thanks,' Mumtaz said. 'Same to you,' and, for the second time that afternoon, hurried down the steps towards the main gate where Sadiq sat in the car. She slowed down only slightly as she spotted Meera at the gate.

'Tell Hafiz I waited,' Meera whispered as she went by.

Mumtaz responded fractionally with a nod of her head and a smile, then got into the car.

'Forgot my pencil-case, sorry,' she told her father as she adjusted her veil.

'Who's that girl?' he asked.

'Oh, she comes to the youth club. Remember? Her mother teaches a cooking class.'

Sadiq stopped at the local grocery so Mumtaz could do the week's shopping. Together they loaded the boot of the car, then in silence drove the few remaining blocks home, where Rashid was waiting with cartons of clothing piled round him.

'I'll have the car loaded in fifteen minutes, boss,' Rashid told his father.

'I'm nobody's boss,' Sadiq said gloomily. He spent a great

deal of his time carting Shehnaaz's products around, and was, Mumtaz knew, begining to feel badgered.

'Thank you, Abagee.' Mumtaz bowed her head with respect, receiving for an answer a smile of love.

The front room of the Sattars' house was now almost entirely occupied by an imposing noisy knitting machine that was turning out a brightly patterned weft of yellow and black material at the rate of one foot every ten minutes. The back room had been turned into a sewing room. There were three large tables against the walls, a woman working at each. One cut patterns, another acted as lock-stitch machinist, whilst the last was an overlocker. Shehnaaz herself put the final trim to the clothing at the end of her production line. Furiously busy with their current output of v-neck sweaters, the women barely acknowledged Mumtaz as she went through to the cluttered kitchen.

'You're late,' Shehnaaz said, following her daughter.

'Sorry. We had Shakespeare.'

'But you did him last year.'

'It was revision. We did the play out loud in class. I had the best part.'

Mumtaz felt a warm glow as she remembered Portia's speech. Mrs Gordon had been quite impressed with her and said so.

'Acting?' Shehnaaz looked at her daughter with a raised brow. It was not a profession Muslims cared for.

'There's a production of *Merchant of Venice* in town next week. Mrs Gordon is arranging a last class outing.'

'Did you remember to pick up those wage slips?' Shehnaaz, worried about business, hardly listened to Mumtaz as she automatically put away the groceries.

'I forgot.'

'But I reminded you several times –' Shehnaaz said, exasperated. 'Well, use notebook paper then. And mark up those price tags. Your brothers are leaving early and they'll need packed food, too.'

Mumtaz simply nodded at these instructions, humiliated at having forgotten the wage slips. She was getting so scatty with all the revision. And then just the fact that college would soon be all over. She felt as though she hadn't experienced it to the full; knew she hadn't.

'Where's Hafiz?' she asked her mother, suddenly remembering Meera's message.

'Resting. Don't bother him. The women are hungry, please start the meal.'

'Amagee – my prayers,' Mumtaz said, giving her mother a searching look. She never let herself stop any more and expected everyone to sail along with her.

'Try not to be too long, then,' Shehnaaz said, barely suppressing her impatience. 'We're hungry.'

Mumtaz found Hafiz tucked up in bed reading a computer manual and looking exhausted and unhappy. She felt his recent ill-health could be directly attributed to the fact that school was ending, and he knew he must come to some kind of decision about Meera. Meera, for her part, loved Hafiz and had confided to Mumtaz that she would convert from Hinduism to Islam. Surely, that should be enough to satisfy Sadiq. But Hafiz was too frightened to broach the subject of his involvement with Meera to himself, let alone his parents.

'How are you feeling?' Mumtaz asked.

'Same,' he replied, continuing to leaf through the magazine.

'Meera was waiting for you this afternoon.'

Hafiz winced and continued staring at the page in front of him.

'Hafiz, you must make up your mind,' Mumtaz said, giving him an imploring look. 'It's not just your life that's in question. There is Meera's too.'

'I know, I know,' her brother replied, slumping deeper into the bed. 'Just let me rest now. Please.'

Mumtaz withdrew, suppressing a desire to seize Hafiz by the shoulders and shake some sense into him. But what sense? What would she do? What had she done? Perhaps her friendship with Adam could have grown into something more if she'd been willing to compromise the Muslim side of herself.

Time alone, reciting her prayers, calmed Mumtaz. Still peaceful, she prepared the meal for the women, and when Sadiq arrived home to find them all eating amidst the debris of the day's work, she tried to fetch him a plate. But, weary and upset, he left before she returned with his food.

The angry whirring of the knitting machine set the tone for the rest of the evening. Sadiq didn't come home until after the workers had left. Mumtaz was in the kitchen washing up and Shehnaaz was in the work room sweeping up scraps.

'They are calling me a battered husband,' Sadiq told his wife without preamble. 'I will not be mocked.'

'We're in profit. You wait and see how quickly they come round.'

'No. I will not be your errand boy or stand on market corners for you.'

'Listen. Things will calm down. I will get the business better organized.' Shehnaaz tried to placate him.

'No, you listen. You tried and you've done well, but it's not working. Your home is in ruins. Your family is falling apart.'

Mumtaz clattered a few dishes in the kitchen, trying to remind them that she was there, but they were oblivious of her.

'What are you trying to prove?' Sadiq asked.

'That I can do it! That we don't need the Astlers!'

'But look what's become of our home. Our life together.'

'I need a different place to work, that's all, proper premises. I need capital.'

'Capital? And where are you going for that?'

'Ask Tariq; ask your brother,' Shehnaaz said.

Sadiq was shocked into silence for a moment.

'Please – Tariq once said –'

'No!' Sadiq raised his voice. 'You are going too far!'

Shehnaaz went back to her sweeping and then when she had finished, she handed Sadiq an envelope.

'This arrived today for Mumtaz from Leicester University.'

Mumtaz watched from the kitchen as her mother gave Sadiq the letter. She could see his irritation replaced by a look of pride and triumph.

'Oh, yes, I thought that would make you happy,' Shehnaaz said, bitterly. 'And is it so different from my wanting to run a proper business?'

Sadiq made no reply, unable to deny the logic of her argument. But here was Mumtaz fulfilling her Muslim duties while his wife was daily changing into a western activist businesswoman.

'If you had only bothered to really lead this family, we'd be all right now,' Shehnaaz sighed.

Mumtaz knocked hesitantly on the open door, and her parents stared up at her, shocked. She knew she was breaking the rule by interrupting them, but the letter was addressed to her.

'I'm sorry, but Hafiz said a letter came for me,' she said, dutiful but determined.

Sadiq hesitated, then handed it to her, and left the house. He needed the solitude of the mosque to put his thoughts in order, or simply to pray. He wandered down Highfield Street, his head bowed, torn between despair for his home and pleasure at Mumtaz's success

'Excuse me,' a voice came out of the darkness as he was passing the synagogue, quickly revealing its owner as old Joe Astler holding out a bunch of keys.

'My eyes aren't so good,' Joe explained, jangling the keys. 'You couldn't find the right one, could you, please?'

Sadiq stared, but it was obvious that Joe didn't recognize him. 'Of course,' he said, and quickly opened the door.

'Thank you, thank you, my friend,' Joe said, smiling wearily. 'Many knock, but few are admitted, eh?'

'God opens to all believers,' Sadiq replied, holding the door open for the older man. He then went round the corner to the mosque, wondering if he and Joe would be praying for the same things. How would it all end?


Adam and Jackie did their revising every evening together in a relatively quiet corner of a pub down the road from the college. They had grown used to the background of loud music, and louder voices over the music, and every night they bent their heads together over their notes and books. Tonight, however, Adam noticed Jackie couldn't quite seem to settle down. She'd already had two halves of lager, and was drumming her pencil on the table in time to the music, her books still unopened.

'Funny to think this'll all be over,' she said. 'It will, won't it?'

'Not necessarily,' Adam said, taking her hand.

'With you swanning it in sunny Cambridge?'

Adam sighed. All this talk about Cambridge. It was bad enough that his family had already decided he was going there, and now Jackie. He still didn't know what he wanted to do. Leicester was not so bad. Joe certainly wasn't getting any younger, and there was Jackie.

'Might just stop here,' he said, leaning over the table to kiss her.

'Great. Have fun.' Jackie gave him a cynical little smile.

'Well, aren't you having fun? Anyway, I thought you were going to the Polytechnic.'

'Stuff the tech,' Jackie said, with the shrug that usually preceded her tough act. 'That place won't get me a job. I'm going back to London. I'll live with my dad.'

'Your "violent" dad?' Adam spoke as casually as she did, refusing to let her rile him.

'Well, he's better than Mum's sex-crazed boyfriend.'

'Has he been giving you a hard time?' Adam could no longer conceal his concern. Jackie rarely discussed her home life yet he often saw the stress of it reflected in her volatile behaviour.

'Just don't take me for granted,' she was saying, calmer now.

'I don't, do I?' Adam asked, as he finished his drink.

'Yes. Hasn't it ever occurred to you to ask me to your home? To meet your family? We've been together for nearly two years.'

'You never wanted to,' he protested. 'I did ask you in the beginning and you just raved on about families.'

'Yeah, once, and then you never asked again.'

'But you said you didn't like the whole concept of the family.'

'Mine,' Jackie interrupted. 'Just mine, that's all.'

Adam digested this change of attitude as he went to the bar to get them each another lager.

'I'll take you to meet my family tonight, if you like,' he told Jackie. 'They're having a party for Joe. Astler's has been in business for forty years today.'

'Tonight?' Briefly Jackie hesitated, and then with an odd smile that was both cavalier and grateful, she said, 'Right. Why not?'

Adam had excused himself from the surprise party his aunt Alex had cooked up on the grounds of having examination pressure. He felt shaky at the prospect of taking Jackie to meet them all without any preparation, but at least it got the whole thing over and done with in one go. If he delayed Jackie might think he was stalling, that he was uncertain, or worse, ashamed of her . . .

'So let's go then,' he said.

They took a cab to Joe's house in Oadby, and Adam let them into the house with his set of keys. The elegant hallway was empty, silent and only half-lit.

'Sure you've got the right night?' Jackie whispered, her eyes widening to take in the antiques and paintings.

Puzzled, and feeling suddenly a bit drunk, Adam opened the living-room door and switched on the lights. Thirty assorted guests grouped around a '40 Years in Business' banner began to sing 'For He's a Jolly Good Fellow', and Adam reeled back, grinning.

'Hi. Thought we'd drop by and join the fun,' Adam said, as the singing quickly petered out.

'I thought you were revising,' Sarah said.

'We got bored. And I wanted to introduce Jackie to the family. This is Jackie. My mother, Sarah.'

'How do you do?' Jackie said, pretending not to notice the sharp glance the woman gave her as Adam continued with the introductions.

'Phil, my dad, and Aunt Alex.'

'I'm pleased to meet you,' Jackie said, her too smooth manner a giveaway of her nervousness.

'Where's Joe, then?' Adam asked. 'Working late?'

Phil nodded. 'Can I get you a drink?'

Jackie and Adam both replied simultaneously, he saying yes and Jackie saying no, though she immediately amended this to: 'A vodka and lime, please.'

Adam was surprised. They never drank spirits, but this, of course, was Jackie being 'grown-up'. 'Er, the same for me,' he told his father and then: 'We're at college together,' he told Alex and Sarah, who seemed to be waiting for some such explanation.

'You model for him, don't you?' Alex said to Jackie.

'Yes, nude mostly.'

There was a stunned silence. 'I meant Adam's costume designs. At least the model resembles you.'

Sarah turned to Adam. 'You never told me. No wonder you've been so busy.' It wasn't clear if she meant Jackie or his designs, but he suspected she meant both. It surprised him that Sarah should seem so thrown by Jackie.

'You're a social worker, aren't you?' Jackie was asking her.

Sarah nodded with a wary look.

'My mum's in local government. She's an economist.'

'Keynes or Friedman?' Sarah asked.

'Karl Marx.'

'Hey, there's Joe's car,' Adam said, grateful to be able to put an end to Jackie's conversation. Her back was up and there was no telling what direction she'd fly off in when she was in a mood like this.

'Come on, everyone. Lights, hiding places,' Alex said, as the front door opened.

'Alex – run me a bath,' Joe shouted from the hall, and his footsteps could be heard going upstairs.

'What about supper, Dad?' Alex called.

'Too tired. I'm going to bed.'

Typical, typical, Adam was thinking. Joe probably knew what was going on and was doing this to be difficult. He switched the lights back on.

'You'll have to get him down here,' Phil said, but Adam was hurrying after Jackie who had suddenly stalked off to the front door.

'Where are you going?'

'I won't be bloody patronized!' she said, proud but clearly hurting.

'Just meet Joe, okay? Please, you'll love him,' Adam said, putting his arm round her.

The door was open to Joe's inner sanctum, a big room that was over-furnished, over-curtained, and heavy with memorabilia. Joe sat at his dressing-table, tired, his eyes shut, clinging to this moment's quiet.

'Opa,' Adam called, rapping gently on the door.

'Adam, my dear boy. Come in. And who is this?' he said, smiling warmly at Jackie.

'This is Jackie, a friend of mine from school. My grand-father, Joe.'

'Forgive me, if I don't rise.'

Jackie nodded, and Adam saw that she was charmed by the old man whose warmth had dissolved her icy anger.

'Look,' he said, remembering the guests downstairs, 'I've got to tell you. There is a surprise party for you downstairs.'

'I know. Why else would I go without my drink?'

'Bad day?' Adam asked sympathetically.

'Rotten. My workers do not love me. I wish someone could tell me why.' Joe shook his head, and turned to Jackie. 'What about you, young lady. Do you understand business?'

'Well, I'm doing business studies.'

'Maybe you could give me some tips. Come and see me.'

'I'd love to.'

'Bring your friend along,' Joe added pointedly. 'I never see him any more.'

'It's just because of the exams,' Adam said, colouring with guilt at his grandfather's half-teasing reproach.

But Joe was already on a different tack. 'So, Jackie, you like my grandson?'

'Yeah,' she said, smiling.

The old man pinched her cheek. 'So do I,' he said, and Adam felt a warmth come over him, having these two people close and loving. Why then did he feel that some shadow of uncertainty was hovering over the three of them? Why had he waited until now to introduce Jackie to Joe? It felt like the ending rather than the beginning. But no, that was just because of school, Adam told himself, and, draping an arm round each of them, he more or less led them down to the party.

Joe was unexpectedly gracious about his 'surprise' party. In fact, he amazed Adam by putting on an act of the utmost astonishment. He even made a stab at circulating and exchanging pleasantries with the guests, but after about half an hour or so he slipped away with his drink. Things at the mill were already getting to him. Adam thought suddenly of the stories he and Mumtaz had written, and wished they could have done some good.

After the party, Adam took Jackie back home with him. He could feel resistance from his parents, though he didn't entirely understand it. How could ex-hippies be shocked by their grown son sleeping with a girl?

'Would you like to phone home now?' Sarah asked Jackie, as they all trooped into the living-room.

'No sweat. I haven't really got one. They don't worry.'

Sarah absorbed this without a word but she did give Adam a penetrating look.

'I'll get a sleeping bag,' Phil said.

'We can share my room,' Adam told him.

'Then I'll show Jackie around,' Phil said hospitably, though Adam knew he was leaving Sarah to deal with the situation.

'How long have you been sleeping together?' his mother asked, as soon as the others had left the room.

'A year or more. Why?'

'Where?'

Adam didn't answer.

'Why haven't you told us?'

Adam couldn't tell if she was simply hurt, or shocked, or what.

'You didn't ask.'

'Did you think we'd object?'

'Mum, I didn't really figure Jackie for your first choice – no.'

'You should have trusted us,' Sarah said firmly.

'I was trying to keep things separate. Like you do. Only now I can't any longer.'

'You'd better go up,' Phil said, coming into the room. 'I think she needs you.'

Mumtaz could see, as the final weeks of college drew on, that Hafiz ailed in direct proportion to the news that came of Meera. When she told him that Meera's parents were arranging a marriage for her, he seemed to rally and grow stronger, emboldened. But this strength lasted only a few hours, and, still unable to confront their parents, he went back to bed.

Mumtaz meanwhile was having her own problems with Sadiq and Shehnaaz. Now that her mother's business was doing well, it was a full-time operation and required a whole staff. Although Sadiq had been proud and impressed that Leicester University was willing to accept Mumtaz, in the end he had withdrawn his support. Shehnaaz needed Mumtaz to help at home and with the business. There was no discussion: Sadiq simply stated these facts.

At first Mumtaz had been too shocked to respond and then instead of arguing her case, she found herself withdrawing from her family. She began to confide in Jackie and Meera, for the first time feeling a need for their support. She felt sorry for her father, and knew he was trying to make the best of a bad situation. Shehnaaz was really running the show, and doing a bloody good job, too, Mumtaz thought. What she couldn't understand, though, was why her mother's success should mean the end of Mumtaz's own struggle for success. She felt Sadiq's concern for her, yet it was as though his bad conscience kept him on every subject but her education.

'We sold all your mother's latest,' he told Mumtaz as he drove her to school. 'Cleethorpes.' He gave a derogatory snort.

'Ama's doing well.'

'She could do with a manager.' It was not the first time he had mentioned this.

'I think Mrs Gordon quite liked my Portia,' Mumtaz said, deliberately changing the subject. 'She said I'd make a good lawyer.'

'You know I don't like this acting business.'

'We were reading, that's all,' Mumtaz assured her father. She hesitated before getting out of the car, trying to decide whether or not to try to get through to him.

'I think I can manage three Bs,' she said, plunging ahead. Sadiq nodded, his head turned away.

'I've tried so hard to put things right. Make you proud of me again.'

'I must go –' Sadiq tried to stop her.

'I've done nothing but study. I've talked to no one. I've helped Ama, and performed my household duties.'

But all Sadiq said, quietly and sadly, was: 'You'll be late for your class.'

Mumtaz got out of the cab without another word. If Sadiq didn't see, there was nothing she could do. She fled from the car into the college and, blinded by tears, collided with Jackie.

'Come along, lovie. You could use a nice cuppa,' Jackie said at once, solicitous and oddly maternal.

'So no university. No law. And you really can't argue with him?' she said as they were on their second cups of tea.

'No. If I agree, he might change his mind. That's my only hope.'

'But you'll get your grant, and you could always get a part-time job.'

Mumtaz raised her head, her large brown eyes dry now. 'No,' she said, not yet ready to take the step of defying her parents' wishes.

'I would, if I had your brains.'

'He's my father,' she started to explain.

'Another good reason for doing your own thing,' Jackie broke in. 'My dad – he deserted us. Nobody owes anybody anything. Your life is your own.' She spoke with a conviction beyond her years, or so it seemed to Mumtaz, but from a different world.

'He wouldn't ever speak to me again. I couldn't live like that.'

'Must be hard being a Muslim.'

'No, it's really very easy. Or it was. I don't want to lose it.'

'Well, you needn't.'

'I would if I lost my family.'

'There are worse things.'

'Are there?'

'With folks like mine, definitely,' Jackie said, and they both laughed. 'But what's your father's gripe? I thought he was the one who let you come here.'

'He was. But now my mother's started a business. She wants me to help.'

'And you will? You'll just give up?'

Mumtaz nodded. There was nothing left to say; no other way that she could explain herself.

Later in the morning when she was working in the library, she was surprised to be joined by Adam. Without a word he put a hand on her shoulder and sat down next to her, his blue eyes filled with concern.

'Don't worry,' he said. 'Your father will come round.'

Mumtaz could feel the colour coming to her face. She stared at him in embarrassment and discomfort, his hand burning her shoulder.

'I must go,' she murmured, and raced off in a pique of anger to find Jackie.

'Why did you tell him?' she demanded. 'And what did you tell?'

'Well, everything, more or less.'

'How could you?'

'He's a friend of yours,' Jackie explained patiently. 'He cares about you. I thought he might cheer you up, the stupid git!'

By lunch-time, Mumtaz had regained her composure, and had numbed herself to her bleak future. She felt better for having spoken to Jackie. She still wished Adam hadn't been brought into it, but now that she had calmed down she saw that it hardly mattered. They would all be moving in different directions soon. At least Jackie and Adam would, while she stayed on in Leicester, working for her mother. Mumtaz paused in the middle of her *bhaji*, suddenly not hungry.

'University isn't everything,' Adam said, sitting down opposite her with his luncheon tray. He gave her an apologetic smile. 'Don't mind if I sit here, do you? Jackie told me I wasn't supposed to know you were upset and that I mortally offended you.'

'Look, I'm not going to university, okay?' Mumtaz said. 'There's really nothing to discuss.'

'I was talking about me, actually, when I said it wasn't everything. I was trying to ask your advice.'

Mumtaz waited, not certain whether or not to believe him.

'Joe's pushing seventy. I'm his only grandchild, and he wants me to take over.'

'But you've got your own life to lead. What about your art? That picture of Jackie in the gallery is brilliant.' Mumtaz blushed as Adam looked at her, thinking of his eyes on Jackie's breasts. How did he see her?

'Well, so have you got your own life to lead,' he was saying.

'It's different for me.'

'Why? Because you're a woman? You don't deserve a career? That's primitive.'

'My family comes first. It has nothing to do with sexism.'

'And my family doesn't? If I joined Astler's I could make my own designs.'

'You're too good for that place.'

'Oh, that's it. A firebrand just like your mother, eh?' Adam asked, and she couldn't tell if he was joking or serious.

'She worked at Astler's for five years,' Mumtaz said. 'She still has friends there who count on her.'

'Yeah, to make trouble by the look of things.'

'Adam, that's not fair,' Mumtaz said, wishing there were some way she and Adam could talk without it turning into a family feud.

'Hey, listen. I agree that the workers should have a union. With or without your mother,' Adam said. 'Anyway, if I stayed here, Astler's would be something for Jackie and me to build on.'

Mumtaz nodded, feeling a small pang at the thought of the two of them working for Joe, together, whilst she'd be in the opposite camp, alone.

The following afternoon Mumtaz left school early so that she could help Shehnaaz with the paperwork involved in her business. She had become inured to the loud clacking of the knitting machine, like the women working round her, and was studying while entering the numbers of finished garments in a log book.

'We should think about starting the dinner,' Shehnaaz began to say when there was a knock at the door. Her mother went to answer, and returned with Jackie.

Mumtaz stared at her friend in mute disbelief, then turned

to her mother, who seemed relatively unperturbed by the un-expected arrival.

Jackie smiled. 'Thought I'd drop in for a natter,' she said, a little shyly.

'How did you know where to come?' Mumtaz still couldn't get over her surprise, and wondered, fleetingly, where Adam was.

'Just asked around.'

'Oh, I see,' and collecting herself, Mumtaz said, 'Ama, this is Jackie – from college.'

Shehnaaz smiled. 'We were about to prepare dinner. Will you join us? Just some rice and curry.'

'Yeah, great, I'd love to,' Jackie replied, put at ease by the woman's gentle hospitality.

'This is Mrs Khan,' Mumtaz said, continuing with the introductions, 'Mrs Begg and Anji. We're all cousins.'

Jackie greeted each woman who continued stitching away industriously.

'Can I do anything?' she asked, turning to Mumtaz.

'My homework.'

'You've got to be kidding,' Jackie said, laughing, but the girls did discuss their assigned essay on *The Merchant of Venice* while Shehnaaz was in and out of the kitchen and sewing-room, putting the final touches to the two separate areas of her life.

'What's that monstrous machine out there do?' Jackie asked, over the loud clacking.

'It knits,' Mumtaz said, holding out one of the bright yellow patterned sweaters currently in production.

'Hey, very smart that is.'

'Put it on,' Mumtaz urged, along with the three cousins, who stopped their sewing to watch Jackie try on the fruit of their labours.

'Very nice,' Shehnaaz said, as she brought in the meal.

'She should model for us,' Mumtaz said.

Jackie went suddenly shy, and the colour rose in her cheeks. 'Oh, come on, Taz.'

'No, I mean it.'

'How much do you sell these for?' Jackie asked Shehnaaz.

'Three ninety-nine.'

'Fantastic. Can I buy it here?'

'No, it's a present,' Shehnaaz said, insisting until the embarrassed Jackie accepted her gift.

The reason for Jackie's unexpected visit became more evident as the evening wore on. Jackie was protesting at the decision to keep Mumtaz from continuing her education. She was touched that her friend would want to help her, but she couldn't help wondering if Adam had a hand in this plan.

'You should've seen the teacher's face,' Jackie was telling the women. '"Are you quite sure?" Mumtaz asks, "because it says here" –'

The audience laughed appreciatively.

'Well, it all comes down to brains, doesn't it?' Jackie went on. 'Mumtaz has got more than her share. She's got a real future ahead of her as a lawyer, everybody thinks so.'

Noting her mother's troubled expression, Mumtaz glared across the table at Jackie.

'That sweater is a real knock-out, Mrs Sattar. How do you make it?' Jackie quickly changed the subject, and to Mumtaz's relief did not say anything more on her behalf. She simply helped clear away the dinner things, thanked Shehnaaz, and went to meet Adam at Astler's.

And how lucky, Mumtaz thought, that her mother hadn't heard where Jackie was off to. Any association with Joe Astler made one suspect in Shehnaaz's eyes. But even more fortunate was the timing of Jackie's departure, for not five minutes later one of her mother's friends from the factory came bolting into the sewing-room, crying curses down on Adam's grandfather.

'Calm yourself,' Shehnaaz said, 'and tell me how it went.'

'He yelled at me,' the woman said, her thin, haggard face in complete contrast to her full pregnancy. 'I just couldn't face the others afterwards, so I left.'

'He can't hold out,' Shehnaaz assured her. 'Not if you all stand together.'

The woman shrugged. 'You couldn't take me on here, could you?'

There was an awkward silence, and then Shehnaaz slowly shook her head. 'I haven't the room or the work.'

The woman rose and went to the door, her dignity returned.

'You are right, Shehnaaz. We must stand together. We must not let him treat us like so much dirt beneath his feet.'

Mumtaz was both frightened and shocked by the approval she saw on Shehnaaz's face as she escorted the woman to the door. Why, she wondered, couldn't her mother back off from Astler's and stick to her own business? And yet she could understand that Shehnaaz found this hard to do. The insult she experienced at the factory had unleashed other resentments over other injustices. Nonetheless, she wished Shehnaaz could forget Joe Astler. And, even more, she wished that she could rid herself of thoughts about his grandson. Mumtaz sighed aloud, thinking that Jackie's friendliness, instead of easing the situation, was making it more complex.

On Saturday, Jackie turned up at the Sattars once again, and asked Shehnaaz to let Mumtaz off work for a bit of a ramble. Sadiq and the boys were out for the day delivering the clothes, and, as Mumtaz had caught up with all the business ledgers, with only the most perfunctory hesitation and deliberations Shehnaaz gave her permission.

As the two girls walked down Highfield Street, Jackie suddenly grabbed Mumtaz's arm and made a dash for the bus across the road.

'I thought you said a little ramble,' Mumtaz complained, once they had got on.

Jackie was fishing around in her bag. 'Here,' she said, handing Mumtaz a bundle of clothing.

'What's this?'

'What's it look like? A bathing suit, of course. I'm taking you swimming,' Jackie declared triumphantly. 'It's a beautiful day, and we're going swimming.'

'Oh, Jackie!' Mumtaz protested. 'I can't swim!'

'I'll teach you —'

'I can't wear this,' Mumtaz went on, holding out the skimpy black leotard.

'What's wrong with it? It's a bloody fortress. I wouldn't be seen dead in it.'

'I'm not allowed to take my clothes off!'

'Please, just for once in your life be bad. For me? Please? I don't want to be alone today.'

There was such a look of entreaty in Jackie's blue eyes, and she stated her needs so simply, that Mumtaz knew she wouldn't, couldn't refuse her.

In the women's changing room, she kept close to Jackie's side. The noise, the bustle and the exposed flesh in this vast public place made her terribly nervous. As did the possibility of being recognized here. She thought of Sadiq and felt the shame of what she was doing, but it was too late now. She put on the skimpy suit and then covered herself with the towel.

'I'm ready.'

'Good girl,' Jackie said. She was unusually quiet as she finished changing into a startlingly small pink bikini, tied her hair in a top-knot, and led Mumtaz out to the big blue-tiled kidney-shaped pool. Something about the scene made Mumtaz think of a desecrated mosque. She shuddered and Jackie put a protective arm round her as they walked down to the shallow end.

'Come on,' she said. 'It's warmer once you're in.'

Mumtaz started down the steps, still wearing her towel.

'I think I'd better take that,' Jackie said with a grin, and Mumtaz thought how much easier everything would be if she could just wrap her head in the towel. Instead, she dropped into the water and stood hugging herself self-consciously as she looked round at her fellow bathers, surprised to find that no one was paying her the slightest attention.

'I mustn't get my hair wet,' she said, backing away as Jackie came alongside her, splashing furiously.

'There's a drier. It's no fun swimming unless you get wet.'

They both laughed and Jackie spent the next hour teaching her the basics of swimming, opening up a new world of purely tactile delights. She dipped in and out of the warm water; floated, floundered, flailed; and feeling, for the first time in many months, carefree and refreshed, allowed herself to forget the rules she was breaking.

'Thanks for bringing me here,' she said impulsively to Jackie.

'Thanks for coming.'

'You never did say what inspired this outing.'

'I wanted to swim. I'm pregnant,' Jackie replied in the same casual tone.

Mumtaz stared at her, speechless, and then turned away; the side of the pool seeming miles distant. She couldn't understand why Jackie was telling her this. What had it to do with her? Suddenly Mumtaz longed for the security of her room, her prayer shawl and the Koran verses.

'Come on. You're cold, ' Jackie said, solicitous as ever.

They went to the changing rooms where Mumtaz sat shivering under a towel while Jackie combed out her hair, and talked. Slowly Mumtaz began to understand how closely her life was intertwined with Jackie's – and how much she cared.

'Don't you remember that first term? Those fights we had?' Jackie was saying. 'You made me feel like a slut. You were so virtuous and proper.' She paused. 'I had never been with a bloke before Adam. It was like you were daring me to.'

'You can't blame me!'

'I'm not. It was great,' she hesitated again. 'But I knew you wanted him, too.'

Mumtaz drew away abruptly, and started dressing. She didn't like the direction of the talk. Had she wanted Adam? She didn't know; she wasn't familiar with that kind of desire.

'There are much more important things to talk about.' Mumtaz's shock, the inner turmoil brought on by Jackie's news subsided, and she felt only the gravest concern for her friend. 'What are you going to do?'

'I dunno.' Jackie sounded weary now. 'What do you think is best?'

'Have you told your mother?'

Jackie shook her head. 'She'll want none of it. Same thing happened to her.'

Mumtaz hesitated. 'And Adam? What does he think?'

Jackie tilted her chin, a stubborn look chilling her blue eyes. 'I'm not going to get in his way.'

Mumtaz was taken aback by her vehemence. 'But Adam has a right to share in your decision.'

'No, he hasn't,' Jackie argued. 'It's mine – ours if you like.'

Mumtaz leaned back against the sink and gave Jackie a long, searching look. It was such a curious thing for her to say, but more curious yet was that in her heart she understood what Jackie meant.

Adam was so distracted by the problems Joe was having at the factory that Jackie's mood swings didn't seem any stranger than usual. She was a temperamental, highly-strung girl, always had been, and he knew that now she was trying to accustom herself to the uncertainty of the future; as indeed he was. He tried to placate her as best he could, while struggling to come to a few decisions of his own. Should he go to university or should he stay with Joe? When he had spoken to Mumtaz, he'd caught a glimpse of an exciting future in, and beyond, university. But somehow his enthusiasm had faded as soon as Mumtaz had gone, leaving in its place an uncertainty that at its worst was like a void. The only way he knew to fill this emptiness was with Jackie. And being with her did, undeniably, bring him comfort.

It was because he wanted to make some kind of reciprocative gesture, to reassure Jackie as she did him, that he insisted she go to the factory so that Joe could show her around and maybe, Adam thought, offer her a summer job. Jackie had been delighted at the invitation, though she shrugged off the likelihood of Joe wanting to employ her.

'This here is all double-knit – t-shirts, sportswear,' Joe was saying, as he took Jackie on a tour of the fabrics section of the factory, a huge room filled with whirring, clanking, computer-operated machines.

'Where do you flog it all?' Jackie asked.

'Aha – Europe, America, Israel –'

'How many shifts do you run?' Jackie asked, and Adam could see how pleased his grandfather was at her intelligent questioning.

'Round the clock,' Joe said. 'There's a five-year waiting list on these machines. That's the state of British industry.'

He opened a sliding door that led them into a hot crowded room that seemed archaic in comparison with the smooth-running production line they'd just left.

'This is the jeans section,' he said, and as they walked through the assembly line, Adam was aware of the hostile glances from the workers. As for the foreman, with his small malevolent eyes, he was standing in his usual place watching his crew. There was definitely something very SS about the guy and Adam couldn't understand how Joe could abide such a Nazi-like presence in his business. Joe quickened his pace, as if he too were aware of the tension in the room, and they hurried on through to the office.

'The jeans I keep for old times' sake,' Joe told Jackie, 'because that's where I started.'

'Adam's got some good new designs,' Jackie said as Adam hung back, embarrassed.

'Are they really good?'

'They're great,' Jackie said, undoing Adam's portfolio. 'Kids will fight for them.'

'Not bad, not bad at all,' Joe said, studying the sketches. 'Forms a little loose but we'll be able to fix that.' He smiled over at Adam, his blue eyes twinkling. 'Designer and Manager. How does that sound?'

'Why not?' Adam said, knowing his mother would have about fifty reasons why not.

'Heard the one about the dog with two tails –' Joe asked merrily.

Adam was thinking that might just be one of his mother's objections, when Alex came in to say there was a deputation of workers waiting to see Joe. Adam wanted to stay and face them with his grandfather, but Joe insisted he take Jackie home.

'Is that a way to treat a beautiful young woman? Take her for tea and drive her home.' he instructed.

'Okay, right,' Adam said, but he remained preoccupied for the rest of the afternoon, his thoughts on the factory. Joe really needed his support there. And some changes must be made. Maybe Mumtaz's mother had started off with a rightful gripe, but now things were really getting out of hand. Too bad he couldn't talk to Mumtaz about Astler's. She was so blindly loyal. Actually, he found it impossible to talk to her at all these days. It was almost as though the friendlier she got with Jackie, the further she drifted away from him.

'Have I mortally offended Mumtaz again? And how this time?' he asked Jackie, thinking of yesterday morning. She had all but run in the opposite direction when she saw him in the corridor.

'What did she say?' Jackie asked, and Adam, sensing at once that she was on the alert, wished he'd never brought it up.

'Nothing. She didn't say anything.'

'I wouldn't worry, then.'

'Oh? About what? What has she told you about me?'

'Nothing –'

'Tell me!' He missed the days when Mumtaz had considered him her friend.

'She's the only one you can think of, isn't she?' Jackie exploded.

'Well, first you tell me her problems and say I should act like a friend, now you get mad if I ask. There's no way to please you!'

'Yes, there is –' Jackie spoke quietly now. 'Just love me.'

'I do,' Adam said. 'Let's pick up your books and study at my house. Maybe there'll be a chance for me to show you how much I love you.'

They spent a quiet time alone together until about six, when Phil turned up, got a drink and settled down on the floor against the sofa with a book, keeping one eye tuned in to Wogan on the box. An hour later Sarah blew in with a lavish Chinese take-away. Adam cleared the dining-room table of the mountain of books and papers they had been studying, while Jackie stood in the kitchen, nervously offering to help his mother. Sarah also felt awkward, and made no attempt to cover her surprise at finding Jackie there. She accepted her offer but left her hanging about while she caught up on the family news.

'Did you have a good day, darling?' Sarah called out into the room.

'Me or him?' Phil asked, briefly looking up from his book.

'Adam. Your days never change.'

'Oh, it wasn't a bad day. Was it, love?' Adam said, determined to include Jackie in the conversation.

'Mmn? Oh, yeah,' she replied, seizing on the support he was offering.

'When do your exams start?' Sarah asked.

'Next week, I think,' Jackie said, sounding vaguer and more unconcerned than Adam knew her to be. She had been swotting harder than him these past weeks, though she'd die if anyone knew it.

'Wednesday,' he told his mother. 'The Shakespeare paper. Then, Monday we have the theatre.'

'Right. That will be a lark,' Jackie said, brightening.

'Adam, I'm free next Saturday. What about driving down to Cambridge?' Sarah said, taking up her favourite subject of the moment. She was determined that Adam should go to Cambridge, and was using about as much subtlety as Joe did in the matter of the private crammer.

'There's time,' Adam replied, unwilling to be pressured or to commit himself, either way.

'It would be a nice break for you,' Sarah dug her heels in. 'Have you got any plans, Jackie?' she asked in a patronizing tone.

'Next weekend?'

'I mean after you finish college.'

'Well, depending on my results, of course,' Jackie began, and Adam could tell she was off in one of her inspired flights of fancy. Her eyes were wide with innocence and sincerity. But if Sarah knew she was fantasizing, she certainly didn't let on, Adam thought. She probably wasn't even listening.

'I have an uncle in Scotland,' Jackie was saying. 'He flies choppers for the oil rigs. He said he might train me.'

'Sounds fun,' Sarah remarked absently, putting plates and silverware on a tray.

'Mum figures it will keep me out of harm's way.'

'Absolutely.' Sarah carried the tray into the dining area. 'Sorry about this take-away. I got held up. Spot of trouble with a nice kid.'

'Really?' Jackie asked, with genuine interest.

'She needs looking after but we haven't the money. County Hall doesn't think we're worth it,' Sarah said bitterly.

'That's the Tories for you,' Jackie commiserated, and Adam was amazed to see a sudden rapport develop between the two.

'Exactly,' Sarah said, doling out the supper.

'What do you think of the expulsions?' Jackie asked.

'Militant?'

'Yes,' Jackie said. 'We do read the news occasionally.'

Sarah was contrite. 'They were necessary, unfortunately.'

'Just seem the wrong victims for socialists,' Jackie mused.

'My wife is a closet SDP,' Phil said, joining them at the table.

'Oh, belt up, Phil,'

'She holds out to annoy the family.' 'He winked at Jackie.

'Right. Everything's ready,' Sarah said, and turned to Phil, who recited a short blessing in Hebrew, which only the uncomprehending Jackie listened to.

'Do you have any religion, Jackie?' Sarah asked.

'I'm an ex-Christian, lapsed several times.'

Adam thought of Mumtaz and the strictures of her Muslim faith, and Jackie's antipathy for people who believed. Well, Sarah believed in things and Jackie seemed to have her fair share of convictions while talking to her.

Mumtaz sat on her bed, wrapped in her prayer shawl, with the Koran open, struggling with the unrest inside her. She hadn't known any peace since Jackie had told her she was pregnant. She hadn't been able to look at, let alone speak to, Adam. It was awful, his not knowing. Yet that was Jackie's business, not hers. She wished she could withdraw and remain in the safety of her Muslim domicile, but there was something between her and Jackie now that could not be severed. Whether it was the baby – 'our baby', Jackie had said – or love for Adam, or guilt, it didn't matter. All Mumtaz could do was give Jackie support, while she struggled to get on with her own life which had never seemed bleaker or more solitary.

'Are you ready, Mumtaz?' Sadiq had come into the room.

'Which verse?' he asked, as he sat down beside her and picked up the Koran.

'I'm sorry. I haven't learned it,' Mumtaz said, too tired to make excuses.

Sadiq looked at her for a moment, then supplied them himself. 'You've been very busy.'

'I've said my prayers.'

'Now this theatre visit,' but Mumtaz interrupted her father before he voiced his objections.

'I don't want to go,' she said. She couldn't imagine spending a night out with Jackie and Adam. Not now. Her feelings were too raw and undefined.

But Sadiq surprised her. 'You should go,' he said, and when Mumtaz didn't reply, he went on to speak of what was really troubling him.

'This new friend of yours, this girl –'

'Jackie.' Mumtaz knew her mother would have told Sadiq about Jackie's visits, and she wished he hadn't waited till now to speak of her.

'Did you ask her here?'

'No. She just came.'

'Do you know what she has to do with Astler's, then?'

'She's the grandson's girfriend,' Mumtaz said, and thought with a pang that Jackie was carrying the Astler heir.

'Does she know Hafiz?'

'Hafiz?' Mumtaz looked at her father. This was the last question she'd anticipated. 'I don't think so,' she replied, thinking how very long ago the market fight now seemed.

'Does she know that Hindu girl?'

'Just from college.' Mumtaz felt cornered by her guilt, almost claustrophobic, as though there were no longer space or air in her room. Had her parents found out about Meera and Hafiz? 'Why do you ask?'

'A social worker came round to the house this morning to ask why Rashid is operating the market stall alone. When your mother explained he was never alone, that his elder brother was working with him, the woman said this was not so. There have been complaints about the boy being left for hours on his own, while Hafiz wanders about with a girl.'

Mumtaz was silent.

'Hafiz has let the whole family down by not fulfilling his god-given responsibilities,' Sadiq said in a morose voice, and Mumtaz thought that she, too, was guilty for her brother's sins.

*

The first person Mumtaz saw at college the next morning was Meera. She was in her usual place, waiting by the school gates though Hafiz rarely came to the college any more.

'I can't go on lying,' Mumtaz told her.

'I know. The whole thing is making Hafiz ill too,' Meera said dejectedly.

'Not as ill as it will. I think my parents have guessed.'

'Oh, no! Please talk to him, please. He knows I would convert.'

'Have you spoken to your parents?' Mumtaz asked, reluctant to bear more messages, but unable to say no.

'Not till he tells his!'

'Are you girls all set for tonight?' Adam asked cheerfully, coming up to them. Mumtaz stared at him, her dark eyes bright with anger, though she didn't realize it.

'The theatre –' he said, puzzled by her look.

'You'll talk to him, okay?' Meera murmured and, gently touching Mumtaz's arm in supplication and farewell, she fled.

'Is she all right?' Adam asked.

'No. Are you?'

'Fine. Shouldn't I be?' he asked, wondering if something more had happened between her mother and Joe.

Mumtaz shook her head, knowing she shouldn't be having this conversation. 'I don't know.' She started to turn away but Adam stopped her.

'Taz –'

Her name spoken like that gave her a sharp pang.

'Taz, what is it?'

'Nothing. Please, I've got to go.'

'But what have I done?'

'Nothing,' she said. 'Nothing at all.'

Mumtaz arrived at the Haymarket Theatre later than the rest of her class. She'd taken her time getting ready, wishing she had a legitimate reason to back out, yet knowing that Meera would be expecting her and some word from Hafiz. But it was Meera who spoke first.

'My parents have found out,' she said, drawing Mumtaz aside.

'How?' she asked, peripherally aware of Adam holding Jackie round the waist as they stood looking at the posters in the lobby.

'Your parents,' Meera said.

Mumtaz felt frightened for her friend, and prayed Hafiz would do something now, lest Meera be forced to live in disgrace.

'Don't worry,' she said. 'It will be all right. I told Hafiz you'd be here.' She didn't add that he'd been despondent and frightened.

'I did it! I did it!' Candy shouted as she ran into the foyer. 'They want me!' She jumped up and down with excitement, hugging them all.

'Loughborough?' Adam asked.

'I was greased shit, man,' Candy replied. 'I'm going to bronze my running shoes.'

'Well, Jackie has some news too,' Adam said, and Mumtaz caught her breath. Was Adam taking Jackie's pregnancy so complacently?

'My grandfather wants her to work at the factory for the summer. She's going to shake out the cobwebs.'

Mumtaz glanced over at Jackie who had wandered away from Adam with a bemused expression.

'Hi. You made it. Good,' Adam said, coming over to Mumtaz. 'How are you?'

'How's Jackie?' she snapped back, unable to look him in the eye. She didn't recognize the sound of her own voice.

'Fine, I think. Why?'

Mumtaz watched him, one half of her heart for him, the other against. He should know about Jackie, and yet the knowledge would separate him irrevocably from her.

'What the hell is going on?' Adam asked.

'Ask her!'

'Christ, Taz!' he protested, aware of Jackie watching them from the corner of the foyer.

'It's not my choice,' Mumtaz replied and ran after Jackie into the theatre as the tannoy gave out the final call.

She hardly heard any of the first act, she was so aware of Jackie's taut, silent presence between her and Adam. It was as if she were a time bomb ready to go off. And go off she did as soon as the curtain came down, sprinting out of her seat and the theatre. Mumtaz rushed out of the theatre after her, into the neon lights and crowds of the Haymarket.

'Jackie!' she shouted 'Wait!'

'I preferred the way you played Portia,' was all Jackie said when Mumtaz, flushed and breathless, caught up with her.

'Listen, you've got to be sensible. We've got to talk about what's going on!'

'I'm all right. I just need some fresh air,' Jackie said, and abruptly strolled off. To a pub, no doubt, Mumtaz thought as Adam came running up to her.

'What is it, Taz? What have I done?' he asked, and once again she found she couldn't meet his eye. She wanted to, but if she did she'd be bound to tell him the truth.

'What?' he repeated. 'What the hell is going on?'

'Jackie is expecting your baby.' She blurted it out, and though she wanted to turn away and run, she took his hand.

'Oh, Christ, no!' Adam murmured, his whole future suddenly falling away. 'Come on, we'd better find her.'

They stopped in five pubs before they found Jackie in a dark corner of a bar, knocking back vodkas and lime. Mumtaz felt curiously numb and relieved now that Adam knew the truth, while he, for his part, was so shocked by the news that he hadn't followed it through. No further than finding Jackie.

'You didn't have to come,' she said, curling up in her corner of the bar.

'Are you okay?' Adam asked.

Jackie turned to Mumtaz. 'You told him. You just had to go and tell him, didn't you?'

'Isn't that what you wanted?' Mumtaz asked. 'Really?'

'Let's go, shall we?' Adam said, helping Jackie up.

'I'll ask them to phone for a taxi,' Mumtaz said, thinking they must be left alone now to talk about things that no longer concerned her.

Jackie was in no state for talking by the time Mumtaz returned, and the air only seemed to increase her drunkenness. Mumtaz and Adam had to prop her up as they waited for the cab, each lost in thought as they murmured assurances to Jackie. Adam now understood the new barrier that had arisen between him and Mumtaz, as if, he thought, religion and the factory disputes were not enough.

As for Mumtaz, she felt that their friendship, innocent though it had been, was definitely affected by Jackie's pregnancy; to her there seemed to be a rift as sharp and cold as the night air.

'Oh, Jesus,' Adam said in a flat, dispirited voice, and Mumtaz raised her eyes to see her father's cab approaching.

'Oh no, oh no,' she murmured to herself.

'Adam, just take me somewhere quiet,' Jackie was saying, oblivious to all that was going on.

Sadiq got out of the car and stared at them, his dark glare resting on Mumtaz for an extra moment.

'She's not well,' she told him, but he merely gave Jackie a look of contempt and opened the rear door.

'Where to?' he asked Adam.

'Astler's.'

'Oadby?' Sadiq asked.

'No —' Adam hesitated for a moment. 'Astler's Textiles, the factory.'

Sadiq nodded and motioned for Mumtaz to get in the front seat.

The drive to Astler's passed in silence though Mumtaz fancied she could feel every one of her father's disapproving thoughts. Sadiq didn't wait to let Adam pay him the fare, but swung the car back on to the road as soon as he and Jackie got out.

'She's my friend. I had to help,' Mumtaz began, determined to talk the incident through honestly and openly.

'She's a whore,' Sadiq replied, with distaste and scorn.

'How can you say that? You don't know her.' Mumtaz had hoped to find a judicious listener in her father. But Sadiq was too tense for reasonable talk. He swerved off the road and braked hard, then turned to Mumtaz.

'And you? What did you drink in there?'

'Nothing.'

'Why weren't you at the theatre?'

'I was. Until Jackie ran off upset. She's pregnant!' Mumtaz

hadn't meant to say it, but then she wasn't protecting either Jackie or herself by keeping the secret, only her father.

Sadiq frowned, regarding her closely. 'And you were helping them?'

'Well, you drove them,' Mumtaz retaliated. 'That's helping, too, isn't it?'

'You can choose better friends.'

'Maybe.' Mumtaz now knew she had never really had any friends until she came to college, and that she was recognizing them as friends too late, just as she was losing them.

'I don't know what's happening to this family,' Sadiq said. 'You, I'm sure, would be better off in Pakistan.'

Suddenly Mumtaz's filial obedience faltered. Loyalty and respect to the Sadiq of the past was one thing, but her father's attitude had surely changed these past months. More and more she felt he was punishing her for Shehnaaz's business, her behaviour.

'No, I don't agree,' she said calmly, opening the car door. 'But if what you mean is that you want me out of the house, I'll go.'

Her father reached out and grabbed her wrist, and stared at her speechless. Tears came into his eyes, and Mumtaz had to swallow hard to rid herself of her own.

'And I'm doing that interview at Leicester University,' she continued. 'I'll move out, get a part-time job. Whatever it takes. I'm not stopping now.'

Sadiq considered her for a moment, then slowly drove back on to the road. When he next spoke it was of Jackie, and his anger had been replaced with bitterness.

'What are her parents doing? She's only a child. What is she, Jewish? Christian?'

'I don't know. She's never mentioned religion,' Mumtaz said.

'She's nothing. Like all of them in this country. That's how you end up – nothing. Like this country.' Sadiq gave her a glance filled with anguish and remorse.

'At least it's home,' Mumtaz murmured, remembering the devastation of Kampala. 'And I am a Muslim, Abagee, and I love my country.'

But her father would not, or could not, speak of those things which mattered most to them both.

One storm of the evening only just settling, Mumtaz and Sadiq came home to find another that was raging still. In the rear living-room Shehnaaz sat sewing, furiously pulling material through the sewing machine as she screamed at Hafiz, who stood visibly shaking by the stairs.

'As though it is not bad enough that you've been involved with a Hindu girl who is despised even by her own people!' she said, her contempt growing more shrill as Hafiz tried to speak.

'Don't you dare interrupt me. In addition to this you allow false suspicion to fall on your sister and you leave your younger brother at the market to do all the work. Does the word honour mean anything to you?'

Hafiz nodded.

'Then you must realize what you've done. You can go now but don't mention computers in this house again. You're working for me.'

'Where have you been?' Shehnaaz greeted Mumtaz and Sadiq with a mixture of anger and relief.

'Theatre was late getting out,' Sadiq murmured.

'You knew about Hafiz, didn't you?' Shehnaaz said, rounding on Mumtaz as she started for the stairs.

'Enough now,' Sadiq told his wife, and as Mumtaz climbed the stairs she heard him say to her mother in a sad, weary voice, 'I don't recognize you any more.'

Mumtaz went straight to Hafiz's room, and closed the door behind her. 'What happened?' she asked.

'I told them.'

'And?'

'And no. She's not a Muslim.'

'But she'd convert. She's said so a number of times,' Mumtaz protested.

'"A Hindu never grasps one God. Think of your children, what will she teach them?"' Hafiz repeated his parents' words in a dull monotone.

Adam opened the door to the factory offices with his set of

keys. He heard the knitting machines in the adjoining warehouse, then the thirty-second bleeper for the burglar alarm which he rushed to switch off. Jackie tottered along after him, laughing hysterically to begin with, then crumpled on the floor, heaving with tears.

'Shit. Shit. Shit,' she moaned. 'Why do I mess everything up? You. Taz. Mum. Dad.'

Adam soothed her with loving words as he guided her upstairs to Joe's office.

'I didn't get pregnant on purpose,' Jackie continued, more sober now.

'It's all right,' Adam said vaguely, at a loss for words.

'But that's what you think?' she asked, watching him carefully.

'No,' he said and took her in his arms. 'I think I never want to leave you.' But Jackie wasn't ready to cuddle and be comforted.

'I'd have got an abortion if I hadn't been so scared.'

'You're sure about all this, aren't you?' he asked, in spite of himself.

'Would I make it up?' she bridled instantly.

'No – I didn't mean that – I meant have you done all the tests, and all that?' he finished lamely.

'Why did you bring me here?' she asked.

'Do you want to go home?'

'God, no,' Jackie replied.

'You haven't told your Mum?'

'God, no,' she repeated.

He hesitated. 'Do you feel okay enough to go to my house?'

'No,' Jackie shook her head, suddenly spent and vulnerable. 'Just hold me. Please don't let go of me,' she said, and as he gazed into her clear blue eyes, her lashes rimmed with tears, Adam knew that he could never let her go.

The next morning Joe and Alex found Adam and Jackie curled up in each other's arms, asleep on the office floor.

'Adam, your mother's been frantic,' Alex scolded, shaking his shoulder to wake him.

Joe found the spectacle amusing. 'When I said join the business, I didn't think you'd take me so literally.'

'I've decided,' Adam cut him short. 'I am joining.' He felt his future had been resolved for him, and he felt oddly relieved.

Jackie sat up, fully awake now. 'No, Adam. Not for me.'

'We're having a baby,' Adam told his grandfather and Alex. 'The business is expanding.'

That same evening there was a family conference. It was inevitable that there would be a clan gathering, Adam thought as he sat close beside Jackie in the Morrises' sitting-room. He was surprised that his grandfather was taking Jackie's pregnancy more calmly and happily than anyone else. He had expected some resistance to the fact that Jackie wasn't Jewish, but then, Joe and Jackie had got along fine from the beginning. His mother, however, was an entirely different matter. For a social worker who dealt with this sort of situation all the time, she seemed to have damn little understanding, not to mention compassion. Maybe what she was reacting to was history repeating itself, since it was her own pregnancy that had precipitated her marriage to Phil. Of course they had a good marriage, but Adam often wondered if they would have stayed together without him.

'It's not the answer, working at Astler's,' Sarah was saying now, as much to her father as her son.

'It's not just for the baby,' Adam said. 'I want to work for Astler's.'

'My dear boy,' Joe began, but Sarah quickly cut him off. 'Don't encourage him in this, Dad.'

'Who's encouraging him?' Joe threw up his hands, offended.

'I mean he's got his whole life ahead of him.'

'Meaning I don't?' Joe countered.

Sarah's green eyes flashed with anger. 'If you hadn't been on at him the whole time about the bloody factory –'

'Sarah, stop it,' Phil broke in.

'It was my bloody factory, young lady, that gave you your bloody education and fancy ideas,' Joe said, and Adam could see the meeting was taking the familiar turn, but Sarah then caught his eye and seemed to recollect herself.

'I didn't mean anything like that, Dad,' she said.

'Yes, but you want the same thing for him – a fancy university,' Joe sighed.

'Well, I don't,' Adam said, tired of hearing himself spoken of in the third person as if he wasn't there.

'Look, Cambridge is not like a private fee-paying school. There are some of the finest professors there,' Sarah entreated him, her voice low and calm now.

'It doesn't feel right,' Adam said. 'I want to stay here where I've got friends.'

'Why not?' Phil backed him up. 'He can go to Leicester. What's the problem there?'

Sarah didn't answer; she had turned her attention to Jackie.

'Are you sure you want this baby?'

Joe rose abruptly. 'No, I've had enough,' he told Sarah. 'I'm surprised at you, talking like this.'

'Well, it's her choice. It's her body, for Christ's sake.'

Joe shook his head. 'Christ, I hope, had nothing to do with it. Remember the *Torah*, Sarah.'

'Things change, Dad.'

'Beliefs don't,' Joe said, and Adam felt Jackie tremble beside him.

'Well, don't pretend you're pleased about it,' Sarah said in an accusatory tone.

'Adam's made an ass of himself; he's made a mess for Jackie. How could I be pleased?'

Adam put his arm round Jackie and pulled her closer.

'I think that's a foul thing to say,' Phil protested, but neither Joe nor Sarah paid him any attention.

'This is Adam's child,' Joe continued. 'It belongs to this family and I won't hear any talk of murdering it.'

'I'm sorry I'm not Jewish,' Jackie murmured, speaking for the first time, and the squeeze she gave Adam's arm told him she was also speaking to him.

Joe managed a smile. 'You are welcome in this family, my sweet. Just call him Joseph, *ja*?'

*

The college entrance that Wednesday was crowded with students pouring in to sit for the exams. Mumtaz walked through the lobby slowly, looking for Meera, and Jackie and Adam. She hadn't seen any of them the day before, and there had been so much friction at home since Hafiz was found out, that she couldn't do anything but fulfil her usual duties. Her heart was breaking for poor Hafiz, but she was more worried about Meera who had put so much more at risk in carrying on the secret liaison with a Muslim. As far as her parents were concerned, the matter was over, and Hafiz would recover in time. But Meera's reputation would be ruined now.

'Taz?' Jackie had suddenly appeared beside her, a duffel bag thrown over one shoulder.

Mumtaz regarded her over-bright smile suspiciously. 'What's wrong, Jackie? Why the bag?'

'I'm going away for a bit,' she said. 'Look after Adam for me, all right?'

Before Mumtaz could reply or catch her, Jackie had moved off through the crowd and disappeared. Mumtaz started to run after her, but the bell signalling the start of the exams immobilized her. She had to sit for the exams; her future was staked on her education.

Adam was at a desk several rows from Mumtaz. He gave her an encouraging smile, and craned his neck around, looking, she knew, for Jackie. She started to get up to go to him, but at a sign from the teacher, sat down again.

She watched, helpless, as Adam, with a worried frown, got up from his desk, left his papers and walked out of the room.

'Adam!' she called, jumping up and nearly following him. The other students stared up at Mumtaz from their papers, reminding her where and who she was. She sat down, for several minutes staring blankly at the empty page before her, fighting off tears.

Later, during the lunch break, she wandered through the college gallery and stood for a long while before Adam's portrait of Jackie. It seemed to her she was saying goodbye to them both.

# NOVEMBER, 1985

Mumtaz left the silent, mausoleum-like law faculty of Leicester University and walked across the grey concrete campus, the November wind blowing back her long dark hair which she now wore loose. In the last four months her appearance had altered in subtle ways, her hair, the make-up that elongated her wide dark eyes, and the simple yet elegantly-cut grey trouser suit. The amount of studying required for her university courses kept Mumtaz thoroughly occupied, and preoccupied, but the experience of being there had bolstered her self-confidence considerably. If she was lonely, she hadn't time to realize it; in fact it suited her that university studying was so serious and solitary.

Mumtaz had planned to stop at the bank but her thoughts, still on work, took her almost a block away before she remembered that she needed to get some cash. Hurriedly retracing her steps, she nearly collided with Adam who was coming out of the university bank, and her heart leapt to her throat, hardly allowing her to speak.

'Adam, what a surprise! How are you?' There was nothing perfunctory in her query.

In the four months since she had seen him, he had grown thinner. His face looked longer and haggard, and his blue jeans and corduroy jacket looked not so much fashionably casual, as worn and uncared for.

'Mumtaz—' He pronounced her name slowly, not from surprise because he had felt they were bound to meet, but from confusion. Now that she was actually there in front of him, he hardly knew what to say. She had changed so much; from an interesting-looking girl to an exotic beauty. 'I'm okay,' he said. 'And you?'

'Fine. Really fine. But what are you doing here?'

'Studying – occasionally.' He couldn't quite believe that she hadn't known.

'But I thought you were at Cambridge,' Mumtaz replied, wondering why, if he'd been here all these months, he had never tried to find her.

'I'm working at Astler's mostly, and then I come here for tutorials.'

'And Jackie? How is she?'

Adam didn't reply for a moment. Whenever anybody asked him this question, he felt suddenly winded, as though he had been given a blow in his solar plexus.

'I haven't seen her,' he finally said.

Mumtaz gave him a quick, searching look. 'What do you mean? What happened? Where is she?'

'I don't know,' he admitted, turning to go, but not before Mumtaz had seen the pain on his face.

'But the baby —' Mumtaz persisted, walking beside him to Joe's old Volvo. 'Please, I don't understand.'

Adam opened the car door, then turned abruptly on her. 'I said I don't know. Okay? Do you really think I didn't try and find her?' He got in the car and then, collecting himself, muttered an apology. 'Look, I'm sorry. It's been a rough time.'

Adam sped out of the car park, leaving a bewildered Mumtaz behind him. He hadn't wanted to leave so soon, but just the sight of her had brought on the confusion she had always evoked in him. And why hadn't she answered the letters he'd written? He had told her everything in his letters; how Jackie had left four months ago; how worried and guilty he was.

Adam was almost relieved to walk into the latest factory crisis, knowing it would at least take his mind off himself and Mumtaz. From a distance he could see Joe working himself up to fever pitch as he tried to talk 'calmly' to one of his Asian workers.

'What have I done?' he was saying. 'I train you for six months and you leave? You don't like me? You don't like the money? Please, tell me what it is with this place? You have a better offer, I'll match it. What is it? A Caribbean cruise with each two dozen pairs? What the hell is it?'

'*Sei ruhig mal*,' Alex murmured. She was standing beside Joe.

Adam, catching his aunt's eye, realized that another worker was leaving. Astler's would really be feeling the pinch soon if something weren't done.

'Oh, go on, get out,' Joe told the woman irritably. 'Don't waste any more of my time.'

'We've really got to stop this,' Adam said as soon as the worker had left.

'Any suggestions?' Joe's anger was deflated now, as was his entire bearing. It hurt Adam's heart to see him slumped like that, so old and defeated.

Adam took a deep breath. 'Yeah. How about letting in the union?'

'Does the union train for me? Does it find me skilled labour? No. It only protects the cretins I don't want. What for? I don't fire them anyway. I'm nice.'

'It would give the workers some discipline of their own devising.'

'Why do I have a foreman?' Joe asked.

'Get rid of him. He's the source of your problems.' Adam was, despite himself, getting worked up now. 'He's a bloody fascist. He's driving the women away.'

'He's been here for twenty years.'

'He's a racist and you can't afford him.'

'Then what? You'll do his job for me? No, just do me a favour now and write me an advert – Overseer. Skilled'. I'm not training again.'

'Then don't bother,' Alex said, looking up from her desk. 'There aren't any.'

'Three-and-a-half bloody million and I can't find workers. Who's to blame? Me?' Joe asked the ceiling, and Adam wondered how this on-going crisis at Astler's would end, and how he and Mumtaz would be affected by it.

Mumtaz hurried through a busy courtyard in the commercial area of Leicester, dodging vans and trolleys as she made her way to the three-storey brick building that would soon house Shehnaaz's factory. She tried to keep her mind on the family meeting that was about to take place, but her thoughts kept drifting back to her unexpected encounter with Adam. Poor Adam, and poor Jackie. Where had she gone? And why?

Mumtaz saw once again the scene at school, Jackie appearing with her bag slung over her shoulder. But Mumtaz had thought she was skipping out on the exams, leaving for a weekend or something. Yet she had told her to take care of Adam, hadn't she?

The breathless pleasure Mumtaz had felt at seeing Adam, the warm glow, was gone. In its place now was a nagging concern for Jackie, a sadness and vague guilt. She wished Adam had told her what had happened. Maybe she could have helped to find Jackie. But she had heard nothing from him. Or anyone else for that matter. She had worked hard through the summer, helping her mother with the business and preparing, at the same time, for university. Both her parents had become quite supportive after she had gone for the university interview.

Perhaps it was simply that the Sattars' family life had passed its crisis. Shehnaaz's business was doing well and Sadiq seemed to have finally accepted it. In fact, they were all meeting with Tariq today in the Imperial Typewriters building to discuss renting the premises.

Mumtaz passed several doors, each advertising one textile firm or another, and made her way to the top floor where an impressive assembly line of industrial sewing machines stood idle. She saw Tariq strolling up and down, inspecting the room, while her family stood nervously watching him.

'How much?' he finally asked Shehnaaz.

'Ninety thousand, to include the lease. Five years.'

'Is that long enough?' he asked.

'We'll be expanding by then,' Shehnaaz said with certainty.

'And you're sure you can staff this place?'

'Tomorrow,' Shehnaaz replied. 'Good people. Skilled and well trained. They're working for me and themselves.'

Tariq took a long moment to absorb this, then began his bargaining. 'Ninety thousand, in five years?'

'Give me two.'

'At fifteen per cent?'

'Tariq, we're family,' Shehnaaz moaned, but he turned his attention to Sadiq.

'So, brother, can you make this work?'

'Of course,' Sadiq replied, uneasy but loyal to Shehnaaz. 'It's working already.'

'So you'll be in charge?' Tariq asked, with a condescending smile. No matter that he had just haggled over the terms with Shehnaaz.

Sadiq glanced at his wife. 'Of course.'

'And this is the whizz-kid salesman.' Tariq gave Rashid a punch, and pretended not to have noticed Mumtaz's arrival.

'Rashid could sell sand to the Saudis.'

'And Hafiz?'

'Floor manager,' Shehnaaz answered firmly.

'What about the computers?' Tariq asked.

'They'll wait,' Shehnaaz replied.

'Till you take over ICI,' Tariq teased.

'Or Astler's, at least,' Rashid said, giving a nervous laugh.

Tariq turned to Mumtaz now, his curiosity obviously having got the better of his contempt, and Mumtaz was gratified to see both her parents move closer to her.

'Well, well, quite a young lady.'

'Hello, Tariq Uncle.'

'Welcome to your new home,' he said, making an expansive gesture, looking something like a dark furry spider hovering around a fly, Mumtaz thought with distaste.

'Is it settled then?'

'What's your job? International contracts?' Tariq asked, amused.

'You must have homework to do,' Shehnaaz told her daughter. 'Go home and start the rice. We'll be along later.'

'Nonsense,' Tariq interrupted. 'I'm taking you all out.'

'Have you signed anything?' Mumtaz's worried question was met with a deafening silence until Tariq roared with laughter.

'There speaks the lawyer. See what you've taken on, Sadiq?'

Later on, Shehnaaz half-heartedly chided Mumtaz. 'How could you speak to him like that?'

'If you're signing contracts you get them checked!' Mumtaz said, unrepentant.

'And in front of your father, too. You know what Tariq's like.'

'Yes, he's a crook,' Mumtaz replied.

'That's enough,' her mother warned.

'I thought you wanted me to help with the business.'

Shehnaaz paused for a moment. 'I've got the boys.'

'Before you didn't want me to study, and now –'

'I didn't like that sixth-form college, and the people you had to mix with,' Shehnaaz said, and Mumtaz knew she meant Adam. 'I didn't want to lose you.'

'You won't,' Mumtaz assured Shehnaaz, returning her unexpectedly tender embrace.

'Ever see any of them? Your friends from college?' Shehnaaz asked.

'No.' Mumtaz didn't want to lie, but she couldn't see the point in telling her mother she had met Adam again, not with the escalating Astler–Sattar feud. Besides, the awkwardness of their chance meeting didn't make others seem likely.

'Good. You can start again then. You've made your choice, just as I have,' Shehnaaz said, for the first time admitting to the similarity of their quests. 'Let's just show them we can do it.'

'We will,' Mumtaz said, touched to be one of her mother's sisterhood.

Several evenings later, Mumtaz stayed late at the university to work in the library and the reading section was very nearly empty by the time she finally put away her notes. As she started to pack up her briefcase she saw Adam slumped across one of the neighbouring cubicles, seemingly fast asleep. She recalled her conversation with Shehnaaz, the talk about making a fresh start, and wondered if she really wanted a new beginning. The emotions Adam had stirred in her again showed that perhaps she wasn't done with her original start, her original friends.

She turned back for one last glance at him from the doorway, wondering again about Jackie and what had happened between her and Adam; wondering, too, how she fitted into this odd equation.

It was a cold night and Mumtaz had every intention of hurrying home, yet she found herself, without volition of her own, waiting outside for the library stairwell lights to go out, and the last readers to emerge. From across the square, she saw Adam and she knew she must give in to the impulse to try to talk to him again. If he still seemed so alienated, why, then she would leave it at that. But it was awful seeing him dishevelled and drained, so unlike himself. If she could, she wanted to comfort him. Just as, in the old days, he had always tried to help her.

'Hello, Adam.'

'Taz. What are you doing here?' he said, startled to find her waiting patiently by his car.

'I was in the library, like you. I thought maybe we could talk, about Jackie.'

'I've already told you everything I know,' he said wearily, 'which is absolutely nothing. I've looked everywhere for her.'

'You saw her mother?'

'She doesn't know anything. And all her father would tell me was that she'd left London and that she didn't want to see me.'

'But the baby?'

'I wish I knew. I suppose she – got rid of it.'

He turned from her, and fumbled trying to get the car key in the lock. His hands were shaking and his head ached. He didn't know why, but somehow everything hurt more, having Mumtaz so near. He swore abruptly, pounded his fists on the roof of the Volvo and broke down in harsh, rasping sobs.

Mumtaz gently took the keys from him and opened the door, bundled Adam into the car, got in beside him, and took him in her arms. It felt so natural an instinct, so right that it was some time before she became frightened of her own passion, even in this guise of consolation. Adam's sobs slowly subsided though he clung to her still, as if his very life depended on it.

'I think about her all the time. I think I can't have loved her enough,' he said in a muffled voice against her shoulder.

His warm breath on her neck made Mumtaz shiver. 'That's not true.'

'Maybe she didn't love me,' he said, knowing there would be relief in the pain if this were true.

'She did. She told me.'

Jackie hadn't told her in so many words, but there was no need. It was perfectly obvious.

'Told you everything, didn't she?' Adam said, and they both laughed, though neither could have explained why.

'God, I've missed you,' Adam said, tightening his arms around her.

'I've been here, you know.' It still puzzled her, and rankled, that he hadn't tried to get in touch.

'Then why didn't you answer my letters?' he asked hesitantly, shifting position slightly so that now she was cradled in his arms.

'What letters?'

'Letters telling you what had happened. And that I was staying here.'

'I never got your letters.' Mumtaz spoke slowly, gratified that he had written, and appalled to think her parents would go to such lengths.

'I thought maybe –' He didn't finish, but Mumtaz understood.

'You thought I was avoiding you.'

'Well, I thought maybe you had to. Listen, I've been feeling like such a shit altogether. I never blamed you.'

'Yes, you did,' she replied, understanding now Adam's restrained behaviour when they first met again.

'A bit, perhaps, but I won't do it again.' He smiled, and kissed her.

'Adam!' she objected, but she too was smiling as she removed herself from his arms.

'Sorry. I'll give you a lift home. It's okay, I finally got my licence. Had to. For the business.'

Mumtaz watched him as he put the car into reverse and backed out of the parking space, the firm jawline with its stubble of whiskers, the thoughtful blue eyes, and the mouth that still tried to smile. Yes, he was a full-grown man now.

'It's a company car,' he was saying. 'Speaking of the company, Joe's not very happy these days. Your mother is pinching our workforce. Couldn't get her to stop, could you?' he asked, only half-teasing.

Despite the reminder that the family feud was still between

them, they drove along in companionable silence, enjoying each other and being together. It made Mumtaz feel somehow disorientated; so much had happened in the past two years, but this special kinship to Adam had stayed the same, become more crystallized, if anything.

Adam pulled the car up to the curb. 'Can I walk with you?'

'No.' Mumtaz shook her head. Only now did she realize she was breaking all the rules she'd been accused of breaking in college.

'Will I see you tomorrow? Lunch-time. In the canteen?'

'Sure,' she told him, gathering her books together.

'Taz, are you okay?'

She smiled. 'I was just thinking of Jackie. The last thing she told me was to look after you.'

'And you are.'

'Goodnight.' Mumtaz leaned over and kissed him, before running into the night, and Adam had the ridiculous notion, the odd sensation that it was the first kiss he had ever been given.

Mumtaz was grateful for the distraction of the move. Her mother was at the new factory overseeing the unpacking while Sadiq and the boys delivered innumerable crates. Though Mumtaz had her hands full with household chores she couldn't keep her thoughts completely away from Adam. One thing was clear: he needed her now. For whatever reasons, Jackie had gone. She probably had decided to have an abortion, which meant Adam was really free; she no longer had that hold on him. And yet wasn't it that very hold which had given him strength? Without Jackie he seemed less confident. What had happened to that ease of his, that innate sense of well-being that used to be so infectious? But it was her own self, Mumtaz thought, that she should be analysing. Could she really still believe, after tonight, that it was only a deep friend-ship she felt for him? It took her a long time to settle down to her prayers and, even then, thoughts of lunching with Adam the next day got in the way. Rules no longer seemed to matter as long as she was with him again.

The canteen was noisy and crowded when they met for

lunch, but Adam found a relatively quiet table by the window where they settled down: she to her packed lunch, and he to a rather suspicious-looking salad. Mumtaz was amazed at how calm and natural she felt. The intensity of the night before had turned into something else, a sort of unspoken intimacy, as if they were already lovers.

'So how's Law?' Adam asked, needing to filter the current between them with everyday words.

Mumtaz half-smiled as she unwrapped her onion *bhaji*. 'Dull and difficult.'

'Think you'll stick it?'

'After all I went through to get here? Of course,' she said. 'But what about you? What happened with Cambridge?'

'I just didn't make it. Walking out of the A-levels didn't help much. But the fact was, I couldn't face leaving Leicester, just in case.'

For a second Jackie's image passed between them, and Mumtaz felt a chill, and a return of the old confusion. Adam, sensing the change, hurried on, 'Anyway, the Fine Art department here is really good. Except it shows up how very bad I am. Joe turned out some of my designs over the summer and I think we'll have to burn them soon.'

Mumtaz laughed with Adam, her heart full to see him like this again. The jokes, and the laughter that brought out the fine crinkles around his blue eyes.

'I love you,' he said softly, as though reading her thoughts. 'Well, you know that, don't you?'

'Oh, Adam.' These words were the only ones Mumtaz wanted to hear, but she could not dismiss Jackie from her mind. Again Adam replied to her unspoken thoughts.

'Yes, I love her, too,' he said. 'Only it's a different kind of love. With you it's like I always loved you, I mean before we even met.'

'I think I know what you mean but . . .'

'No, it's not a problem,' he interrupted, taking her hand and gazing into her dark, liquid eyes. 'Really it isn't, Taz.'

'Isn't it?' she asked sombrely, and then stopped herself. This was all too soon. 'I've got to be going now.'

Neither of them noticed as they threaded their way past the

crowded tables to the door, the girl who so haunted their thoughts. At the farthest table at the other end of the room sat Jackie, watching them both as she nibbled absently on a sandwich. When they left, she rose too, and followed them out. A series of emotions crossed her face as she watched them walk across the square arm in arm: relief, a wry amusement, and a profound wistfulness.

Jackie had a sort of windswept healthiness about her now. She carried her seven-month pregnancy well, neat and snug beneath a tight-fitting jacket, and moved with assurance, every now and then giving her taut stomach a loving rub as she wandered through the park and down to the canal where she and Adam used to come. She sat in their special spot on the riverbank, her eyes smarting from the winter cold, and skimmed stones over the water's top, a frown of uncertainty creasing her brow.

The afternoon light was beginning to fade, it would soon be evening, and still she had no place to stay. She must decide what to do next. That morning, as soon as she got back to Leicester, she had gone to her mother's house. It was a mistake, of course. Her mother had been too shocked at seeing her, and her belly, even to speak. Not so the boyfriend, of course.

Jackie had experienced a terrible sense of *déjà vu* when she heard his voice in the background, demanding to know who was at the door. She had turned and fled, and though her mother started to run after her, the pull of the man in the house had been stronger, and she had given up pursuit.

Jackie hadn't planned to go to the university. She just found herself headed in that direction. And then the temptation to have a look around for Adam and Mumtaz was just too much. So she sat in the canteen hoping that they might come in. She didn't want to speak to them; no, not at all. She only wanted to see if – well – if they were together. And now what? she asked herself. Slowly, she got up from the riverbank and returned to the city centre and sat below the town clock, absently watching the Christmas shoppers hurry by as she tried to plan her next move.

Not until the clock chimed five did she reluctantly get up and join the crowds.

Sarah Morris was closing up the Social Services office for the night when she heard the front door open.

'Come in. Sit down,' she called from the supply room. 'I'll be right with you.'

Jackie paced about the office nervously until Sarah came in, recognized her and froze.

'My God, it's you!' she cried, her professional reflexes deserting her.

'Yes, it's me. I'm not a ghost,' Jackie said, refusing to let herself be intimidated.

'Where have you been?' Sarah's voice was harsh, strident. 'Have you any idea of the hell Adam has been going through?'

'Has he?' Jackie replied, the vision of Adam and Mumtaz still fresh in her mind.

'What do you mean, has he? Why did you run off like that? Why have you refused to see him?'

'I didn't want to get in his way,' Jackie replied simply. 'You thought I would. Don't pretend you didn't.' She paused. 'I'm sorry he didn't get to Cambridge. I wanted him to go. My plan didn't work, did it?' Jackie said, her confusion making her look like a little girl.

Struggling with her emotions, Sarah gave her a sudden hug. 'Are you all right?' she asked, her tone now warm and concerned.

Jackie nodded, the other's unexpected affection bringing tears to her eyes.

'How's the little one?'

'Kicking,' Jackie said, patting her stomach with a smile.

'Have you see Adam yet?'

The smile disappeared from Jackie's face. 'No. I only want a place to stay.'

'You and Adam can stop with us until you sort yourselves out.'

'You don't understand. I don't want to see him. I can't face him.'

'Then what are you here for?' Sarah asked, perplexed.

'Supplementary sodding benefit. I can't get it in London.' She took a deep breath. 'I've got to be sensible for the baby.'

'So what can I do?'

'Help me find a place. And, please, you won't tell Adam, will you?'

Sarah drove Jackie to the girls' hostel – a big white house that was several streets from the Social Services offices. She tried to regain her professional poise as she itemized the help Jackie could get: from the medical to the financial. And yet, as they entered the deserted reception area of the hostel with its overflowing ash-trays and bleak fluorescent lights, she couldn't keep the personal side of their relationship completely muted.

'Are you sure about this?'

'This is really what I want. I'm sorry. I shouldn't have come to you. I should've seen another social worker.'

Sarah hesitated a moment. 'It is his baby, isn't it?'

'Do you really think I'd say it was if it wasn't?' Jackie asked wearily. 'Yes, it's your grandchild. Now, please, take us to our cell.'

Sarah led the way upstairs, across the landing and into a cramped double bedroom with two beds; one unmade, with a coffee cup on its side-table, set on top of a pile of books, beside a family photograph. Clothes were scattered untidily about the room, and there was a chill draught.

'This is great,' Jackie said, putting her duffel bag down on the spare bed. 'Thanks a lot. I'll be fine.'

Sarah hesitated, unsure as to what more she could do or say. 'Try to get a good rest. And remember the clinic tomorrow,' she said, and reluctantly left.

Alone, Jackie paced around the room a few times, taking in her new surroundings. She checked the view from the window – an alleyway – then paused to inspect the photo of the Asian family by her room-mate's bed, swinging round as she heard the door open.

'Christ, it's you?' she exclaimed, as Meera came in the room.

'What are you doing here?' Meera asked, equally surprised.

'I'm your new roomie,' Jackie said and the two girls hooted with laughter and disbelief.

Meera reached out to feel Jackie's tummy. 'So, where's Adam?'

'I just want to do something on my own,' Jackie said with a shrug. 'What about you? Left home?'

Meera glanced away for a moment. 'They threw me out. They found this bloke for me, bald he was, with spots. I said it wasn't fair on him.'

'Not pregnant, are you?'

'No!'

'I thought this might be the banged-up lock-up.' Jackie laughed and embraced her old friend.

'And Hafiz?' she asked, after a moment.

Meera lowered her eyes. 'I haven't see him,' she said.

As Shehnaaz expanded her factory, Astler's was faced with the possibility of a strike in its jeans section. Joe insisted on tackling the problem head-on by talking to his workers, and both Adam and Alex attended the meeting on the shop-floor. Alex hovered beside Joe, anxious to protect him from his unfriendly staff, while Adam sat taking notes.

'We're a small firm,' Joe began. 'I started working with my hands before these sewing machines were invented. And in '45 let me tell you this country didn't have much to offer –

'Anyway, we're a family business,' Joe continued at his leisurely pace, despite the unresponsive, stony-eyed audience. 'We can pay good wages because we know our job. We work hard and those computer jobs in the annex are making us a bit over the odds.'

'Are you saying that jeans aren't profitable?' one Asian woman interrupted, and Adam knew she was thinking of Mrs Sattar expanding her business on the strength of jeans.

'Let me finish, please, then you can ask what you like,' Joe said. 'Jeans are a washout is the short answer. Now if we bring in some fancy union from London, I'm going to spend all my time talking to them instead of selling jeans, which is what I'm good at.'

'Couldn't you sell more?' the same woman asked.

'Sure, if you people would work faster.'

'On time rate? Why should we?' another woman stood up and shouted.

'You wouldn't pay any more,' someone else called out.

'You don't listen,' the first woman said.

'I don't understand,' Joe said, then tried to lighten the mood. 'Like you, my English isn't too good.'

Adam saw at once that his grandfather's joke had misfired badly; management and labour were further from a reconciliation than ever.

'If jeans don't pay, how come the Sattars are expanding, eh?' a worker called out.

'That's their business. If you want shoddy goods, go and work there.'

'All we're saying is, give us a share in running this place and we'll improve it,' the original speaker said.

'And then take it over; thank you very much,' Joe replied.

'Take us seriously, why don't you?' someone else cried out.

'I do,' Joe said, his face turned a deep red with frustration. 'I train you and you desert me. I should use only English, with no talent.'

'That's racist,' a woman stood up and protested.

'You call *me* a racist?' Joe asked in a loud, rumbling voice.

'You meant us, didn't you? The Asians.'

'You think that's racism?' Joe shouted over the uproar. 'Okay, I take it back. No offence meant.'

Adam was watching Alex who was suddenly boiling over with rage on her father's behalf. He tried to catch her eye, but it was no use.

'How dare you! How dare you people talk to him about racism?' she broke in.

'Alex, it's okay,' Adam said, but she didn't even hear him.

'Do you know what racism did to him? Do you know all he lost? Not just a home. Not just a good bloody production line. His family. All of it. Mother, father, brothers, sisters. That's racism and if it happened here we'd be the first ones with you.'

'Alex, enough. Leave. Now,' Joe ordered, and Adam was relieved to see his aunt obey, though she still trembled with anger.

'Listen, please,' Adam said, rising and trying to make himself heard to the roused crowd. 'Let's carry on. There's no need to stop talking. You haven't understood!' But no one listened. The women were already heading out of the door, voices raised in protest and anger.

Mumtaz had already heard about the dispute at Astler's when Adam saw her the following day at university; and the version she heard had a definite anti-Joe Astler slant, as he had anticipated.

'That remark he made, it was stupid. But he meant it as a joke against himself. How could it have been anything else?'

'That's not the way I heard it,' Mumtaz said calmly.

'He was trying to explain, that's all. Joe gets nervous and worked up. Then he speaks too quickly without checking his words.'

'Adam, it's not a slip of the tongue. It's an attitude. And it smacks of racism.'

'You can accuse him of a lot of things, but not that.' It was bad enough that the factory workers misunderstood Joe, but Adam couldn't bear Mumtaz to share their views. 'He's stubborn, I don't deny that. But Joe went through a hell of a lot to get where he is today. He's proud of his company.'

'It's their company, too, Adam. They work there,' Mumtaz said evenly.

'Yes, but Joe can't let go. He's too insecure, even now.'

'He's going to have to, one day.'

'In his own time,' Adam said. 'And maybe you'd tell that to your mother.'

Mumtaz sat up straighter, and gave him a sober, steady look. 'She's only helping. Those women come to her for advice.'

'Yeah, and then throw it back at us.' Despite himself, Adam spoke with a tinge of bitterness.

'She's been cleaning up your mess,' Mumtaz said loyally, though she couldn't help but think of the family mess that had developed in the process.

'Oh, so it's mine now.'

'I didn't mean *you*.'

'No?' Adam couldn't stop. 'You've always meant me. I'm responsible. Remember?' They weren't talking about the factory any more, but about their relationship, and Jackie. At least, that's how it seemed to him, and there was no point in pursuing this line of discussion. Mumtaz meant too much to him. He'd be responsible and shut up, to preserve their friendship and whatever more they might have.

'Adam, please. Please,' Mumtaz was saying, her large dark eyes opaque with distress.

'It really doesn't have anything to do with us,' Adam told her, wishing with all his heart this were true.

That night, when the family gathered for dinner at Joe's house, Adam tried again to get through to his grandfather. There had to be a satisfactory remedy to the labour situation at Astler's, if only Joe would listen. But it was, Adam reflected, an even more tense gathering than usual. Alex was in an agony of remorse for her outburst at the factory, while Joe seemed filled with a dangerous, cocky belligerence. Sarah was unusually quiet and distracted. Only Phil offered Adam any support.

'Opa, let's talk to them once more at least,' Adam said when his grandfather announced he'd let the workers carry out their strike.

'When they come back, fine,' Joe said stubbornly.

'They won't come back. They feel insulted,' Adam explained yet again.

'You weren't talking to them.'

'Perhaps he should have been doing the talking,' Phil said quietly from his end of the table.

'It's only the jeans workshop that's striking anyway.'

'For now,' Alex added.

'Well, who needs them?' Joe shrugged. 'There's plenty unemployed where they came from.'

'Opa, you can't do that. They're on strike.'

Joe bridled. 'Adam, I appreciate your vast business experience but –'

'Dad, stop it,' Alex interrupted again, glancing over at Sarah who remained silent and withdrawn. Joe followed her gaze, suddenly aware of his main opponent's unusual silence.

'Have you nothing to say, for once?'

Sarah didn't even rise to the bait, but looked at him vaguely for a moment.

'I was just thinking – if you won't be busy – I think I'll take Adam to Israel for Christmas. He needs a break.'

Adam looked at his mother sharply; it was the first he had heard of the plan. And how unlike Sarah, to want to leave her work and politics. She had been so distracted lately, he was sure she was involved with a new case. Now, here she was talking about a trip to Israel that he didn't really want to take.

Adam knew, even before seeing Mumtaz the next day, that she was the reason for his reluctance to leave Leicester. There were other contributing factors, like Joe, of course. But, for the most part, he did not want to be separated from Mumtaz yet. He had only just found her again, and with her an ease, a rightness within himself. He strolled across campus with her to the law faculty, luxuriating in this sensation as he watched Mumtaz's face, memorizing the tilt of her head as she asked a question, the quick gleam of intelligence in her dark eyes.

'A trip to Israel would be so fascinating.'

'Yeah, well, I don't like to leave Joe. He's on a short fuse.'

'He'll get by. He's got your aunt.'

'Yes, but I'd keep wondering what was going on. I wouldn't want to be out of touch right now.'

'If there's a strike, there's nothing to be in touch with.'

'So they're going ahead with it?' He wasn't really surprised, but he was disturbed, and worried about the consequences. 'Perhaps it can still be averted.'

'Perhaps,' Mumtaz said, then stopped and gave him a long, direct look. 'I don't mind talking openly about things but I won't be your mole, you do understand?'

Adam laughed. 'Thanks. I'll watch what I say.'

'I don't tell them anything,' Mumtaz reproached him. 'How could I?'

Adam put his arms around her and though at first she resisted, her body of its own volition yielded to him, and he thought how perfectly matched, how beautifully moulded it was to his.

'Tomorrow,' he murmured, breathing in her heavy sweet scent.

'Right, see you tomorrow,' she said, freeing herself with a slow smile.

*

Later that afternoon as Mumtaz sat in her mother's office typing letters, a crowd of women from Astler's factory came pouring in, pleading with her mother for work. She thought of Adam – touching her lips where his warmth lingered still – and wished her mother would not involve herself in their business. Perhaps Adam could avert a strike, but not as long as these women kept coming to Shehnaaz for advice.

'I'm full up,' Shehnaaz was telling them. 'Every machine's taken.'

'Start a second shift.'

'I can't sell what I've got. Stay and fight Astler's.'

'Why?' asked one woman. 'You didn't.'

'Because no one backed me,' Shehnaaz explained. 'Look, I'll do what I can to give you all some piecework while you're out.'

'What do you mean?' asked a woman.

'Mum, let them sort out their own problems,' Mumtaz said. 'It's none of your business.'

Shehnaaz ignored her. 'Out on strike. I thought you women were walking out.'

Mumtaz's chair scraped the floor as she quickly stood up. She shot her mother a disapproving glance, then bolted from the office. She didn't like to hear what was going on between the two rival businesses; it tainted her friendship with Adam. But it was getting harder to avoid since Adam had become so active in Astler's. Harder still, for the fact was that she really did support her mother's views, or most of them.

Mumtaz hurried out of the warehouse and into the street, so absorbed in her thoughts that she didn't see Meera until she stepped directly into her path.

'Oh, Meera!' Mumtaz gave her a warm embrace, guilty that she had neglected her since starting university.

'I was in the area so I thought I'd catch you for a minute.'

'I'm sorry I've not been round,' Mumtaz said. 'But between university work and helping my mum –'

'No problem,' Meera shrugged, but continued to look at her as if she wanted to say something more, or hear something more.

'Hafiz hasn't said much. To anybody,' Mumtaz volunteered.

'Yeah, it's not that,' Meera said, then paused awkwardly.

Adam then? Mumtaz wondered. How could Meera of all people object? 'I've got to get home and start dinner. Sorry,' she said, the chimes of a nearby church bell reminding her of the hour. 'I'll come to see you soon, okay?'

'No, better not. Look, it's just –'

'There's my bus,' Mumtaz interrupted and, giving her a kiss, dashed down the street. Only later, reflecting on the other girl's preoccupied air, her elliptic conversation, did she wonder why Meera had sought her out.

Mumtaz was still thinking about Meera when she met Adam in the Mandela Lounge of the Student Union the following day. She had told Hafiz of their meeting, but he pretended not to hear. She supposed his attitude meant that he had really barred Meera, even by name, from his life. But she'd never be able to tell her that. How sad it all was.

And she couldn't help but feel that Meera somehow blamed her, if only because Hafiz wasn't available to take the blame himself. Mumtaz took a sip of her orange juice, and looked over at Adam. Were they, too, with their different backgrounds, destined to end in sadness?

'What are you thinking with those deep dark soulful eyes of yours?'

'I think that Meera blames me for Hafiz. You know, it comes of trying to help, playing message carrier.'

'Come on,' Adam said, grabbing her hand and pulling her up. 'You need some fresh air to clear all these whirlygigs out of your head.'

Adam bundled her into Joe's old Volvo, took a few turns through the city centre and, in minutes it seemed, they were driving along a country road. Mumtaz fancied she could hear birds over the hum of the engine, even though it was winter.

'Where are we going?' Not that it matters, she thought, her spirits rising. The space and peace made her feel so free. Free, and yet at the same time somehow united to Adam. Being with him was both the most easy, natural thing in the world, and also the most exciting.

'Where we're going is a secret,' he said.

'Come on, tell me.'

He gave her a mischievous grin. 'I'm kidnapping you. It's the Revenge of the Astlers. Young heiress abducted and never heard of again.'

Mumtaz pushed him, making the car swerve and they laughed as Adam recovered the wheel.

'But she really does have it in for us, your mum,' Adam said, after a moment.

'She's running a business.'

'A bloody Jihad. First she pinches our staff. Now she's stealing our customers.'

'She's not,' Mumtaz exclaimed, startled at this latest development.

'Are you sure? Honestly?' Adam asked, seeing the uncertainty in her eyes before she looked away. 'I still love you,' he said, his deep voice a caress. 'Can't help it; I just do.' Mumtaz moved closer to him and he put an arm round her. Neither spoke again till they came to a small vegetarian bistro set in a bower corner of a village. The restaurant was cosy and dark, done up in mahogany wood booths and soft, dim lights. An enormous Christmas tree stood crowding the lobby, twinkling with coloured lights.

'It's charming. But I'm not a vegetarian, you know,' Mumtaz smiled, wondering if this was his interpretation of a Muslim.

'I think they'll probably let you in,' he teased.

'I've never been in an English restaurant,' Mumtaz confessed, and Adam stared at her for a moment, then, laughing softly, hugged her to him.

'It doesn't mean I'm a peasant, Adam,' she warned. 'Only a Muslim.'

In his enthusiasm, Adam over-ordered, and they were served a feast of experiences new to Mumtaz: quiches, pizzas, esoteric salads of carrots and raisins and nuts.

'I don't suppose you want a drop?' he asked, holding up the bottle of wine.

Mumtaz shook her head, then burst into giggles as he knocked over his own glass of wine. He was oddly fidgety, and had hardly touched his food.

'Are you all right?'

He grinned. 'Yes, fine. But I think I'd better get this over with.' He reached into his pocket and took out a small blue velvet box. 'Your Christmas present. I couldn't find any decent wrapping paper in time for tonight.'

Mumtaz hesitantly took the box and found inside a diamond ring. She stared at it for several moments, deeply moved and mesmerized by its sparkling beauty.

'Oh, Adam,' she murmured. 'It's truly beautiful, but I can't accept it. My family –'

'They'll get over it. Families can and do get over anything.'

She realized then, for the first time, just how serious Adam really was. She had seen the ring as a gesture of intention; romantic, but harmless. Now she understood it had been a proposal for action and complete commitment.

He reached across the table and took her hand in both of his. 'It's not about strikes and trying to put things right. It's about you and me.'

'And what about Jackie?' Mumtaz asked. She still felt her presence between them. It was impossible not to. Jackie had played so big a part in Adam's past. And her own.

'I've thought about it,' he replied slowly. 'And I'm certain she's not coming back.'

Mumtaz was silent. She couldn't be so positive; she knew how Jackie had loved him. But that was not the only problem.

'I guess I'm not worth it, am I?' Adam's blue eyes clouded over with uncertainty.

'Adam, it's not a – a business deal.'

'If you loved me it wouldn't matter.'

'I do love you and it does matter,' Mumtaz explained, her voice calm though her heart was beating hard and quickly. 'I couldn't ever not be a Muslim.'

'I'm not asking you to give it up.'

'Then you'd convert?'

'No.' Adam's reply was quiet but firm.

'Islam and Judaism are very close. We share the same god, the same prophets. You'd be welcome,' Mumtaz said.

'I can't believe in God.'

'Then you've nothing to lose.'

'You think there's nothing else to believe in? I'm Jewish,' Adam said. 'I wouldn't change that if I could.'

They looked across the table at each other, helpless but in perfect communion.

'I want to make love to you,' Adam whispered, caressing her hand.

Mumtaz cast her eyes down, staring at the table. 'You haven't got a very good safety record,' she replied, smiling, trying to diffuse the strength of her response to his desire.

That evening Mumtaz stayed late at the warehouse office. She was determined to find out if Shehnaaz was, as Adam claimed, taking away Astler's clients.

'Who is J. M. Goldberg, then?' she asked, coming upon yet another new name.

'New customer,' Shehnaaz answered tersely, busy with her own paperwork.

'From Astler's?' Mumtaz probed, but her mother didn't answer. 'Is that why you pushed for the strike? So you could get their customers?'

Shehnaaz stopped writing and looked up at Mumtaz. 'I have to make this business work. People depend on me. I've got ninety thousand to pay off. Before even thinking about your dowry.'

Dowry. The archaic though by no means unfamiliar word threw Mumtaz completely off balance. Were her parents thinking of her marriage now? It was intolerable.

'I saw Meera the other day. You know, the Hindu girl,' she said suddenly. 'Why didn't you let them marry? Hafiz is miserable, and Meera is living in a hostel.'

Shehnaaz put down her pen and regarded Mumtaz closely. 'Don't fall in love,' she said. 'It never works. Not till you're married.'

'And what if I did?' Mumtaz asked, knowing she had.

Shehnaaz got up and went over to the filing cabinet. 'I thought you were here to help me,' she said, firmly putting an end to the discussion.

The next day Mumtaz went to see Meera at the hostel, gravitating there from a new sense of identification with her friend. But Meera, sitting on the edge of her bed, seemed intensely ill at ease. Or perhaps it was simply the bitterness brought out by any discussion of Hafiz.

'If he had wanted me, he could have come and got me from here.'

'What will you do now?' Trembling slightly, and staring at her hands, Mumtaz realized this question was addressed as much to herself as her friend.

Meera started clearing up the tea things. 'Marry. Take a typing course. I don't know –' she said, and turned nervously as the door opened.

'Give me a hand, will you?' Jackie said, and stopped short as she saw Mumtaz. The two women stared at each other in disbelief. Jackie turned as though to bolt, and then, changing her mind, came into the room, banging her parcels down angrily.

'I didn't know she was coming,' Meera told her anxiously.

Unable to wrench her eyes away from Jackie, Mumtaz said to Meera, 'This is why you came by the factory that day? Why didn't you tell me?' Oh, Adam, she thought, with a sudden shiver of fear and pain. If only Meera had told her, things with Adam wouldn't have gone quite as far. 'So you decided to turn up at last,' she said quietly to Jackie. 'Why here? What are you doing here?'

'Having my baby,' Jackie replied, in a manner that was at once casual and aggressive.

'Adam looked for you all summer!' Mumtaz said angrily.

'Yeah, I was just seeing how long he'd last. Not very, apparently.' She gave Mumtaz a shrewd look.

'That's a shitty thing to say. He's talked of nothing else.'

'Yeah, he's good at that.'

Mumtaz could restrain herself no longer. 'I'm bloody bored hearing about you and your baby. You shouldn't have gone. You broke his heart, his spirit.'

'Not so's you'd notice.' Jackie put down the tea kettle with a shaking hand.

'You set us up, didn't you?'

'Yes, I did,' Jackie said quietly. 'You and Adam are right for each other. I'm not.'

'Then why bother to come back?' Mumtaz asked, beside herself.

'Because I wasn't brave enough,' Jackie burst out. 'Don't you understand anything? I just wanted to be near you.'

Mumtaz, her anger and frustration spent, moved towards her friend, full of remorse.

'No, sod off,' Jackie repelled her advance. 'Go back to your bloody university. The baby's mine. I'll let you know if you can see her – him, I dunno. Now push off! No, wait, Taz,' she called in an anguished voice as Mumtaz, confused, hurt and a bit relieved, started for the door. 'Come here!' She held out her arms and they embraced, each hiding her tears from the other.

'Here, want to meet the baby?' Jackie placed Mumtaz's hand on her stomach. 'Got to be still. Annoys her otherwise. Him. It's driving me crazy.' She looked into Mumtaz's eyes, her own filled with wonder. 'Feel anything?'

Mumtaz nodded and tried to smile, though the kick she felt seemed to go straight to her heart. Here was Adam's child. He could never turn his back on it, or Jackie.

'You don't know how much he's missed you,' Mumtaz said, remembering the look that came into his eyes when he spoke of Jackie.

'Yeah, well, missing's the best bit.'

'I hope so,' Mumtaz murmured, and turned to go.

Jackie caught her by the arm. 'If you get like that, I'll be off again! He's yours now. Probably always was. This is the way I want it.'

'No,' Mumtaz said. 'You don't know what you're saying.'

'Why not? I thought you loved him. And me.'

'Yeah. I think that's the trouble.'

'Never mind. Give us a hug, both of us,' Jackie said and this time they both wept openly, for one another, and themselves.

Mumtaz arranged to meet Adam in a café near the hostel that same day. She didn't want to have time to think about any of it. She simply wanted him to see Jackie and for them to get back together again; for the new ordeal to be over. She felt desperately sad and nervous as she sat opposite Adam, stirring her coffee. Just as she had felt when she first knew Jackie was pregnant and he hadn't had a clue. Only now it was worse, of course. They had become so much closer.

'Are you all right?' Adam asked.

She nodded, studying his face, the square, obstinate chin, the blue eyes soft with love, memorizing every detail.

'Adam,' she began, and then faltered as she glimpsed Jackie approaching the café. So there needn't be any difficult farewell speech, after all.

'I've got to go.' Mumtaz stood up quickly. 'I love you,' she said quietly and ran, before Adam could get to his feet.

'Taz! What is this? Wait —' Adam started after her, and froze as Jackie entered the café.

'You!' he said, staring in amazement.

'Right, me,' and her defiant look told him she was as startled as he.

'We'd better sit down,' he said, the shock of seeing her after all these months giving way to anger and despair.

'Sorry. Wrong number,' Jackie said, flip as ever, and quickly left.

Adam sat down and systematically finished his coffee, unaware that it had gone cold. He was trembling all over, as if his warring emotions were playing out their battle on his nervous system. The major point was that Jackie had kept the baby, was very pregnant, and he knew his only course was to stay with her. He put some coins on the table and left, half-hoping he'd be too late to catch her.

She was about fifty yards down the London Road when he spotted her, and realizing she must be headed for the railway station, he broke into a desperate run, all his apathy suddenly dissipated at the thought of her disappearing again. He raced into the station just as she was going down the stairs to platform four.

'Jackie!' he shouted, and in answer heard the doors of a train slamming shut.

Still senselessly calling her name, he started chasing after the train, only to see her sitting on a bench, her head in her hands.

'Don't ever do that again!' he shouted, standing over her, torn between relief and rage.

'You can hit me,' Jackie replied. 'We're both pretty fit.'

'I don't want to hit you.'

'I'd have got on the train,' she was saying. 'I'm just too tired. Sorry. I'm so sorry.'

Adam sat down beside her, put his arms round her, and pulled her head down against his shoulder. 'Why did you do it, disappear like that?' he asked. If only she had stuck it out everything would be so much simpler. Now there were so many complications.

'Don't ask questions, not yet,' came the muffled reply.

'God, I thought something awful had happened to you. Leaving me like that and never a word from you,' Adam continued, recalling the anguish of those months when he searched for her.

'I'm sorry.'

'Just never do it again. Swear you won't.'

'I swear I won't!' Jackie said, acquiescent.

Adam looked down at her large, rounded stomach and gently touched it. 'Why didn't you stay with me?'

'Two of you?' Jackie replied, patting her stomach. 'Give me a break.' But she quickly relented when she saw the confused look in his eyes. 'I never wanted to hold you to it, that's all. It's my own lookout.'

'But I was happy,' he protested. 'We were happy.'

'Yeah, you and the lost tribes of Israel,' Jackie said, her flip tone back.

'They were trying to help. They wanted you in the family.'

Jackie drew back from his embrace. 'You're not taking me over, Adam. You can come and see me sometimes. Change some nappies, and then piss off before you get bored. That's the way it's going to be.'

'But I thought –' Adam began, and wondered what he had thought. That he'd go back with Jackie while loving Mumtaz the way he did?

'Yeah, well, I'm different now,' Jackie said. 'Now go and find Mumtaz. You look nice together.'

Adam stood up and stepped back, regarding Jackie as

though distance might give him the necessary perspective to see into her mind. What worried him was that she acted without understanding herself any better than he did.

'Can I give you a lift?' he asked. 'If that's not an imposition?'

'Still driving Joe's Volvo?'

He nodded warily. 'How do you know?'

'I saw it when you came to my dad's.' She paused to let the words sink in. 'I just didn't want to see you, that's all.'

It was a deliberate, painful thrust, and for a moment it took Adam's breath away. 'I see,' he said. 'On second thoughts, you can take the bus. Give me a ring when you feel like it or if there's anything you need –'

He walked away, his head throbbing, his heart pounding and his thoughts reeling. He didn't understand Jackie's hot-and-cold game. All he knew was that she had driven Mumtaz away, and that in only a matter of weeks he would be a father.

That evening in the middle of a conversation with his mother, watching Sarah watching him, Adam suddenly realized that she knew about Jackie. It explained everything. This was why she'd been so distracted recently; this was the special case that had been absorbing her. He simply could not believe that she had kept it from him.

'So you knew Jackie was back,' he said.

Sarah sighed. 'Yes, but only these past few weeks.'

'Why didn't you tell me?' he asked, hoping for some adequate explanation, though he knew there could be none.

'She came to me as a social worker. In confidence. If she wouldn't tell you, I couldn't force her,' Sarah explained, taking minimum responsibility.

'Of course you couldn't. Especially with me packed off to Israel for Christmas.'

Sarah gave another sigh. 'Adam, I did try. I asked her to move in with us. She wanted the hostel.'

'And that was it? A clean business deal?'

'It wasn't my secret.'

'Couldn't you have lapsed, just for once in your life?'

'No, especially not for you. It's her pregnancy and her choice,' Sarah reiterated. 'And, yes, all right, I was protecting you.'

'If only,' Adam laughed. 'She meant you to tell me.' Didn't he know Jackie's ways and games better than anyone, no matter how they perplexed him.

'Darling, she doesn't need you,' Sarah was saying. 'We'll look after her at the Social Services, you know that.'

'The problem is now I've gone and really fallen for someone else.' He hadn't intended to say anything about it, not now, but out it came.

Sarah stared at him, surprised. 'Who?'

'You don't know her,' Adam replied, instantly regretting his outburst.

'Why can't you tell me who it is?'

'It's not my secret!' Adam replied, and his heart ached as he thought of Mumtaz giving him that final assurance of her love.

Mumtaz spent the evening barricaded behind a stack of textbooks, furiously jotting down notes as if the words could blot out the image of Adam. She kept telling herself she would simply return to the way she was before they met at the university. She would live for her future and that meant studying law. She would also learn to live with the fact of Adam and Jackie, and their child. They would remain friends and she would share in their happiness.

'Can I hear your verses?' Shehnaaz said, coming into the room.

'Where's Aba?'

'He's out delivering. He asked me to listen to you.'

Mumtaz frowned. 'Haven't learned them. I'm afraid my mind's not on it.'

'Well, it's not too late,' Shehnaaz said, giving her an affectionate pat on the arm.

'Mum, can I have those letters you intercepted?' Mumtaz asked. It was her way of showing her mother, and herself, that the Adam affair was over. Shehnaaz stopped, confused by her daughter's calm, non-accusatory request.

'I just want to throw them out. If you haven't already,' Mumtaz went on, though she longed to read them, just once.

Shehnaaz remained silent, trying to read her daughter's passive face.

'I don't think you had any right to keep them from me. But it doesn't matter. I don't mind. Not now.'

'What has that boy said to you?' Shehnaaz finally asked.

'He talked about the strike,' Mumtaz said, determined to reveal nothing more.

'Blaming me, I suppose.'

'Should he?' Mumtaz said coolly. 'You're only taking what's yours. By the way,' she added, as her mother reached the door, 'you didn't show the letters to Aba, did you?'

Shehnaaz shook her head, and Mumtaz, breathing one sigh of relief among many of despair, covered her head and opened the Koran.

It was nearly the end of term before she saw Adam on campus again. She had shifted the level of her emotions; they were not so personalized now. She was serene again, quite ready to be a friend to both Adam and Jackie. Or so she told herself as she crossed over to the entrance of the law faculty where he was standing.

'How's Jackie?' she asked cheerfully.

'I don't really know.'

Surprised by this answer, and his belligerent tone, she hesitated before saying, 'It must be nearly time for the baby.'

'Yes, very nearly,' Adam said, still standing stiffly, refusing to be a part of her casual, friendly pretence.

'Well, I've got to go. See you next term.'

'Maybe sooner,' he said, still unsmiling. 'We're taking you to court.'

'What?' Mumtaz cried. 'What for?'

'Sharp practice. Incitement to strike.' Adam ticked them off his fingers. 'You'll understand the legal aspects, I should think.'

'It's not our fault,' Mumtaz protested, but Adam was suddenly standing closer, his voice low and tender.

'Nothing's changed, you know,' he said. 'Pretend if you like, but it hasn't.'

'I'm not pretending.'

'Christ, stop acting,' he implored. 'What do we do now?'

Mumtaz threw her arms round his neck and kissed him. 'Please don't say any more.'

'Can't we talk a little? Don't go,' Adam held on to her arm, but, seeing the tears gleaming in her dark eyes, reluctantly released her and watched helplessly as she ran across the campus.

Though she ought to have been at her studies, Mumtaz went to the girls' hostel the next afternoon. She had promised to stop in to see Meera who, now reconciled with her family, was leaving to return home. But the real reason which she couldn't hide from herself was to talk to Jackie; to find out what was happening between her and Adam.

'Did you want Meera?'

Mumtaz was half-way across the reception area of the hostel before she recognized Sarah.

'Yes. I think she's expecting me.' Mumtaz felt strangely tongue-tied at seeing Adam's mother, and wondered what she thought about Jackie being there.

Upstairs Mumtaz found Meera taking a last look around her corner of the room. Dressed in her traditional Hindu garb, she looked young and innocent, quite at odds with the bleak surroundings. Mumtaz gave her a hug and slipped a small Christmas parcel into her hand, while Jackie came over from her bed with another present for Meera.

'Go on, you old cow. Best of luck to you.'

Meera gave her friends a look that was at once hopeful and doubtful. 'I've got to give it a try, right?'

'Right. I'd do the same, if Mum asked,' Jackie assured her. 'Just don't get bulldozed into anything, okay? Remember, it's your life.'

'So how have you been?' Mumtaz asked Jackie, once Meera was gone.

'I'm doing fine.'

'What's going on between you and Adam? Why are you giving him such a hard time? Don't you know he wants to be a part of all this, to share the responsibility?' She surprised herself, not by the directness of her questions as much as the passion with which she asked them.

Jackie began folding baby clothes and repacking her hospital suitcase.

'Responsible is the one thing I never wanted him to feel –'
She broke off as someone rapped on the door.

'Hello, Jackie. I just wanted to see how you are,' Sarah
said, remaining in the hall. 'And to remind you about Christmas. We don't do much, but Adam thought you might change
your mind and join us.'

'Why doesn't he ask me?'

'You haven't exactly encouraged him.'

'Well, tell him from me –' Jackie began, but the older
woman cut her off.

'I don't take messages. I'm a social worker. Let me know
about Christmas.'

'She's a cool one,' Jackie murmured admiringly, after Sarah
left.

'You're another,' she smiled at Mumtaz. 'Thanks for
coming here,' she said, embracing her.

How could they all have each other and be so lonely because
of it? Mumtaz wondered.

'Just keep him happy,' she murmured.

Jackie stared into her dark eyes for a moment, then nodded
gravely.

Adam managed to persuade Jackie to come to the Morrises
for Christmas dinner when he played down the significance of
the day – after all, the Morrises were Jewish – and played up
the menu – highly nutritious for an expectant mother. Jackie
had been alternately warm and remote in the past week, perhaps responding, Adam thought, to his own uncertainties.

Take today, for instance: here she was acting affectionate
and looking so pretty and what was he doing? Wishing he
were somewhere else. Not to be away from Jackie especially,
he thought, eyeing the remains of the turkey dinner littering
the dining-room table, only the clutter of it all. But no, wasn't
that another of the lies he kept telling himself? If he were
going to be honest, he'd admit that missing Mumtaz was his
problem.

'So Jesus says to God, "But I thought –"' Joe's joke was
drowned by a chorus of protest. 'Let me finish,' he said. 'It's a
good Jewish joke, like celebrating Christmas.'

Jackie smiled at Adam and then got up to help Sarah clear the table.

'No, don't you dare move.' Sarah's admonishment was gentle, almost tender, Adam thought. He had noticed a new understanding between his mother and Jackie. They still gave each other a lot of space but now it seemed to be mutual respect which prompted this.

'Honestly, I need the exercise,' Jackie said, but Adam sat her down again beside Joe. He knew his grandfather enjoyed her company, and if anyone could draw Jackie into the warmth of a family it was Joe.

'So what do you call him?' Joe asked, pointing to her stomach which was now bigger than Adam could ever have believed possible, though she still carried the weight buoyantly.

'Her,' Jackie said. 'I don't know yet.'

'I can think of some nice Hebrew names,' Joe said, patting her affectionately on the cheek.

'Dad, that's enough,' Alex warned.

'I'm teasing. She knows it.'

'So have you two made any decisions yet?' Alex asked Adam as he laid out the dessert plates.

'No.'

'Not yet,' Jackie murmured.

'There's no rush,' Sarah said, and Adam didn't know whether she was protecting Jackie or himself.

'Isn't there?' Phil asked quietly, as Sarah turned off the lights and brought in the flaming Christmas pudding.

'Get married,' Joe said and blew out the flames. 'Get married and then you can come and work for me at Astler's, okay?' he said, taking Jackie's hand.

'With the baby?' Alex asked.

'Sure,' Joe said. 'Once the strike's over. And that won't be long. We have them by their necks now.'

'Oh, yeah, Mumtaz told me,' Jackie said, and Adam felt himself go rigid.

'Who's Mumtaz?' Alex asked, as Sarah turned the lights back on.

Jackie stared at Adam in disbelief, and the colour rushed to his face, even as he justified his position to himself. How could he mention Mumtaz's name at home when their families were feuding, were in a cut-throat competition. Didn't Jackie understand anything that was going on?

'You mean you've never talked about her?' Jackie asked, regarding him with an incredulity that verged on contempt.

'Maybe now isn't the time.'

'What's wrong with now?' Joe asked. 'So who is she?'

'You met her once at sixth-form college. Parents' day. Mumtaz Sattar.' Adam dropped his small bombshell to a deadening silence.

'The daughter of our trouble-maker,' Joe murmured after a bit.

'Mumtaz is at university, reading law. We're friends.' Adam glanced at Jackie. 'Is that enough? Satisfied?'

'So what haven't you told us about her?' Alex asked.

'That's none of your business, Alex,' Sarah said, coming to his support.

'You knew?' Joe asked.

'Not exactly,' said Sarah.

'I really don't think that Adam's friends are any concern –' Phil started, but Joe immediately cut him off.

'It helps to know who's talking to whom.'

'Those people have been out to get us for years,' Alex said.

'For God's sake,' Sarah sighed, and started to clear the unfinished dessert away.

Jackie was already on her feet and rushing to the door. 'I'm sorry. I shouldn't be here. You've all been very kind but I'd better go now. Sorry if I caused any bother. I didn't understand, that's all.'

'Jackie,' Sarah called after her.

'It's not you, darling,' Alex said, but her words were lost to both Jackie and Adam as he followed her into the hall.

'I'll drive you.'

'No, you won't.'

'Look, I'm not running from anything!'

'No one would notice with you,' Jackie said, and let herself out of the door.

\*

Adam didn't see Jackie again in the week before New Year's Eve. With the baby due at any moment, he found it impossible to concentrate on anything but their seemingly insoluble situation. He went to the hostel several times to see her, but chose the hours she was least likely to be there, overcome with apathy as soon as he took any action. And yet he felt if they could only speak to each other honestly, they'd be able to work it out; to come to some sort of living arrangement for after the baby.

Sarah continued to assure him that Jackie was perfectly capable of following through on her decision. She was strong, his mother said, and moreover had a perfect right to make her own choices, and lead her own life. He wanted to believe her, but the sudden revelation of her own fierce protectiveness for him made Adam suspect her.

Despite the crisis at Astler's, Joe gave his annual New Year's Eve bash and the family, too, acted as if it had been a fine year and the next would be the greatest ever.

Adam knew he was drinking too much, but he found it overwhelming to think that the only definite thing the new year held for him was fatherhood. He kept watching the door in case Jackie decided to turn up. But as midnight approached, it became clear that she was ignoring his invitation. Too bad, it would have been a good thing, he thought, to sort themselves out for the new year. Still, after that fiasco of a Christmas dinner, he wasn't exactly surprised. They never did make out well at his family gatherings. Of course, tonight was different, Adam thought, looking around at the loud, drunken party, and as the doorbell chimed, he hurried towards it, convinced it was Jackie.

But Joe had got there first. '*Shalom!*' he said with a flourish, and Adam gaped. His grandfather was speaking to Mumtaz's father.

'*Salaam,*' Sadiq replied.

'And a Happy New Year!' Joe said. 'Someone leaving already?'

'Your grandson.' Sadiq caught Adam's eye. 'I was told to find you.'

Adam felt a huge lump in his throat, and tried to swallow. 'What is it? What's happened? Is Mumtaz all right?'

Sadiq looked him up and down. 'I have come to take you to the hospital, to the maternity ward.'

'Right.' Adam felt instantly sober and yet everything had the slow unreality of drunkenness. 'Thanks.'

Stunned and shaken he followed Sadiq out to the cab, and sat dumbly on the edge of the back seat while Sadiq sped through the streets oddly quiet on New Year's Eve.

'So, you're at university with my daughter,' he said.

'Yes,' Adam murmured, first refusing, then asking for the cigarette Sadiq had offered him.

'You're going to be even busier now,' Sadiq told him. 'It's an absorbing experience, fatherhood.'

These words stayed with Adam as he followed Sadiq through the hospital lobby and up to the third-floor maternity ward, but they, too, had no reality. Only when he saw Mumtaz walking down the corridor towards him did he feel himself on solid ground again.

It took him a long moment to register the fact that she was walking alongside a trolley, on which a red-faced, sweating Jackie lay.

'Get away from me, you bastard!' she screamed at Adam. 'I don't want you here. Just sod off and leave me alone.'

Mumtaz tried to restrain her, casting Adam a glance of apology and understanding.

'Your idea, was it, Taz?' Jackie cried as the two nurses rushed her down to the labour ward. 'Thanks for nothing.'

Adam stood with his arms hanging at his sides, gazing at Mumtaz, overcome by a rush of sadness and embarrassment. 'It was good of you to let me know. Thanks for asking your father to get me,' he said, thinking how ironic it was that both he and Jackie should need Mumtaz. Was it because one loved her so well, or because one felt well-loved by her?

'Sorry, Adam. I didn't think it would be like that,' she said quietly. 'She needs another woman now,' and pressing his hand reassuringly, she returned to Jackie.

Adam lost all sense of time as he waited. He paced the quiet hospital corridor, the pounding of his heavy shoes the only sound. Every five or ten minutes he would stop to stare out of the window into the black night as if there was something out there to guide him. Sadiq, waiting for Mumtaz, sat half-dozing on a bench, his open newspaper still clasped in his hands. And Phil, on call, was in and out; awkwardly offering his paternal support.

'Adam.' He swung round from the window as Mumtaz gently touched his shoulder.

'The baby?'

'Not yet. But it shouldn't be long. She wants you there now,' Mumtaz said, her voice husky though she held herself in perfect control. 'Come.' She took a firm grasp on his arm and led him down the corridor to Jackie's room.

'Wait.' He held back from the door for a moment, looking into her eyes, which seemed darker, larger with unspoken thoughts.

'You're such a good friend,' he murmured ineptly, and quickly kissed her cheek before he went into the room.

Jackie looked exhausted, bathed in perspiration, but flushed with near-victory.

'Mind if I stay with you?'

'Mind if you don't,' she grinned at him, with a return of her old spirit.

'How is it?'

'Beastly! What'd you expect?' She hissed with pain and slumped back. 'Ouf,' she said, then held out a hand. 'Come here, you.'

Adam sat down by the side of the bed and Jackie grabbed hold of his hand. 'Don't let go,' she said between clenched teeth, as she felt the next contraction come on. 'Please, don't let go.'

Adam walked up the narrow staircase of the terrace house where the law centre had its offices. His clothes on the scruffy side, his forehead creased in thought, he might have been any one of the neighbourhood clients, except that he was not Asian. Though his step was quick and resolute, his blue eyes had a vague, faraway look. He was, in fact, lost in the absent reverie which had become his only defence against reality over the last fifteen months. Only when Adam saw Mumtaz at the reception desk in her faded jeans and a sweater, her long black hair flowing loose, did his eyes brighten. He took a seat at the back of the waiting-room and gave himself over to the pleasure of watching her as she talked to a client.

He hardly ever saw her when she wasn't busy, or about to be. She had continued her law studies at university, was working now part-time as a general assistant for the solicitors at the law centre, and also managed to be very involved with the students protesting against apartheid in South Africa. The busier she was, the more relaxed she seemed and the more beautiful she became, Adam thought, as he waited for her.

It was true that Mumtaz had changed over the past months. She had learned to immerse herself in life as she found it. This meant Adam too. He was now only part – though still an unresolved part – of the whole. The Muslim–Jewish situation that had prevented their coming together was just one of the many problems. The Sattar–Astler feud had intensified, and as for Adam's relationship with Jackie, it not only continued but was more complex than ever. Adam saw her and their daughter, Fina, regularly, though Jackie, still insisting on independence, shared a flat with Meera.

Yet Mumtaz and Adam were closer now than ever before. They had learned to accept the love that had always been between them; and the fact that there was no possibility of a future together. With this acceptance had come the ability to enjoy what until now they had denied themselves: a consistent, staunch, friendship that had made them as comfortable as brother and sister, and as intimate as lovers.

Adam leaned back in his chair, enjoying the play of expression on Mumtaz's face – the gentle humour in her gaze, the warmth of her patient smile – as she spoke to an aggrieved, middle-aged Asian woman.

'If you decide to take legal action,' she was saying, 'one of our solicitors – '

'But he's my husband. I can't. Would you?' the woman interrupted. 'What are you, a Christian?'

Mumtaz regarded her client with a proud smile. 'I am a Muslim like you, if it matters.' Aware of Adam waiting for her, she thought how many times they had had similar conversations.

'Anyone for me? Who's next?' A tall, dark, good-looking Asian man in his mid-thirties came out of his office and glanced round the queue, making Adam realize just how conspicuously out of place he was.

'Can I help you?' he asked pleasantly to Adam, his dark eyes questioning.

'No, thanks. I'm – er – waiting.'

'For anyone in particular?'

'Mumtaz Sattar,' Adam replied, noting the man's surprise. He wondered why he had assumed the solicitors she worked with were all scholarly men her father's age.

'Nasreen!' Mumtaz was now warmly greeting a friend of her mother's at the head of the queue. 'Can I help you?'

'I don't think so,' the woman replied in icy tones. 'It's your mother. After two years, we're worse off with her than we were at Astler's.'

'Mumtaz.' Said approached her and spoke in a low discreet voice. 'There's someone to see you.'

She gave him a startled glance, realizing from his tone that he had expected to take her out for a meal. It was a habit they had fallen into when they both worked through the lunch-hour together.

'A friend from university,' she murmured. 'Come, let me introduce you. Said Farrukh – solicitor, this is Adam Morris.' Watched by the entire waiting-room the two men then shook hands, hastily and awkwardly. Then Said turned to Nasreen. 'Please, come right through.'

'Ready?' Adam asked Mumtaz, whose gaze was fixed on Nasreen. 'Or did you forget we're having lunch after your meeting?'

'Of course I hadn't forgotten,' she said, hurrying ahead of him to the street where she unlocked her pushbike from a lamp-post.

'Then why did he seem surprised to see me?'

'I sometimes have lunch with Said. He runs the place.' She dropped the bike chain in her bag. 'Single-handed most days, too.'

'Really?' Adam said, feeling a spark of jealousy at her praise.

'Yes, really. He'd be earning a fortune in practice.'

'Then why doesn't he?' Adam asked, lifting the bike on to the roof rack of his car.

'Because he has a conscience. He knows where he's needed. And he's on the council, a prospective MP,' Mumtaz added.

'Oh, God, one of them,' Adam moaned.

'He's very genuine!'

'Yeah – like all politicians,' Adam said derisively, though in fact he was driving Mumtaz to the university where she was doing her own politicking. They drove in silence; Mumtaz's thoughts on the disturbing meeting with Nasreen at the law centre, and what it might mean to her mother; Adam wondering whether or not Said might be a rival for Mumtaz's affections.

He was still musing over this as he sat in the lounge of the student union, idly sketching Mumtaz who was holding a meeting across the room. Why shouldn't she go out to lunch with Said when he, for God's sake, was still involved with Jackie? But then what did logic have to do with love? he wondered.

'I've had an answer from the ANC,' he heard Mumtaz say. 'Marule will be in London next month and he has agreed to come to Leicester to speak about apartheid in South Africa.'

'Well done, Taz,' several members spoke at once.

'I've suggested the sixteenth,' she continued, her face animated and glowing with excitement. 'So we should be hearing something definite next week.'

Adam put all thoughts from his mind and concentrated on his drawing for the next half-hour – a twenties-style revolutionary sketch, executed in bold clear lines.

'I look like a cross between Joan of Arc and Mother Teresa,' Mumtaz laughed. Finished with the meeting, she had come up behind the absorbed Adam and was leaning over him.

'Keep on like this,' he said, grinning as he rose to embrace her, 'and you might end up being just that.'

Jackie and Meera shared a small second-storey flat above an electrical spare-parts shop on Evington Road near the bottom of Spinney Hill. 'What could be more convenient?' Jackie said. 'We're next to a pub, a gospel church and more Asian take-aways than you can count.' Once a fortnight or so, Mumtaz would join her old college friends for a take-away meal and gossip; the strength of their love for each other dispelling the awkwardness. Somehow she and Jackie and Adam had grown accustomed to the odd situation, Mumtaz thought, as Adam drove her to the flat that evening. They were even content to have it remain so. It was the hint of changes that upset the tenuous balance. But, then, it always had been that.

'Bout bloody time,' cried Meera, who was waiting for them at the window. 'Where's the grub? I bet it's all cold now.'

Adam held up his steaming carrier bag as he and Mumtaz crossed the street to the narrow green door beside the shop entrance. The door opened as they got there and Jackie stood beaming at them both, her fifteen-month-old daughter in her arms. She had put on a bit of weight with motherhood and looked both stunning and relaxed. She greeted Adam with a friendly kiss.

'Hiya,' she said. 'Say hello to your dad, grizzlebum,' she told the laughing baby.

'Oh, that's horrible. Grizzlebum,' Adam moaned, looking to Mumtaz for confirmation, but she hadn't quite yet adjusted to the occasion. It always took a while to get used to being with Adam the father and Jackie the mother, and their child who looked so like both of them.

'Taz, come here, you old rotter!' Jackie cried. 'How've you

been?' She gave her a big growling bear hug with the baby, and didn't let go until Mumtaz laughed.

Watching, Adam thought Mumtaz looked sixteen again, but his pleasure in the scene was tinged with sadness and nervousness.

'She's grown, hasn't she?' Jackie said, thrusting Fina at Mumtaz. 'Here. Take a load off my hands.'

For a second Mumtaz hesitated. She felt apprehensive with their child, for no matter what Jackie had said all those months ago about the baby being 'theirs', nothing could have been more untrue. The baby was hers, and Adam's, and the Astlers'.

'She weighs a ton,' Mumtaz said, taking Fina in her arms.

'And now you can change her nappy,' Jackie said mischievously, and watched as Adam supervised the changing of the baby on the bathroom floor.

'No, other way round,' he said, watching Mumtaz's deft but overly cautious moves.

'My word, Taz,' Jackie said. 'That's good. I think you've been practising in secret.'

They all laughed, but it was an odd strained moment. Mumtaz knew that soon she ought to be changing her own baby. But how, when all she wanted was to have Adam's?

'Has Fina been baptized?' she asked, trying to deflect her thoughts from Adam.

'Sore point,' he warned, with a wink.

'Joe says Fina's Jewish. But I wanted her christened,' Jackie explained.

'You did?' Mumtaz was surprised that Jackie, who professed to believe in nothing, would take a stand on this point.

'Well, not really,' Jackie admitted. 'It was just to set a precedent. I mean, I couldn't face the circumcision thing if it's a boy next time.'

Mumtaz froze and though she didn't, couldn't look at Adam, she could feel how tense he, too, had become. Naïve fool that she was, she'd no idea that they were sleeping together. Yes, she was a fool, and a jealous fool at that.

'So Fina's nothing,' Jackie was saying. 'Just a little pagan like her mum.'

The atmosphere mellowed considerably as they sat down and helped themselves to Adam's mammoth take-away and wine, all save Mumtaz who still unobtrusively abstained. No one bothered her about being a teetotaller any more. Though she chatted and laughed, and seemed as relaxed as the others, she kept thinking of Jackie and Adam together, wondering how often they were still making love. It amazed her that after all these years of being part of an acknowledged triangle she could suddenly feel such a seething, hot-blooded jealousy.

'Did you see Candy on the box?' Meera asked. They'd all been following her career as a professional athlete with the greatest interest and pride.

'No. When?' Mumtaz asked.

'Last week. Four hundred metres. She really made it, greased lightning. To absent friends,' Adam said, raising his glass.

'Yeah, absent bloody friends. God bless 'em,' Meera said. And asked, right on cue: 'How's Hafiz?'

'Away mostly, selling,' Mumtaz replied, her tone apologetic. Perhaps Meera's feelings for Hafiz were no different from her own for Adam, she thought. Perhaps she couldn't let go either. Meera had returned home for a year, hadn't been able to get on with her parents and had moved out. But Hafiz, Mumtaz knew, had played no further part in her life, even if the damages of two years ago remained.

'Is he happy?' Meera asked.

'I don't think he knows,' Mumtaz lied, for lately Hafiz had been seeming much more like himself. 'We're so busy with my mother's business. Things are a bit rough.' She stopped. Now that Jackie was working for Joe, she was speaking in front of two members of the competition.

'Look, I'm sorry about the jeans war,' Jackie began, looking over to Adam for support.

'It's about the last thing we need,' Mumtaz murmured.

'Joe's gone ape. He thinks he's Goliath. An eye for a bloody eye and all that.'

'I know,' Mumtaz said. 'And then Mum retaliates. On principle.'

'Yeah, Joe's chuffed all right. Anything for a nice punch-up. The man's on self-destruct.'

'Don't exaggerate,' Adam interrupted, still coming to his grandfather's defence.

'Well, he's got us selling at a loss just so he can undersell Sattar's. You think that's good business?'

'He wouldn't do that.'

'Listen, mate, I work for the man. I know,' Jackie argued.

'Why not just bring home the account books while you're at it,' Adam said, and Mumtaz flushed with embarrassment. Surely he couldn't think she'd ever repeat or use anything he said about Astler's. They had discussed the family business a number of times; and considered themselves no real part of the fight.

'Oh, stuff your smutty little family secrets,' Jackie cried impatiently. 'Why shouldn't Taz know? What do you two talk about while you're holding hands in class?'

'Almost anything else,' Adam said, while Mumtaz played with the crumbs on her plate.

'Oh, I see.' There was just a touch of venom in Jackie's voice. 'Mustn't disturb your honeymoon, or rattle the ivory tower, eh? Well, why can't you two just knock their bloody heads together?'

'My mum won't listen. It's gone too far,' Mumtaz said quietly. She hadn't even told Adam how serious the problems at Sattar's were becoming, what with Nasreen turning up at the law centre for legal advice, and Tariq putting on the pressure for his money.

'How bad is it?'

'We've got a loan due in six months. Then there's the mortgage on the new house.' But she really couldn't regret that shiny semi-detached building that always seemed overlit and somehow soulless.

'And?' Adam was saying. 'What happens if you can't get the money?'

'It's owed to my uncle. He'll take over, I guess. Put his son in charge as manager.'

'Would that be Cousin Hassan?' Meera squealed with delight. 'You husband-to-be?'

'Oh, Meera.' Mumtaz stared at her in shock. Only once had she ever mentioned her obnoxious cousin, and that had been in the strictest confidence when they were at college.

'That way you'll keep it in the family,' Meera continued. 'Very neat, and very Muslim.'

'Like hell,' Jackie said, and came over to give Mumtaz a hug. 'You're a self-made woman now and there's no looking back.' She might have been speaking for herself as well, Mumtaz thought sadly, but what could either of them do when their present lives were based on the past?

The talk of business problems and marriage contracts brought the evening gathering to a rather abrupt end. Meera went to her room, laughingly claiming her foot was too big to fit in her mouth, and Jackie put Fina to bed while Adam cleared up the supper with Mumtaz's distracted help.

After what seemed hours Adam drove Mumtaz – and her bicycle – to Stoneygates, as far as he was allowed to go. From here, as usual, she would ride her bicycle home.

'Why didn't you tell me you're still sleeping with her?' The question burst out of Mumtaz as soon as he had parked the car.

He didn't speak for a moment. 'How could I explain? You wouldn't understand and I don't expect you to. In a way, I guess, it's for old times' sake. I mean, she's the mother of my child, isn't she? And I still care for her. You know that.'

'And it's to be a boy next, is it?' Mumtaz continued, unable to dismiss what she could only irrationally think of as his infidelity. At the same time she knew she was lucky Jackie didn't mind the amount of time she and Adam spent together.

'It's the first I've heard about that,' he said, colouring. 'I don't know why she said it. You know how Jackie is sometimes.'

'I'll go to bed with you, if that's what you want.' This, too, burst from Mumtaz. She would be breaking all the rules, but she had already been breaking them by continuing her friendship with Adam. They had become as close as two people could be, why wait any longer? She didn't mind sharing his company or even his affection, but she was tired of holding herself back. What or who was she waiting for, if not Adam?

'Taz,' he was saying, his eyes brimming over with love as he gazed at her. 'Oh, Taz, I wouldn't ask that of you.'

'Well, sod you then. I'm jealous!' Mumtaz cried out, not

unaware that her outburst sounded like Jackie. 'I hate it. Sure, I love her and I love you. But I hate it.'

'Then marry me,' Adam said quietly.

'Oh, yes. With the in-laws knifing each other at the wedding. And Fina yelling blue murder –' She didn't dare think what Jackie would do.

'We'll sort them out.' And as if reading her thoughts, he added, 'Jackie, too. Don't worry. I'm sure she'll be okay.'

'My parents couldn't take it.' Mumtaz spoke calmly now. How could she get mad at Adam for sleeping with another woman when she wouldn't marry him?

'Then forget about them, for Christ's sake.'

'I can't do that,' Mumtaz murmured. 'I want to be useful, to be who I am. I can break rules but I'm not going to cut myself off.'

'Okay,' Adam said after a moment's pause. 'Then I'll go. It's the only bloody answer in the end.'

'No. Don't you dare.'

Adam wrapped his arms around her tightly and Mumtaz gave him a long fierce kiss.

'Now go back to Jackie,' she said. 'It's all right, go. At least I'll know you're not miserable.'

'Oh, will you?' Adam asked, and as he watched Mumtaz ride off in the night, he tried to remember when their days hadn't been tinged with misery.

Later, at home, he tried to write an essay on Leonardo da Vinci's notebooks, but it was impossible to think of the old master. Instead he sat idly sketching Mumtaz's face while his mother flicked through her casebook, taking copious notes, and Phil sat in front of the mute television set, listening to Beethoven's Ninth on his headphones.

'Have you and Jackie fallen out again?' Sarah asked.

'No,' Adam replied. He knew his mother monitored the time he spent with Jackie, and was oddly protective of the girl she was so opposed to his marrying.

'Do you still see the Sattar girl?'

'Yes.' He wasn't going to elaborate on his relationship with Mumtaz. His mother had discussed the hopelessness of the situation more than once already.

'How long, oh lord, how long?' she said, giving an exaggerated sigh that made Adam throw his pen down with irritation.

'Well, it just seems so pointless,' Sarah continued, as Adam packed up his books.

'And not very fair on Jackie,' she added.

'What's fair?' Adam had to bite his tongue lest he reveal how unfair the situation was for Mumtaz, and him. He frowned, clenching and unclenching his right hand, and was immensely relieved when his father took off his headphones and, oblivious of the subject under discussion, smiled benevolently at his family.

'Klemperer, have a listen.'

'Thanks, but I'm off,' Adam replied. He didn't know if it was because of what Sarah said, but driven by guilt and an equally desperate need for affection, he decided to go back to Jackie.

She was in bed but still awake when he got to the flat.

'Left your date and come back to your old lady, have you?' she asked, in an unsurprised, affectionate tone.

Wordlessly, with a small, rueful smile he turned out the light and sought refuge in her outstretched arms. Although their love-making did not have the passion that charged every kind of exchange – verbal, tactile, and emotional – with Mumtaz, there was undeniable comfort in being with Jackie. Perhaps it was because she had been his first lover and only lover, he thought, or maybe it was simply that they'd been together for so long now.

'You weren't by any chance thinking of her, were you?' she asked when they lay spent, holding each other.

'No.'

'But you are now?'

'Yes,' Adam confessed. There was no need to lie. Jackie understood how he felt about Mumtaz. In fact, it was her own bloody ambivalence that had fostered it.

'You two been to bed yet?' she asked, as if she wouldn't know if they had.

'No.'

'You should,' Jackie said. 'Get it over with.'

Startled by the turn of the conversation born of their intimacy, Adam said nothing, wondering what would be got over. If he slept with Mumtaz it would be another beginning, not an end.

'I wouldn't mind. Honest, it wouldn't bother me in the least.'

Adam stroked her hair, wondering if she realized what she was saying. She never seemed to know, or at least never showed, how much things got to her until she was ready to hit the roof. If she really did understand his love for Mumtaz, how could she speak about bed as something to be got over with?

Adam drove Jackie to Astler's the following morning after they left Fina at the Day Care Centre. She was working full time now and Joe, delighted with what he called her 'business nose', referred to her as his executive secretary. Her own choice of job title bordered on executive gopher, but she loved the work, including all the finagling and hassling. It was also one way to be involved with Adam's family without tying up everybody in knots, matrimonial and otherwise. The only truly negative side to the job was Joe's on-going war with Sattar's. But Jackie had learned to keep her opinions to herself on that score, at least as far as Joe was concerned.

Jackie went directly to her desk by the window and started sorting through the morning post while Adam, anxious to see if what she had said about Joe cutting prices was true, started tapping into the computer. Alex was perched on Joe's desk, frowning as she read the *Leicester Mercury*, and Joe was muttering to himself, half-way to rage, as he tried to light his cigar.

'Blacklegs. She steals my workers. Then, after one whole year of a so-called strike when I hire new ones, she calls them blacklegs!'

'Coffee?' Jackie asked, filling up the kettle.

'Yes, please. I'm glad you're here, darling,' Joe said. 'You, too,' he added to Adam. 'You want coffee?'

'No, I've got to run. I have a lecture on Inigo Jones at ten,' Adam said, still concentrating on the computer.

'And for all those insults, she gets her picture in the paper like a hero. Read it out loud,' Joe commanded his daughter. 'I want my grandson to hear.'

'Announcing the recruitment of a third shift, to provide work for up to forty new employees, Mrs Sattar said, "The Astlers of this world no longer have it all their own way. In future, private firms will think twice before tolerating racism."'

'You hear that?' Joe spluttered, incredulous. 'You hear what she said about me?'

'She doesn't name you directly, Dad,' Alex said, but the silence from Adam and Jackie showed she might as well have done.

'Will you leave that bloody computer alone?' Joe shouted at Adam. 'We have serious business problems.'

Adam continued staring at the screen. 'I know. You're giving the jeans away.'

'We were out for a year. I have to get the trade back from them,' Joe said, jabbing at the newspaper.

'By selling below cost?'

'Adam, either you work here or you don't.'

'Look, if it makes any difference, the Sattars are not doing as well as they make out.' Adam hoped to diminish his grandfather's anger and worry, but instead he increased it.

'I know that,' Joe said. 'How do *you* know?'

Adam saw Jackie's warning frown, but ignored it. She was the one who had so disapproved of his having kept his friendship with Mumtaz a secret. And now she was encouraging him to do exactly that.

'Mumtaz told me.' Adam met his grandfather's gaze.

'Ah, your Arab mole,' Joe said with contempt.

'Joe, this is not the West Bank, and Mumtaz is not an Arab. Please let's try and talk to them.'

'What for? More insults? She can apologize, then maybe I'll talk.'

'He's right about that,' Alex said. 'She shouldn't have made such remarks to a newspaper.'

Torn, Adam tried to be fair. 'It's just that Mrs Sattar has been under a lot of pressure.'

'Yes, and that's because I'm finally hitting back. Let her squirm a little.'

'That's sick,' Adam said, turning away.

'Oh, so you think I'm sick, do you?' Joe said. 'Well, clear off then. Run to your little friend.' He gesticulated wildly towards the door. 'Go on, and don't come back until you know which side you're on.'

Adam stared at him in disbelief. It was almost as if their roles were reversed. Joe was now the angry unreasonable child, and Adam the rational adult. He walked out of the office, attempting composure though this rift with Joe left him trembling and heart-broken.

'Thought this was a family business,' Jackie told Joe, and getting in the last word, she followed Adam out.

Mumtaz didn't hear about the newspaper article until she saw Adam at university, and, even then, they hadn't had time to really speak; only to acknowledge that the feud was now completely out of hand. Mumtaz promised Adam, and herself, that she would try to talk sense to her mother. It was clear that if Shehnaaz and Joe didn't stop fighting now neither of them would have anything left to fight for.

Shehnaaz was in the kitchen preparing the dinner she would not be home to serve. She was working with the brittle efficiency of someone under enormous physical and mental pressure, and hardly noticed when Mumtaz came in.

'Hello, Mum.'

'Oh, Mumtaz, it's you,' was the vague reply.

She didn't have to find a tactful way to bring up the newspaper article because her mother had it prominently displayed on the noticeboard, and she read it with a sinking heart. Adam hadn't exaggerated. 'Isn't this being rather too confident?' she hazarded, knowing how careful she must be.

'People like success stories,' Shehnaaz, the businesswoman, replied. 'It's very good for the order book.'

'But that reference to the Astlers,' Mumtaz began, then hesitated as Shehnaaz turned from the stove to stare at her.

'Yes? What about it?'

'Well, why go on at them? Surely that doesn't do anything for sales.'

Shehnaaz took a deep breath. 'Wherever the boys go they

come sniffing around, underselling us. I just want them to understand that we won't put up with it.'

'Then why not say that? Why this racism business?'

Shehnaaz glared at her. 'Have you forgotten why I left Astler's?'

'Amagee, that was years ago!'

'That foreman is still there.'

'But you're not.'

'So that's the end of racism?' Shehnaaz asked. 'No, I don't think so.'

Mumtaz sighed. 'Mum, isn't it time to stop all this? It's not helping us. Or them.'

'Oh, you know that, do you?' Shehnaaz asked, giving her a shrewd look.

'Yes, I know.' Mumtaz reminded herself that she was no longer a child. 'I run into Adam Morris from time to time at university and we both think it's gone far enough.'

'Oh, you run into him, do you?' Shehnaaz said, seizing upon her admission just as Mumtaz had feared.

'Don't twist what I'm saying. We're simply worried about what's happening to our families, and their businesses.'

'Well, thank you for telling me,' Shehnaaz said coldly, and turned away from Mumtaz with a dismissive shrug.

'Said Farrukh thought I should warn you. You're heading for trouble,' Mumtaz went on, reluctantly but steadily. 'Nasreen has been down to the law centre, and they'll walk out, contract or no contract.'

Shehnaaz threw down the dough she was kneading, now truly enraged, though her anger was no longer directed at Mumtaz. 'This is *their* business! How could they walk out?'

'Is it really theirs?' Mumtaz asked. 'How can you say that when you've just cut their wages?'

'I have capital to repay. Do they want Tariq instead of me?'

'If he'll pay more, probably yes. Settle with Astler's and then you'll be able to pay more. Stop this stupid jeans war,' she urged her mother, but Shehnaaz was lost in her own thoughts, her brow knitted in a concentrated frown, and Mumtaz knew it was pointless to go on.

That evening she met Adam in the library, and when she

felt the warmth of his smile, she felt like weeping. She ought never to have mentioned his name to her mother. How could their love survive in a climate of such hatred?

'Adam, I tried. She won't forgive your grandfather. It's as simple as that.'

'But to keep up this business of calling him a racist,' Adam said, shaking his head. 'Isn't that going too far?'

'Not *him*. It's the foreman. You know that.' She paused. 'Then again . . . maybe Joe too. If you suffer from racism, it can make you racist. I never liked Candy much.'

Adam looked at her, shocked and affronted.

'It comes from Uganda. My family were British colonials. I suppose they were right to chuck us out except that was racist, too. Do you see what I mean? God, it's all such a mess. Why can't people just get on?'

Adam took her hand in both of his, and again Mumtaz felt herself close to tears. She was exhausted by it all, and looking at his drawn face, the dark circles under his eyes, she knew he was too.

'Look, why not meet my family? Someone's got to make the first move.'

'I couldn't,' Mumtaz said. 'It would be not only disloyal, from my parents' point of view, but a terrible betrayal. I've done so much I shouldn't already. Please understand.'

'Can I see your parents, then?'

Mumtaz leaned over the table and kissed him. 'It wouldn't work. You know that.'

'What, then?' Adam asked, but Mumtaz was silent. They had come to the usual end of their conversation. Nothing was resolved, but the way Adam gripped her hand told her it could not continue this way much longer.

Though Joe had apparently calmed down since their confrontation, Adam felt extremely nervous about taking Jackie and Fina to his house for the family Sunday lunch. It took a lot of persuasion from Jackie before he agreed.

To his relief, Joe didn't bring up business. His face wreathed in smiles, he concentrated his still considerable energy on his great-granddaughter: playing the piano for her, giving her rides on his back and bouncing her on his knee until both he and the baby were red in the face and laughing helplessly.

'See? I told you it'd be okay,' Jackie said, watching them play with a serene, maternal smile.

And Adam had to admit she was right. It was an unusually peaceful family gathering, what with Phil passing round the sherry and Sarah quietly reading the Sunday papers.

If only, he thought afterwards, if only Alex hadn't shown Sarah the article in the *Leicester Mercury*.

'This is contemptible,' his mother had cried. 'Why didn't you phone me?'

'What for?' Alex asked.

'To draft a reply before they spread any more lies.'

'It'll pass,' Joe said.

'This kind of thing doesn't pass.'

'Let it rest, Sarah,' her father said, his smile fading.

'The tabloids could pick this up and publish even more muck.'

'Wouldn't go down too well with the Labour Party, would it?' Adam wondered if that was worrying Sarah.

'It's not me, Adam. It's Joe,' she said indignantly. 'If you're not a racist you must say so and say it very loud. Otherwise this rubbish could lead to a witchhunt.'

'And you should know,' Adam murmured under his breath, relieved to see that Joe was turning his attention to Jackie.

'When are you two going to be sensible and make an honest woman out of this little one?'

'I think they say that of the bride,' Phil said, with a smile.

'Yes, her too,' Joe agreed. 'You're too nice to him, *schätzchen*. He's a scoundrel. Make him pay for his pleasure.'

'I thought I did.' Adam tried to join in the game, though his heart wasn't in it.

'After all you've done for this bloody place, Dad. Good God! The work you've brought to this town!' Sarah was now saying, her voice loud above the others.

'The money I've made,' Joe said, giving her a curious glance. 'I thought you disapproved of capitalist pigs.'

'Dad, we may not agree about Israel,' Sarah said. 'But Zionism isn't racism. You don't deserve an attack like this.'

Adam could feel the tension grow, not the least of which was in himself, as Joe, trembling slightly, handed the baby back to Jackie.

'Can't we please let it go?' Adam asked his mother. It had taken several days for Joe to recover his equilibrium and now she was getting him all upset again.

'Why let it go?' Sarah gave him a searching look.

'I really don't think any malice was intended.'

'Oh, you don't?' Joe asked, his tone taking on the same timbre as Sarah's.

'You wouldn't have a personal interest in this, by any chance?' Sarah challenged Adam.

'You know damn well I do,' he replied. 'Mumtaz Sattar is a friend of mine. And I happen to know they're in trouble.'

'They are?' Joe said. '*They* are? Well, what about us?'

'They're dropping their wages.'

'And she tells you about it, does she?' Alex asked, raising one eyebrow.

'Yes, of course. We're lovers, more or less.' He had startled even himself with his simple declaration, and for a moment there was utter silence. Then like a stone dropped in a pool, the ripples began to spread.

'This is infantile,' Sarah said.

'I don't think this is exactly the place or time,' Phil said, while Joe, shocked and incredulous, shook with rage.

'I never thought to hear such a disgusting statement from my own grandson. And you?' he said, turning to Jackie. 'You know about this?'

'Yes. And I love Mumtaz too. Why should we change? Why don't you try to get along with people instead of fighting them?'

'I think this is going to take some talking about.' Phil spoke calmly, but there was nothing controlled about Sarah.

'How could you, Adam?' she screamed. 'Aren't things complicated enough for all of us? I think you'd better go now.'

Adam regarded his mother silently, struck by the irony of the situation. All his life he'd been the one backing Joe, trying to make up for the arguments between his rebellious mother and her father. Now here they both were, up in arms against him. But what bothered him most was Sarah's motive. He couldn't help but suspect she was less upset about her father's business than his involvement with Mumtaz.

'Yes, go!' Joe was saying, between gritted teeth. 'Take the bastard with you and don't bother coming back with the next one.'

Adam stared at him in shock, while Jackie, without a word, swept Fina up in her arms and ran from the house.

'Right then,' Adam said, with a bitter glance round at his family as he followed her. 'We're going. As far as we can get.'

Once roused, Sarah would not or could not calm down. She claimed her father had lost too much time in replying to the Sattar attack and that she must do what she could.

Arriving at work the next morning, she made a call to an associate in the Low Pay Unit department of the Social Services Centre.

'This isn't anything that concerns my department,' she began. 'But I thought you should know. Are you familiar with Sattar's? Well, they're dropping their wages, according to one of the workers. She sounded very upset. I thought it might be something you people should look into.'

Sarah herself hadn't realized how profoundly disturbed she had become over Adam's entanglement with Mumtaz. She had hoped it was an infatuation that he would get over. It could never work with their different backgrounds, never. And, if that weren't trouble enough, there were Jackie and Fina. Adam was too young to know what or whom he wanted. She had no choice but to confront Mumtaz's mother, speak to the woman openly. She knew Mrs Sattar didn't want Adam for her daughter any more than she wanted Mumtaz for her son.

That night on her way home she stopped at the Sattar factory. Finding the door unlocked, she went right in, through a deserted hall and into a large workroom where the rows of sewing and knitting machines stood still and silent.

'Anyone in?' she called.

Shehnaaz was alone in the office, working on her books when she heard the call. She rose slowly and went out into the workroom.

'Yes,' she said, staying to the far end of the room once she had recognized who her caller was.

'Could we have a word?' Sarah was businesslike.

'I've nothing to say to you.'

'It's about your daughter.'

'Be careful,' Shehnaaz interrupted, taking a few steps forward. 'You can lie about my business if you must but –'

'I don't care about your business.' Sarah cut her off. 'I'm worried about my son.'

'And so you should. For a social worker you're remarkably inattentive.'

Sarah ignored the jibe. 'Just keep her away from him.'

'If you had any concept of parental care, you wouldn't need to be here,' Shehnaaz retorted.

'Your daughter needs help.'

'Not from you,' Shehnaaz said proudly.

'It could never work between them. He has a child by another woman. Besides which they have nothing in common.'

'Quite so. Why don't you tell this to him?'

'You agree then?'

'Absolutely. So does my daughter.'

'But I thought –'

'I'm sure he's a nice lad,' Shehnaaz said frostily, 'but he's out of his depth.'

'Don't think we objected because –' Sarah stopped abruptly, hesitating to bring in the issue of race.

Shehnaaz stared at her, her black eyes shining, then suddenly burst into laughter.

'I came here as a mother,' Sarah explained, with an unexpected humility.

Shehnaaz nodded and smiled. 'Can I offer you some tea?'

'No thanks. I'm double-parked and I've got an appointment,' Sarah lied, not wanting to prolong the interview. She'd had her say, and heard what she wanted to hear.

'Another time, then.'

'Perhaps.'

'Give my regards to your father,' Shehnaaz said, her amusement slowly turning back to worry as she watched the other woman go.

The next days were unusually quiet at the Morrises' house. Sarah spoke neither of the Sattars nor of Adam, but immersed herself in her casework and chores for the Labour Party. Phil, on the other hand, was sorely troubled by Adam's continuing absence, and by the way they had parted. He, too, kept silent and waited, hoping to see or hear from Adam. But after four days with no word, and Sarah's easy acceptance of the situation, he began to suspect his wife of keeping information from him.

'Have you seen Adam?' he asked as they ate supper.

'No,' Sarah replied without looking up from the notes she read as they ate.

'Expecting him?' he asked.

'Not really.'

'Goddammit, he's my son!' Phil raised his voice in unaccustomed rage. 'He walks out, we don't see him or hear from him and you sit there studying somebody else's problems!'

'Sorry, sorry,' Sarah murmured in a soothing voice.

'All right, just tell me what's going on, will you?'

'I'm helping him, or trying to.'

'And what does that mean? What have you done?' Phil asked quietly.

'I went to see Mrs Sattar.'

'Oh, no.'

'The girl's at risk. Adam could ruin her. I've seen it happen a million times in my work. Muslim girl, western boy, it's a disaster.'

'And you're sure you couldn't ruin the girl yourself?'

'Darling, we're responsible!' Sarah replied, her pale face colouring slightly. 'Anyway, Mrs Sattar knew already. According to her, the girl doesn't even like Adam. The mother laughed.'

The day Sattar's employees walked out was the worst time Mumtaz could remember since her family was forced to flee Uganda. Shehnaaz was beside herself: hurt, angry, and helpless to meet her workers' demands. Mumtaz knew from her book-keeping that there wasn't enough money to pay higher wages. When the workers asked to be cut into the profits, Shehnaaz had to admit that there were none; the jeans price war with Astler's had taken care of that. Their final demand, that the factory be turned into a workers' co-op, as Shehnaaz had always promised, also had to be denied. The company was still Tariq's in all but name, and not hers to share.

Mumtaz was relieved when her father arrived at the factory to take his place at Shehnaaz's side. She left him to comfort her mother as only he could, and hurried over to Jackie's to share the burden of her worries with the ones who understood her best. There, she sat drinking tea with Adam and Jackie as she brought them up to date with the latest, somewhat mystifying developments.

'I don't know who's been stirring things up,' she said. 'But it's not the law centre. Said has been desperate to cool things down.'

'Taz, look, there's something you should know,' Adam said. 'I told my family the truth about us.'

Mumtaz looked from Adam to Jackie with a sharp intake of breath. 'What happened?'

Jackie rolled her eyes. 'What didn't? Adam chose his moment well – Sunday family dinner.'

Adam gave her a small smile. 'Fall of Man. I'm banished from the Garden of Astler. Out.'

Mumtaz felt her heart turn over. 'And how long until it reaches my parents?'

Although Mumtaz was extremely apprehensive about a confrontation with her parents – now inevitable – she tried to hold her fears at bay, giving her time and thoughts to the anti-apartheid society and the arrangements for Mr Marule's speech at the student union.

On the night of his visit, when she went into the living-room to say goodbye to her parents, she found Sadiq reading a book while Shehnaaz, her lips pressed together in concentration, sat at her desk with note-pads and a calculator.

'Could you check these for me?' she asked Mumtaz. 'I can't make them add up.'

'What are they?' Mumtaz asked, flipping through the pages.

'Projections,' her mother replied wearily. 'Maybe you'd pull up a chair and keep me company.'

'Not tonight, Mum, I can't,' Mumtaz said, looking at her in surprise. 'Don't you remember? I've got that speaker from the African National Congress coming to the student union.'

'Well, then, you'd better run along.'

'I'll do it first thing tomorrow,' Mumtaz promised, trying to placate her mother, and assuage her own guilt. But Shehnaaz was not in a mood for being put off.

'Go! Just go!' she flared out. 'You've left us anyway so what difference can it make?'

'I'll help,' Sadiq intervened. 'You get along, Mumtaz.'

But Mumtaz, stunned by her mother's outburst, stood still, her eyes lowered, wondering what was to come next.

'Go,' Sadiq repeated. 'You'll be late. I'll collect you when it's over.'

'Thank you, Aba,' she murmured, and walked slowly away.

'Hush, it will be all right,' she heard Sadiq say to her mother who was weeping now. 'We'll get the business straightened out.'

'It's not that.'

'What then?' Sadiq asked. 'It's Mumtaz, isn't it? But, what's wrong?'

Mumtaz paused in the hallway, torn between wanting to hear Shehnaaz's reply and to run away.

'Nothing you couldn't have guessed,' she heard her mother say bitterly.

It was an obvious reference to Adam and, her heart heavy, she fled the house.

Adam was waiting in front of the student union, watching for her when Mumtaz arrived and she experienced an overwhelming sense of relief and warmth as he took her hands in his. It came to her then that partly what she felt was freedom. She was free now that her parents knew about Adam. No more evasions, hiding or subterfuge. She and Adam needn't hide their feelings for each other from anyone, any more; not even themselves.

'Trouble?' Adam asked, puzzled by her silence.

Mumtaz gave him a kiss, not caring who might see. 'My mother found out. But I don't care as much as I thought I would. It will be all right. As long as we can be brave.'

'That will be the easy part,' Adam said, ushering her into the building.

The lecture room was packed by the time Mr Marule arrived and Mumtaz felt a thrill of pleasure at the deafening applause as she escorted him to the podium. He was a small, unassuming black African, dressed in a neat grey business suit, but his dark eyes were filled with purpose, a determination and dedication that had already captivated many.

Mumtaz approached the microphone, flushed and nervous, but when she spoke her voice was steady and clear.

'It's an honour to welcome, on behalf of the students' union and the anti-apartheid society, Mr Marule of the African National Congress, who is here to talk about the state of emergency in South Africa, and what the resistance movement is doing.'

The question and answer period after Mr Marule's lecture extended far beyond the allotted hour, and then almost everyone – the speaker included – adjourned to the Mandela Lounge for further discussions over drinks.

'Congratulations. A very successful evening,' someone said at Mumtaz's elbow, and turning she saw it was Said Farrukh.

'Thought I'd come and surprise you,' he said, smiling.

'Well, you have,' Mumtaz told him, returning his smile, though she was puzzled and touched to see him there.

'I'm impressed with the way you organized this. Well done.' He hesitated a moment, glancing at his watch. 'Can I drop you off anywhere?'

'Thanks, but I have a lift.'

'Well, then, see you Saturday.'

Mumtaz watched Said go out of the door, then hurried over to Adam who was clearing up behind the bar. 'What did you think?' she asked. It was his opinion she'd been wanting to hear all night.

'Frankly, I was a bit shocked at all that anti-semitism.'

'Anti-Zionism,' Mumtaz corrected him. 'Israel is arming South Africa. It's a fact.'

'So what do I do? Join the PLO?' Adam asked, smiling.

She squeezed his hand, wanting to stay with him, close to him, but knowing that she must leave. 'I'd better go. Dad will be waiting.'

'Stay with me,' Adam said, grabbing her hand and pulling her back to him with sudden force.

'I've got to go home and face them,' Mumtaz said. If she chose to be free, she must meet them as an adult.

'Taz, listen. Just talk to them.'

'I may not be given the opportunity,' she said, with a rueful smile.

'Then leave. Call me. I'll be at the flat. I'll come and get you. We'd get by all right, you know.'

Mumtaz kissed him. 'I do love you,' she whispered and, hurrying from the lounge, she made her way down the drive to the main road.

It was a cold dark night and she felt uneasy as she stood there, scanning the passing cars for her father. It was unusual for Sadiq to be late. Perhaps he wasn't coming, now that he knew the worst. She stepped back as a battered car slowed down.

'Wanta ride?' A tough-looking boy, no older than Rashid, stuck his head out of the window. 'Get in.'

'Christ, it's another damn Indian tart,' his companion said.

'Pack up your bags, Paki,' the yob at the wheel shouted viciously, and putting his foot down, roared away.

Shaken, Mumtaz started to run back up the drive, and then stopped, relieved, as she saw the lights of Sadiq's cab turning into the drive.

'Hey, you!'

Her welcoming smile turned to a grimace of fear as the car accelerated towards her and spun round in a U-turn. The thugs were back.

'Figured we wouldn't pass up a free dish of curry.'

A stocky skinhead had got out of the car and was standing in front of her, holding his arms out.

'No, you don't, bitch,' he said, as she tried to bolt past him towards the union.

'Come on, Paki whore, we ain't got all night even if you have.' A six-foot bearded youth had got out of the car and was coming towards her while a third thug in black stood holding the rear car door open with mock civility and a vicious leer.

She began to scream then, wild sobbing cries as she struck out at the men who were trying to drag her into the car.

'No, no! Leave me alone! Get away!' she screamed, kicking at them as they tightened their grip on her arms. She thought she was done for when she heard a wild yelling that was not her own and suddenly Adam was there, laying into the yobs with a crazy, mindless courage. He knocked down one of them and as Mumtaz, forgotten, lay in a helpless heap, the other two closed in on him with a lethal battery of kicks and punches.

'Adam! Adam!' she screamed again. The beating lasted only a few minutes, but it felt like hours before they had done with Adam, and were piling back into their car.

Less hurt than shocked, Mumtaz crawled over to Adam and took him in her arms. His face was bruised and already badly swollen. There was blood coming from his mouth and nose and he lay with his knees doubled up, clutching his abdomen in pain.

'Oh, Adam,' she cried again, and held him tightly, moaning with his pain.

Sadiq found them like that twenty minutes later and for the first time in his life broke every traffic regulation speeding to the hospital. Horrified, holding himself responsible, he telephoned Sarah and Phil Morris, and then sat waiting, his lips moving soundlessly with prayer.

It was an hour before he, and the Morrises, were taken into the casualty ward.

Adam, pale and shaken, but cleaned up and bandaged, was laughing softly as Mumtaz adjusted the patch over his eye.

'I feel like Captain Hook.'

Neither of them was aware of their parents until Sadiq cleared his throat.

'They say you can leave now.'

'You're both going to be just fine,' Sarah said. 'Thank heavens it wasn't worse.'

'You needn't have come. We're fine,' Adam said stiffly and put his arm around Mumtaz.

'How exactly did it happen?' Phil asked. 'Do you know who they were?'

'Just a car-load of thugs. They went after Mumtaz. Taz, my parents, Phil and Sarah. You met at college once,' he said with a defiant glance at his mother.

'Yes, I remember. Hello, Mumtaz,' Sarah said, holding out her hand. 'I'm so sorry you had to experience this terrible thing tonight.'

'If it weren't for your son –' Sadiq said, and broke off. 'We are deeply grateful to him for rescuing her.'

'Has Mrs Sattar been told, then?' Sarah asked.

'Not yet. I didn't want to alarm her. But now we will go home and explain everything,' Sadiq replied and waited for Mumtaz to join him at the door.

'Mumtaz and I are going to Jackie's,' Adam said, calm but resolute. 'We'll make our own way.'

Sadiq continued to gaze at Mumtaz, his dark eyes burning.

'I'd like to look after him, if nobody minds,' she explained, returning his look and trying to smile.

Sarah shrugged, nodded at Sadiq and left.

'Give me a ring tomorrow, Adam,' Phil said, following her out of the room.

'I will take you in the taxi,' Sadiq said, cold and formal, and didn't speak again.

'I'm sorry, Abagee,' Mumtaz said when they arrived at Jackie's flat, and tried to take his hand. 'I can't leave Adam like this.' Her eyes pleaded for understanding, but Sadiq turned away.

'I'll be back tomorrow, if you want me,' Mumtaz said, and winced at the resentment in her father's eyes.

'I know. I'm sorry,' she murmured again, and quickly got out of the car.

Jackie made Adam and Mumtaz recount the events of the night over coffee.

'The bastards, the bloody bastards,' she kept repeating. 'I should have been there.'

'Listen,' Adam finally said. 'I'm dropping. Where's the sleeping bag?'

Mumtaz looked down at the floor, suddenly self-conscious now that sleeping arrangements were to be discussed.

'Just get to bed,' Jackie told him. 'Go on.'

'I'll stop in here,' she told Mumtaz when they were alone.

'No. I will.'

Jackie sighed. 'Come on, it's late. There's room for everyone in that big old bed.'

Fina's soft senseless chatter woke Jackie early the next morning. She gazed at Adam sleeping soundly beside her, then glanced on her other side where Mumtaz lay fast asleep. With an odd sad smile she crawled out of bed, and picked up Fina.

'Come on, dumpling, we're going to visit your granny.'

Mumtaz was awakened later that morning by the sound of the birds singing outside. For a moment, disorientated by the unfamiliar surroundings, her dark eyes registered puzzlement, then, fleetingly, shock as she realized Jackie was gone and she and Adam had rolled into the middle of the bed. She felt him warm beside her and didn't know whether to draw away or move closer. He stirred slightly, and she turned towards him and gazed into his face, seeing none of the bruises, only the love reflected there.

She knew after their first kiss that they had reached the point of no return; but she didn't want to go back to the way things were. When Adam pulled back slightly to give her a look of warning, she adjusted his eye patch, covered his other eye with her fingers and pulled him back to her. She felt shy of his eyes, yet was made bold by the touch of him. Their love-making was very gentle, all the more sensuous for its very caution and slowness. It was unlike anything Mumtaz had ever imagined and she knew this was truly the culmination of their love.

They got up just before noon and went into the kitchen to prepare breakfast as if they'd been living together for ages. They hardly spoke. But there was so little need for words now, Mumtaz thought. Each caress or kiss they stopped to exchange as they moved about the kitchen became more articulate.

They were just about to sit down at the table when Mumtaz heard the front door open below and Fina bawling. She looked over at Adam, suddenly embarrassed and nervous, but he smoothed down her hair, smiling reassurance.

'Smells good,' Jackie said, coming into the kitchen, carrying the howling baby. She hesitated a fraction as she took in Adam and Mumtaz's state, then thrust Fina into Mumtaz's arms.

'Dying for a pee,' she said. 'You don't mind, do you? It was a long bus ride back from my mum's.'

Mumtaz floundered, not knowing what to do with the crying baby, and a bit frightened of Jackie.

'What brought all this on?' Adam called to Jackie, as he took the child from Mumtaz.

'She didn't like the bus conductor.'

'So how was your mum?' he asked casually when Jackie emerged, slightly pale.

'Fine,' she replied distantly, and went into the front room.

'No rude comments?' Adam asked, following her, trying to ease the growing tension between the three of them. He glanced at Mumtaz for help, and she gently pushed him out of the room and closed the door.

'What can I say?' she began, sitting down beside Jackie.

'God, I'm sorry, Taz,' Jackie said, slowly dissolving into tears. '*You're* sorry?'

'It wasn't that I minded you two being together. I just couldn't bear being alone.'

'What happened?' Mumtaz asked, growing alarmed.

'Nothing, nothing.' Jackie burrowed into Mumtaz's arms like a child. 'How was your morning? Was it nice? Christ, at least tell me it was all right.'

'It was wonderful,' Mumtaz said quietly, feeling both grateful and guilty as she wiped the tears from her friend's face. 'Now tell me.'

'I couldn't stay here, could I? Didn't want to. So I took Fina to my mum's. Only she wasn't there. But Richard was.' Jackie sobbed as she pronounced her stepfather's name and Mumtaz tightened her hold around her.

'He invited us in for tea. Said it might be easier without mum around since we never seemed to get on when she was. So I said fine, we'd stop in for a quick one,' she paused. 'And that's just what I had,' she said in a muffled voice.

'Oh, Jackie, no. Oh, my dear,' she said, trying to comfort her friend, while her own new world came tumbling down. It was so like Jackie – her wild, ambiguous gestures. This shameful act of giving in to her mother's man was merely a cry for help; a cry for Adam to come and save her. Mumtaz felt her heart breaking, not only for herself, knowing that she must give Adam up, but also for Jackie who could never let him go.

'My mum came home just as we were leaving,' Jackie was saying. 'She clocked the scene in one minute.'

Mumtaz continued holding her until the sobs subsided. She thought how brave Jackie had been all these years with Adam. She had been independent to the point of rebuffing him, always hoping to make him take a stand. But when she considered that he might really choose Mumtaz, she had made an impetuous, desperate move for his attention. Mumtaz sighed, and slowly rose. It was time for her to leave them alone together. She had her night of love and she would hold it in her heart for ever. The rest was up to Adam.

'Where's Jackie? What happened in there?' he asked, when Mumtaz came into the kitchen.

'Please talk to her.'

Adam grabbed hold of her hand. 'Taz, don't run.'

'Go to her.'

'No regrets?'

Mumtaz shook her head and he kissed her. She held on to him, embracing him tightly, and he smiled, relieved. He brushed the hair back from her face, the touch of his hand an intimate caress, kissed her once more and left. Mumtaz looked blankly round the kitchen, then went to the bedroom and got dressed to go home.

Jackie was folding a pile of laundered baby clothes and Adam could tell from her swift precise movements that she was trying to be busy. He watched her, wondering what to say, how to pick up the pieces.

'Listen, I know it doesn't make much sense, but, in a way, I love you more now. Can you understand that?'

'Would you do the same for me?'

He tried to be honest. 'I don't know.'

'Was it better with her than me?' she asked, getting straight to the point.

Adam hesitated. 'Different,' he said. The intimacy and passion they had experienced surpassed anything he'd ever known. He couldn't imagine wanting or having anyone else now.

'There's something I should tell you,' Jackie said slowly, her eyes filling with tears again.

'Whatever it is, it's okay,' Adam told her, but he was completely unprepared for the halting, remorseful story she told him.

'Why did you let him do it? Why now?' he demanded, suspecting it was because of Mumtaz, even though Jackie herself had encouraged, in fact arranged, their early morning together.

'I don't know,' Jackie insisted, and he had to accept this for the truth.

'And Fina was watching, I suppose?' He felt his guilt giving way to anger.

'No!'

'What did you tell her? Mummy's going upstairs for a minute. Or did you do it on the kitchen table?' he asked, unable to stop.

'Just leave! This ought to make it easier.'

'Did you tell Taz?'

'I need a friend too!' Jackie said defensively.

'Oh, Jesus!' Adam looked at her with disgust. 'You wanted to get rid of her, didn't you?'

'I don't know. I really don't.' Jackie met his accusing gaze. 'Please don't go on at me any more.' Adam continued to stare at her for a moment, as though seeing her for the first time, and then he left.

Sadiq had driven around Leicester for hours after leaving Mumtaz with Adam, while Shehnaaz fretted all night. Now that he had told her all that had taken place, far from being reassured, she was nearly hysterical.

'Why couldn't you have phoned?' she kept demanding.

'I didn't know what to say.'

'She's really unharmed?'

Sadiq nodded. 'Barely a scratch.'

'And you just let her get out and walk away with the Astler boy?' Shehnaaz asked in disbelief.

'His woman lives there. She's got a child. Do you think she's going to let anything happen?' Sadiq reasoned, though he himself felt unsure.

'Then why are you so upset?'

He merely shrugged.

'Why didn't you stop her?' Shehnaaz persisted.

'How? She's an adult!' Sadiq argued. 'What was I to do, scream and shout? Drag her home by the hair? He saved her life. Don't you understand?' He watched his wife who was frowning. 'What is it? What do you know?' he asked, realizing he was not alone in his knowledge of Mumtaz's secret love. 'You knew, didn't you?'

'And you've always known!' she replied with an accusatory glance, though she doubted that either one of them could have changed the course of her daughter's heart.

Mumtaz arrived home in the early evening after walking around the city for most of the afternoon. She didn't know where she'd been. Her legs felt numb, her heart sore, but her head was quite clear. There was no way for her to hang on to Adam, she now knew, because hanging on is just what it would be. Jackie needed him more. What she had done today showed how much she really did want Adam in spite of her cavalier manner. It also showed that she couldn't really take care of herself.

Rashid came bounding downstairs as Mumtaz closed the front door.

'The heroine returns!'

Sadiq quickly appeared in the living-room. 'Properly discharged from the hospital? If you had phoned, I would have come for you.'

Mumtaz coloured, realizing he had invented this explanation of her night's absence for her brothers.

'You're a real tigerwoman,' Rashid said proudly.

'Sure,' Mumtaz replied, trying to adopt a cocky tone.

'And look who else is home?' Rashid said, as Hafiz, looking handsome and well, came downstairs. He went straight over to Mumtaz and gave her a warm hug. She felt herself on the verge of tears, and tried to laugh instead.

'You look terrific,' she said. 'The business is really beginning to agree with you.'

'It went quite well. Manchester isn't a bad town.'

'How's the Astler kid?' Rashid asked. 'Dad said he rescued you like Superman.'

'Sounds like he put up quite a fight,' Hafiz said, giving her a quizzical look, but Mumtaz turned away.

'Abagee, do you think you and Ama could spare a minute?'

Sadiq nodded. 'You sit down. I'll get your mother. Perhaps you boys could manage a cup of tea.'

'Yeah, sure,' Hafiz and Rashid replied in unison.

Mumtaz faltered slightly when Shehnaaz entered the living-room, but her mother was past anger, her dark eyes were filled with love and concern.

'How are you feeling?'

'Awful,' Mumtaz replied, quite honestly.

'It will pass,' her mother promised.

Mumtaz looked at both her parents and took a deep breath. 'I know you'll be surprised, but I want to get married.'

The tense glance her parents exchanged alerted her to the ambiguity of her remark. They thought she meant Adam, when that was exactly what she didn't mean. 'I ought to be settled. I want to work. I want someone to look after me. I think father should find me a husband. Someone who'll accept me as I am.'

'Mumtaz, you've had a very nasty shock,' Sadiq began, but she interrupted him. She wanted the business settled now so that she could get on with life.

'Why not speak to Uncle Tariq?'

'Not Hassan, never,' Shehnaaz intervened.

'It would help the business,' Mumtaz countered. 'It would be a good move.'

'I'll sell first.'

Sadiq started pacing the room, shaking his head. 'She shouldn't be thinking of marrying at all, not until she qualifies.'

'Please, Aba,' Mumtaz beseeched him. 'Look at all our friends.'

'You're different,' her father replied, and Mumtaz wanted to scream her denial.

'I can't do it any more. Don't you see? I just want to be a good Muslim. Please. That's all.'

'Will you tell her now?' Shehnaaz asked Sadiq. He closed his eyes, pressing his lips together with reluctance, then spoke.

'We have received a marriage proposal through the Imam.'

Mumtaz looked up in surprise. 'Who from?'

Her father hesitated. 'You've no idea? He's very well-connected. The Imam was very impressed.'

'Who?'

'You know the man,' Sadiq said. 'His parents made it clear that this was his idea. He wanted to do things properly.'

'Not Said?' Mumtaz asked doubtfully.

Her father nodded.

'How long have you known?' she asked, stunned.

'A couple of months.'

Mumtaz laughed and shook her head. It might work. She certainly respected Said, and they had much in common. 'Why didn't you tell me?'

'I didn't want you to be bothered,' Sadiq replied. 'You're young still.'

'Yes, think about it,' her mother advised. 'There's no rush.'

'None,' Sadiq assured her. 'It's clearly not what you want right now.'

'But it is,' Mumtaz insisted. She thought fleetingly of Adam, knowing that their perfect love-making had made her impure. 'I'm just not sure it's fair on him,' she finished, wondering if she could ever learn another kind of love.

Adam spent a long time walking along the riverbank after he left Jackie, hoping to outdistance his anger; to understand her action, and his own mixed feelings which had precipitated it. Yet all it did was remind him of the hours they had once spent by the river. Those days seemed so far away; he and Jackie were different people now. If it weren't for their child, would they have stayed together this long? Not that Jackie had ever wanted him to be a full-time parent. Or had she felt – maybe rightly – that he wasn't ready for it?

He couldn't fault her for what had happened with Richard. It was himself he blamed for that.

But why had she always been so ambivalent about *him*? Why had she always insisted that he and Mumtaz belonged together?

Well, she was right about that. His heart filled with the memory of the early morning, those few tender, passionate hours with Mumtaz obliterated all other thoughts. If Jackie had a need for him, it was inconsistent, ambiguous. But there was no question, there never had been, of how much he and Mumtaz needed and wanted each other.

They belonged together. It was with her he felt most truly himself. There was so much they had to speak about; so many plans to make. He glanced at his watch. There was still time; he'd go to her house now. They'd settle things between them and then tell her parents. He turned back to his car, walking faster until this new urgency made him break into a run.

Rashid opened the Sattars' door and Adam tensed slightly as he saw the other's hesitation.

'Is Mumtaz in?' he asked, trying to feel as if his calling there were a natural thing. It was his right. Whatever else had happened they were truly bound to each other now.

Rashid slowly extended a hand. 'Come in. And thanks for helping my sister last night.'

'Who is it?' Shehnaaz called from the hallway.

'It is Mumtaz's friend, Adam.'

Adam listened anxiously for Mumtaz, but the footsteps he heard were her mother's.

'I hope you aren't too badly hurt,' she said gently. 'I wanted to call and thank you.'

'Is Mumtaz all right? Could you tell her I'm here?'

Shehnaaz hesitated. 'One moment, please,' she said, and left the room as Hafiz came in.

'Welcome,' he said, smiling at Adam. 'We are grateful to you. Sorry they messed you up, but I hear you did a good job on them, too.'

'Worse than our market day, eh?' Rashid said.

Adam tried to respond to the two brothers' good-natured banter, but he was bewildered by their high spirits. He understood that they were pleased with him for protecting Mumtaz, but he had anticipated, if not actual fireworks, at least hostility over his involvement with her.

Shehnaaz came back downstairs, smiling apologetically. 'Mumtaz sends you her greetings and says please excuse her, she is resting now.'

'I see,' Adam said, bewildered. It was the last thing he had expected.

'She's somewhat overwhelmed.' Shehnaaz spoke casually, though she watched his face. 'Today she had an offer of marriage.'

Adam felt the blood rush to his head. 'What? She what?'

'A good man,' Hafiz interjected. 'She's done well.'

'He's a big-shot lawyer,' Rashid said, strutting across the room. 'One of the fat cats.'

'Rashid, it's a secret,' Shehnaaz scolded her son indulgently. Then she turned to Adam. 'He is one of Mumtaz's colleagues, Said Farrukh.'

'Please, couldn't I talk to her?' Adam tried to hide his desperation, speaking slowly and calmly. 'Just for a minute?'

'I think not today.' Shehnaaz guided Adam towards the door. 'Please give my regards to your grandfather. Our differences don't count for much, do they? Not after last night.'

Adam broke away from her gentle grasp on his arm and ran to the staircase.

'Taz! Come down! Please!'

There was a hush of surprise and apprehension as everyone waited, but no response came from upstairs.

Shehnaaz hurried to Adam's side. 'Please go,' she gave him a beseeching glance. 'Mumtaz is so fortunate.' But he waited, still gazing at the stairs.

'Taz!' he called again, his voice breaking.

'Think of her,' Shehnaaz pleaded. 'You've protected her so well. You're a good friend.'

Suddenly drained of energy, his legs gone weak and unsteady, Adam allowed himself to be led to the door. Once outside, he stood for a long while staring at the upstairs windows, waiting for a sign or message that never came.

# OCTOBER, 1987

The Mandela Lounge was packed for the term's first student union meeting. Six union officers stood at the front of the room, Mumtaz in the centre at the microphone. She wore an exquisite silver and blue *shalwar kameez* and her long black hair was pulled back in a loose plait.

'I'm sorry you couldn't vote for us, but here we are,' she told the freshmen. 'If we do a lousy job, you can throw us out at the end of term. You may not find anyone else to take over, but you can try.' She smiled. Next year at this time, she'd be done with university, and someone else would be standing here. She'd be a practising lawyer, maybe a practising mother, always a practising Muslim. 'And now, if you'll excuse me,' she concluded, glancing at Said who waited at the door, 'I must go. I'm getting married this afternoon.'

The room broke out in friendly cheers as Mumtaz joined Said and she felt proud and secure. For once she really knew what she was doing, what was expected of her, and she'd got it right. She had told Said everything about herself and Adam and from that point on, hadn't looked back. With Said she had, day by day, built a close and solid relationship. They liked and respected each other and shared many common interests. If at times she wondered if that was enough, if she experienced a fleeting sense of nostalgia for the past with Adam, she quickly tamped it down by studying harder, or distracting herself with her political activities.

'Taz!'

She and Said were in the lobby, trying to make their way through a crowd of well-wishers, when Adam pushed his way to them.

'Wait, Taz!'

Her heart skipped a beat at the sound of his voice. She hadn't known he was back from Israel.

'Adam. Nice to see you,' she said, smiling brightly, though she was stunned at the sight of him; the fortnight's stubble shading his fair pale skin, his scruffy clothes, and the mauve smudges of sleeplessness beneath his eyes.

'I just got back,' he said. 'Heard your little speech.' His blue eyes searched her face.

'I'm sorry. We really have to dash,' Mumtaz said. 'I'll see you around.'

'No, listen –' Adam stood in their path, staring at Said.

'Adam, this is Said Farrukh,' Mumtaz said, tightening her hold on his arm. 'My fiancé.'

'Yes, we've met,' Adam said. 'A long time ago.' He stared at Mumtaz, puzzlement mingling with pain as he tried to match this present woman to the inner image he had been carrying around. Then he turned to Said.

'I'm her lover,' he said. It was a challenge, but the older man merely took out his car keys.

'I'll be waiting in the car,' he told Mumtaz.

She studiously avoided Adam's gaze until Said had gone, then she rounded on him. 'Did you think I hadn't told Said?' she asked, furious that these past carefully constructed, disciplined months should be threatened.

'I thought you were waiting a year to marry. After finals, remember?' Adam said, as if it were an arrangement Mumtaz had made with him, not Said. He felt warmed, just by the familiarity of her anger.

'It's just the register office,' she found herself explaining. 'The wedding will be next summer. It's simply a form of engagement.'

'Pretty bloody final, if you ask me. And legal.'

'Well, it's none of your business, and no one's asking you.' She wouldn't let him interfere with her life again.

'Do you love him?'

'Yes,' she snapped at him defiantly.

'Be honest!' Adam said, seizing hold of her hand.

'You're telling me to be honest,' Mumtaz said, drawing her hand free. 'It's time to grow up, Adam. You've got a child and a woman who needs you. What the hell are you doing?' she asked, her fingers still burning from his touch.

'Missing you,' he murmured. 'Loving you.'

Mumtaz bit down hard on her lip trying to keep the warmth

of his words from enveloping her. 'I don't understand you. I don't know what you stand for.'

'What I've always stood for,' Adam replied. 'Us.'

Mumtaz gave a deep sigh. 'It couldn't have worked. You know that. Each time we got close to trying, you saw how much damage was done.'

Adam shook his head, not listening to her. 'Are you sure you're not using him?' he asked.

'How?' In fact, Mumtaz worried about this all the time. She had never felt worthy of Said's love.

'Is it *him*? Do you want *him*? Or the Muslim life?'

'Both.'

'Does it work in bed?' Adam asked, his gaze so intimate Mumtaz felt the colour rise to her cheeks.

'It will, when we choose.' Said did not expect her to sleep with him until they were married in the Muslim ceremony, and meanwhile she tried not to give the matter too much thought, for the very idea of love-making evoked memories of Adam.

'Well, I'd hate to be him if it doesn't,' he said, turning to go, and his words and bitter tone caused Mumtaz to stumble slightly as she hurried to the car.

Said made no reference to Adam as he steered the car through Leicester's busy traffic, but Mumtaz felt weighed down by the unspoken presence. She watched Said who kept his eyes fixed on the road, his mouth set and serious. He wasn't the sort of man to put up with such scenes. He was a politician who needed a hard-working, respectable wife.

'I think we'd better call it off,' she said.

'Is that what you really want?' Said asked, jolted.

'I wanted you to be proud of me.'

'But that is just what I am. Very much so,' he said, giving her a warm glance. 'Now can we be happy?'

Mumtaz smiled and leaned over to kiss him on the cheek. 'Yes, please.'

The fact that she was getting married scarcely penetrated her consciousness, so intently did Mumtaz concentrate on the details of the register office procedure. It wasn't until later that night, during the festive celebration at her home that she began to realize the truth of what Adam had said. Register office or not, it was final and legal. Even as she recalled his words, she told herself she must put the memory of him – past and present – out of her mind. She had an important new role to perform and the two families, the Imam and a few friends were there to witness as well as celebrate it.

'Mumtaz, check the oven before everything burns.' Shehnaaz, in charge of the proceedings, was glowing with pride in her moment of triumph. The marriage was not, however, the only reason for Shehnaaz's high spirits. Said's father had offered to take over her business loan from Tariq. Much to Mumtaz's discomfort, for she felt it added new strings to an already complicated marriage contract.

'Come on, featherhead,' Shehnaaz teased her as she slowly removed some trays from the oven. 'They'll be starving out there.'

Mumtaz tested the *samozas*, and put the trays back in. 'Can't make them bake any faster.'

Shehnaaz took the oven glove from her. 'I'll do it. You go and get ready.'

On her way upstairs, Mumtaz heard the voices of the men, especially that of the Imam, congratulating himself on 'this most illustrious match'.

'Sadiq, you're so old-fashioned. Why not marry them and have done with it?' he asked.

'I'm not having Said ruin my daughter's education.' Sadiq's reply brought a round of indulgent laughter.

'Ah, yes,' the Imam said. 'I myself have nothing against the education of women.'

'Is that so?' Sadiq asked, as incredulous as Mumtaz who had paused on the stairs to listen.

'Not with such a happy ending,' the Imam replied. 'She'll make a good wife.'

Mumtaz stopped smiling. Wife. What would it mean? She'd done all right as a daughter, and after a rough beginning, had done well as a student. But it was easier to imagine being a lawyer than being Said's wife.

'Think how much longer you'll have to wait for your grandchildren,' the Imam said, and Mumtaz felt a moment of unease. She was grateful that Said hadn't tested the physical side of their relationship. Their kisses tended to be little more than affectionate, but then Said was a very moderate man. He didn't have the emotions, the passionate nature of Adam. Mumtaz caught herself up short at this thought and slowly went to her room.

After his encounter with Mumtaz, Adam had returned to the Mandela Lounge where he drank to her marriage, for her marriage and against her marriage until the bar closed late that night. Then, unable to face his family or his loneliness, he headed for Jackie's flat, where he found only Meera left in residence.

'You didn't know, then?' she said. 'Well, how would you? Haven't exactly kept in touch, have you?'

'Where are they?' Adam's words were still slurred, but finding Jackie and Fina gone had considerably sobered him.

'Her mum finally broke with the lech and she asked Jackie to come back home. She's dotty about Fina. She takes care of her while Jackie goes to work.' Meera paused, examining Adam closely. 'You don't seem in such great shape. Look, I know how things are with your folks. So if you want to camp out for a while in Jackie's old room it's okay with me.'

Adam told himself it might take a few days to get used to Mumtaz's marriage and to get himself reoriented to Leicester again. But for the next fortnight he did nothing except brood in the afternoon, drink too much at night, and sleep it off all morning.

It was nearly three weeks before he appeared at Jackie's house – clean-shaven and freshly dressed. He knew he had a lot to make up to her. If it could be made up. There was no real excuse for the way he'd just taken off for Israel without giving her and Fina a second thought. Yet, even in his absence, she had proved her loyalty by sticking with Joe. Mumtaz was out of his life now – he'd learn to accept that – and his place was with Jackie and Fina.

'Hi,' he said as Jackie opened the door. Her face was thinner, more finely chiselled around the cheekbones, her hair a bit longer and wilder, but the sultry blue eyes that gazed into his were the same. Evocative and provocative.

'Thought you'd forgotten us,' she said casually, holding the door open to him.

Adam followed her into a cluttered living-room. Clothes were drying on a rack by the heater, toys were scattered about the floor, and Jackie's mother sat in an armchair dressing Fina.

'Look who wandered in, pumpkin. It's your daddy,' Jackie said.

'Hi, Fina.' Adam, feeling a surge of love and guilt, stared hard at his daughter, hardly able to believe she was already two-and-a-half. Blond ringlets and big round blue eyes, she was the very image of Jackie.

'I'll go get us tea,' Jackie said, while Adam gave Fina the Star of David he had bought for her in Jerusalem.

'She's really grown,' he told Jackie's mother.

'It would be more apparent to you than us,' was the cold reply.

'Look, the last time we met – when Jackie left Leicester – well, I'm sorry for the way I talked.'

'You needn't be,' the older woman said. 'It was all true. I was a rotten wife and a rotten mother. But I'm quite good as a grandmum, aren't I, petal?' She cuddled Fina who chortled delightedly.

'Thanks for looking after them.'

'Jackie's really fine now,' her mother said with a meaningful look. 'We all are.'

Adam nodded, then reached for Fina. 'May I hold her?' He had a desperate need to feel the warmth of family.

'She's your daughter.'

Adam pressed Fina to him, breathing in her talcy baby smell, and it all felt very right to him. He wondered why he'd stayed away so long.

When Jackie returned with the tea, her mother announced she was taking Fina out for a stroll and Adam, left alone with Jackie, felt tongue-tied. He had no idea where or how to begin. There was, he knew, bitterness on both sides.

'Mumtaz has got married.'

'I know,' Jackie replied, without expression.

'I wanted to get over it. That's why I didn't come sooner,'

he said, and cursed himself for a fool to start that way. 'What I really want to say is – I'm sorry. I shouldn't have left you like that last summer. As soon as I was gone, I wanted to come back.'

'Why didn't you?'

Adam was silent for a moment. 'I just didn't know how,' he admitted. It was the same reason he hadn't been able to face his family yet. He'd got over his anger at their behaviour over the Mumtaz affair, but it had been replaced by a feeling of failure. He felt that he had failed everyone. Joe, for not saving the business; Sarah, for not being a prize student and activist; Phil for not being like him; Mumtaz, Jackie – the list was endless.

'Christ, you're worse than Joe,' Jackie murmured fondly. 'You know, he really misses you. They all do. I hope you'll go round and see them soon. They know you're back.'

'I mean to – just as soon as –' He left the sentence unfinished. He didn't want to see them until he felt whole again and he didn't seem to be doing too good a job of putting himself back together.

'Things are really bad at the factory,' Jackie was saying. 'The damn Sattar rivalry has the business in lousy shape. Joe's taken to his bed and is threatening to close down.' She gave Adam a penetrating glance. 'He feels beaten. Says he's going to announce his retirement on his birthday.'

'He always says things like that,' Adam said, not wanting to think of his grandfather giving up.

'This is different. He really doesn't care any more. Alex says that Sarah hasn't spoken to him or her since you took off.' Jackie hesitated. 'Without his family behind him, Joe doesn't give tuppence for the business.'

'Really that bad?'

Jackie nodded. 'I tried to talk to Mumtaz's mother. You know, make a peace treaty.'

'What happened?' Adam asked, admiring her pluck. Joe couldn't have known about it, of that he was sure.

'I told her the jeans war had got out of hand and that the competition was hurting us both. I suggested we negotiate and Astler's would carry their knitwear and they'd take our jeans.' Jackie shook her head and sighed. 'But she didn't go for it. She didn't believe Joe was ill. I think she wants him to come crawling, actually. Anyway, she said she knew Astler's was folding and she was in the market to buy.'

'Is Mumtaz still involved in the business?'

Jackie gave him a shrewd look. 'I think not, but you can always try to stir things up.'

Adam coloured. 'I really am getting over it. I mean it just takes a little getting used to. You know how you always said Taz and I were right together –'

'I bloody well talked you into it,' Jackie admitted.

'Maybe you were wrong about it all. You and I have grown up together. I don't want to lose you or Fina.'

'You won't'.

'I'd like to live with you. If you'll have me,' Adam went on. 'I don't mind where. The flat, your mum's or Joe's. We might just survive.' He paused. 'I'd suggest marrying but I think you'd laugh.

Jackie was hardly laughing. She looked down on Fina's toys, concealing the hurt she felt at so half-hearted and dismissive a proposal. 'No, Adam. Thanks all the same.'

'Is there someone else?'

'Not yet,' she replied quietly.

'Well, why not me, then?'

'I want to move on,' she said, meeting his gaze with candour and entreaty.

'Oh, right. Well, with Astler's gone, I guess there's no use in hanging round me.' He lashed out in pain.

'Astler's is not going under. And that's cheap,' Jackie protested.

'I'm sorry. I didn't mean it. Look, can't we talk this over?' Adam pleaded, suddenly feeling desperate. 'I thought you and I . . . well, I hoped things hadn't changed that much between us.'

'I'll always love you,' Jackie said. 'You took care of me when I was very messed up.' She held out her arms to him. 'You'll always be my first, my best, but it looks to me like we've gone as far as we can.'

Adam stepped back from her, his emotions in check. 'Right. I understand.'

'Please go and see your family. And start your painting again. You're so good.'

Adam nodded absently, still thrown by his unexpected dismissal. 'Christ, I'm sorry. I've really cocked it all up.'

Jackie took his face in her hands and kissed him. 'Come and see us again soon. Fina needs you.'

'Sure,' Adam said, and left quickly, afraid he might make a real ass of himself and cry. He couldn't imagine being truly without Jackie, any more than being without Mumtaz. Not to mention the sad fact that Joe and his family were now beyond his reach, too. Cocky public schoolboy loses it all, he thought, turning into the pub on the corner.

Adam spent the winter months in a drunken haze. He hardly attended any of the classes he had signed up for. When he did go to the university it was only to prop himself up at the bar in the Mandela Lounge. Art no longer meant anything to him, he decided, because life itself was without meaning. The only worthwhile pursuit was oblivion, he told himself. Unfortunately, booze didn't always work.

It wasn't working on Friday night when the lounge turned into a raging disco. He didn't much care for the punk band, nor for the half-dozen unappetizing lads who were his fellow barflies, but still he attempted to win them over with his rather limited repertoire of jokes. He'd run out of all but one-liners, and was preparing to order another drink, when he saw Mumtaz in the crowd.

'Taz!' he cried with drunken delight.

Mumtaz nodded at him and kept going. She was devastated to see him in such a condition, but with her pain there was anger that he should have allowed this to happen to himself.

'Taz, Taz.' He pushed through the crowd towards her. 'Fancy a dance?'

'No,' she said, stepping backwards and casting a glance round for Said.

'Jackie dumped me.' Adam gave a hysterical little laugh. 'Funny, isn't it? Well, laugh, for Christ's sake! Certainly you must see the joke of it.'

'Excuse me, I must go,' Mumtaz said, steeling herself against his words and the feelings they evoked.

'Well, sod you, then,' Adam cried out in drunken despair. 'Some bloody friend.'

Several days later Adam's grandfather, bundled up in a thick dark overcoat against the winter cold and looking as grey as the morning, hailed Sadiq's cab. He didn't recognize the driver, so consumed was he by thoughts of Adam. He had decided to pay him a surprise visit. It was either that or not see him at all. He couldn't bear to think of the boy drifting further and further away from them all. Adam had come to see him only twice since he'd returned from Israel. And how unlike himself he'd been; so guarded, so withdrawn. Weeks had passed since then.

'Driver, please wait,' Joe said, as the cab pulled up at the flat.

Meera's face fell when she opened the door and saw Adam's grandfather.

'Hello, Mr Astler.' She spoke in an uncertain voice, not knowing whether to let him in or what to say. She had had just about enough of Adam's messed-up selfish phase. He neglected his grandfather so the old man came to him. And how was she supposed to tell him his grandson was still in bed – with a girl, a naïve fresher who had fallen for his good looks and sad stories?

'Forgive me,' Joe said, with a formal European bow. 'May I speak to Adam?'

Meera gave him an apologetic smile. 'He's not in.' Better a lie than the truth.

'Ah, well,' Joe sighed.

'Would you like a cup of coffee?' she asked impulsively, not wanting to send him back out into the cold. Maybe it would do Adam good to come into the kitchen and find his grandfather drinking coffee.

Joe hesitated, but only for a moment. 'Another time.'

Back in Sadiq's cab, he slumped against the seat, an expression of sadness and defeat on his face.

'Home again?' Sadiq asked, concerned for the old man in spite of Shehnaaz's vendetta against him, or maybe because of it. He didn't know which, only that he felt an odd sympathy and identification with him.

Joe nodded and sat absently looking out at the leafless trees of Spinney Hill passing by.

'Do you have family?' he asked, glancing into the rearview mirror to catch Sadiq's eye.

'Yes.'

'I lost mine. In Germany.' But Joe was thinking of Adam as well.

'My parents died in Uganda,' Sadiq confided. 'They stayed too long.'

'Ah, they're the lucky ones,' Joe murmured despondently, and they drove on in silence.

'Any children?'

'Three,' Sadiq replied, thinking how odd it was that this man who had changed the course of his family's life didn't even know who he was.

'Proud of them?'

Sadiq raised an eyebrow. 'Their life is so different.'

Joe nodded sympathetically. 'Grandchildren?'

'My daughter is getting married. I hope she's done wisely,' Sadiq replied carefully. Mumtaz still seemed too young for the Muslim ceremony to take place after she finished at the university.

'They never do,' Joe said cynically. 'But tell them? Don't even try.'

'How is your grandson?' Sadiq asked impulsively.

Joe looked into the mirror, startled. 'Why? Why do you ask?'

'You don't remember me, do you? My name's Sattar.'

'So why are you driving a taxi?'

'Just staying out of trouble.'

Joe gave a shout of laughter. 'I like it.'

'Your grandson was in love with my daughter.' Sadiq was relieved to be discussing the matter in the open.

'I know,' Joe said quietly.

'It just wasn't possible.'

'We agree, my friend,' Joe replied. 'We should have talked sooner.'

It was almost noon before Adam tried to come to grips with

another rude awakening. The girl he had brought home burst into tears when he told her he had things to do and they weren't spending the day together. As she furiously pulled on her clothes, he tried to remember her name, but his recollection of the previous evening was hazy.

'Listen, love, don't be like that. It was a great night. Honestly.' What did these women want, anyway? Adam wondered, dragging himself from the bedcovers. He made a feeble attempt at going after the girl, then stopped to pull on a skimpy dressing-gown Jackie had left behind.

'Wait a minute, will you?' he yelled, as she ran down the corridor to the door. 'Have a coffee at least.'

But she was gone, and he stumbled into the kitchen where Meera greeted him with a disdainful, disapproving look. 'Paying half the rent doesn't entitle you to use the place like it's your private bordello.'

'Sorry, sorry,' Adam said, and took his coffee back up to bed, promising himself he'd start the day all over again.

Though he was successful in restarting the day and placating Meera, that night was a repeat performance of the night before, and the night before that. He stayed out drinking till closing-time, then found himself bringing home new friends, too far gone to recognize the old friend who was sitting in the front room with Meera.

'Hello, Adam,' she said, and he found it just as hard to recognize her subdued voice.

'Jesus Christ! It's Candyfloss, Superstar. Great to see you,' and as one of his fellow revellers put on the music, he reached for her hand. 'Let's have a dance, for old time's sake.'

'I can't.'

'Oh come on, Twinkletoes,' Adam said, trying to pull her up.

'No really,' Candy resisted firmly. 'I can't.'

'Christ, another loving friend!'

Meera gave him a look of utter contempt. 'Don't you ever stop thinking of yourself?'

'I can't use my legs,' Candy explained coldly. 'Botched them up bad in a motorcycle accident. I was pissed and showing off.'

Adam stood staring at her, his eyes glazed with a shock he

was too drunk to handle. 'Oh God, I'm sorry, Candy.' He turned away to try to quieten down the rowdy bunch he'd brought home, and when he looked again Meera and Candy had left.

The next morning Adam woke up with a bad hangover, and an even more painful conscience when he recalled the scene with Candy.

'You're disgusting,' he told himself, repeating the phrase again as he wandered into the front room and saw the wreck he and his friends had made of it. Full of self-loathing and remorse he went to find Meera.

'I'll move out,' he told her without preamble.

Meera gave him a long, hard look. 'I don't even know you any more, Adam.'

He sighed. 'Don't know myself. I'm sorry about last night; about Candy.'

The doorbell rang then, and he hurried to answer it. But the relief he felt at getting away from Meera's scrutiny turned to alarm when he opened the door and saw Hafiz.

'What's wrong? What happened? Is Mumtaz all right?' Adam asked, then coloured at the incomprehension he read on her brother's face.

'Oh, I guess you want to see Meera,' he said, suddenly remembering what Mumtaz had told him of their clandestine romance. It had been over for ages, he knew that. And he knew they had both survived the break-up.

Meera had a job in a Leicester travel agency, and was doing well with it. Hafiz, for his part, had become happily involved in the sales department of Sattar's. As he led the way to the front room, Adam couldn't help but compare himself with Mumtaz's brother and he wondered if he'd ever be able to pull himself together as Hafiz had.

'What do you want?' Meera asked in a shocked, though not unkind, voice as Hafiz walked into the room.

'I wanted to see how you were.'

'Isn't it a bit late?' she asked, then relented. 'I'm very well, thanks, And you?'

'I, too, am quite well. But I'm sorry for everything. I wanted to tell you that.'

'Hey, you did me a favour,' Meera said coolly. 'Sit down, if you like, and I'll get tea. Would you like some, Adam?'

'No thanks.' He felt he'd already heard more than he should have. 'I'd better start cleaning the place up. Thought I might go and see Candy afterwards.'

Candy's family lived in a council flat in Highfields, a seedy hovel on the top floor of a rundown building. When Adam asked for her, a scowling middle-aged man took him into a small corridor and left him there. He could hear a gentle piano sonata coming from one of the rooms, and from another the cries of a baby, and the raised voices of other children at play. The music ceased abruptly and Candy hobbled into the corridor, leaning heavily on her two canes.

'How'd you get here?' she said, giving him an apprehensive glance.

'Meera gave me your address. I thought you might fancy taking a drive.'

'Why not?' she asked wearily.

'I was an ass last night.'

'Forget it,' she said, hobbling down the rickety stairs, flight after flight, while he watched, appalled at her misfortune – impressed at her acceptance and courage.

'Was that you on the piano?' he asked, once he'd got her safely tucked into the car.

'Yeah. Thank God, I always kept it up.'

'I'd forgotten you played,' he said, recalling the one time he had surprised her in the middle of a Chopin étude in the music-room.

'I was the tough, loudmouthed Candyfloss. Classical music wasn't my thing, was it?' She laughed. 'And you, man, you were a real spoilt prick, if I remember correctly.'

'Yeah,' Adam grinned, relaxed by her honest humour and somehow bolstered by her strength.

'How much longer till you're better?'

She looked out of the window and didn't reply for a moment. 'I won't ever be able to compete again.'

'Well, at least you'll walk,' Adam said, and suddenly gave voice to the plan that came to him in her dim, dingy hallway.

'Why not move in with Meera and me? You could bring the piano, and I'd coach you into getting back on your feet.'

Candy gave him a sceptical glance. 'Looking for a hot and heavy romance with a cripple?'

'Of course not.' Perhaps he simply felt he could learn a lot about living from her. He had to pick up the pieces of his life somewhere, sometime.

'Not playing the martyr, are we?' Candy was saying.

'Nope,' Adam laughed. 'I think I've already done that. So what do you say?'

'I won't put up with any of your shit,' Candy warned, her dark eyes serious.

'That's what I'm counting on,' Adam replied, feeling better than he had in months.

Although Mumtaz's life was busier than ever before, she hadn't managed to separate herself from Adam as much as she pretended. She had kept a close eye out for him at the university, marking his progressive decline with anxiety. Her last encounter with him at the lounge had, once she was alone, reduced her to tears. From what Hafiz said about his visit to the flat, Adam was still following the path of self-destruction. She wished that somehow she could help him, but the only thing she could think of doing – more for herself than Adam – was to arrange to meet Jackie at the café they used to frequent in their college days. She felt an aching nostalgia as she sat waiting for her, but Jackie, when she arrived, was reserved and greeted her coolly.

'So what's all this about Adam?'

'He's not well, is he?' Mumtaz began awkwardly.

Jackie gave a sarcastic smile. 'And how would you know, pray tell?'

'I can't help it. My life is very different now,' Mumtaz defended herself unconsciously adjusting the veil that covered her head.

'Oh, no one's knocking you,' Jackie said. 'Not even poor old Adam. We all know that your own people are more important to you than anyone else.' Jackie paused, and took a sip of her coffee. 'Maybe we all learn that sooner or later.'

'Jackie, you know it's different for me.'

'Sure, but for God's sake, we're friends. We were kids together. Don't you think we deserve a bit more?'

'Like what?'

'Oh just be nice to Adam. Give him a little human kindness, can't you? He feels like a leper. And you treat him like one, according to the grapevine.'

'I have a new life,' Mumtaz protested.

'So do I. And Meera. Even Candy. But that's no reason to dump the past.'

'There's no way to fit Adam in.' Mumtaz didn't say it hurt too much, but that was as much a reason as any. 'I've had to wipe the past out.'

'Can't be done.'

'Well, I've done it!'

'Sure,' Jackie said, patting her hand. 'That's why you phoned me.'

Of course, Jackie was right, and in her heart Mumtaz had known it all along. If it would help Adam, she had no choice but to confront the past again. She kept recalling what Jackie had said about the rift between Adam and his family, suddenly seeing the true depths of his loneliness, even if it were self-imposed. But it was also the desire to purge herself of guilt for the past and rid herself of Adam's unhappy ghost, that finally propelled Mumtaz to his grandfather's house.

A bewildered Joe received her in the living-room, where he and Alex were working on some accounts. Mumtaz introduced herself, and quite candidly stated the cause of her visit while her hosts listened, too stunned to comment.

'I know how much trouble I caused, and I'm sorry for all the unhappiness. There really isn't very much I can do now,' Mumtaz concluded. 'But I know Adam still needs his family, whatever he says, and however he may act. I know that I did. That is what I wanted to tell you. Now if you'll excuse me, I'll go.'

'Stay for a coffee,' Alex suggested.

'You know him so well,' Joe added, giving her a yearning look.

'Please don't. It hasn't been easy talking about the past,' Mumtaz confessed.

Joe nodded sympathetically. 'I know. I'll see you out.' He took her arm and escorted her to the door. 'Thank you for coming. Thank you very much.'

Not an hour later, Joe picked up the phone and ordered Sadiq's cab. If he were going to try to confront his grandson again, he'd go there with someone whose presence he found congenial.

'I'm nervous,' Joe complained on the way to the flat. 'He should be nervous, not me.'

'Maybe he is,' Sadiq said.

'He doesn't know I'm coming,' said Joe. 'It's the only way, but you wouldn't understand. Your children respect you.'

'Do they?'

'Your daughter came to see me, to talk about my grandson. She's a fine girl. You must be proud of her. She behaved very honourably.'

'She always does,' Sadiq murmured, with a tinge of apprehension. He was shocked to hear what Mumtaz had done, but then, he had never completely trusted the quiet conclusion of her affair with the Astler boy; nor believed in her total absorption in her new life. The constant activity allowed no time for thought. Maybe now the past would take its proper place in time.

'Of course, she couldn't know I'd immediately tell,' Joe was saying, with a cautious glance into Sadiq's mirror. 'I hope I haven't made a mistake.'

'Of course not, my friend.' Sadiq was grateful for the other's candour. The two families were far more alike than Shehnaaz would ever want to know.

'It goes no farther, then,' Joe said with finality. 'Now please, tell me more about Kampala.'

For the rest of the drive, Sadiq recounted their flight from Africa; the urgency, the bribery, and the escape at dawn that led only to an intern camp in northern England; a story that was not dissimilar to Joe's own experiences.

'What do I owe you?' he said, as the cab pulled up at Adam's flat.

'I've put it on account,' Sadiq said, shrugging.

'You must let me buy you lunch sometime.' Joe had forgotten for a moment that his friend was the husband of his business rival. He remembered only as he added, 'My regards to your wife.'

Sadiq smiled and raised an eyebrow.

'No, I suppose not,' Joe agreed. 'Well, *shalom*.'

'*Salaam*,' the other replied.

The scene of companionable domesticity in the flat was much better than anything Joe had been prepared for. Meera was in the kitchen, Candy sat at the piano which was on the half-landing, and Adam and Fina could be heard playing in the front room. Joe seized on the music to ease the unexpectedness of his entrance, stopping to listen to the Schubert sonata Candy was playing.

'Very good,' he said, squeezing on to the bench beside her. 'But lean on this phrase more.' He played the crescendo with a special Viennese lilt that was sentimental and haunting. 'Ja? There's the pain, there. Hear it?'

Adam came out of the front room with Fina, and stood staring at his grandfather in surprise.

'Let me try,' Candy said, unaware of the guarded looks Joe and Adam exchanged.

'Better, much better,' Joe said, but his attention was on his grandson, and his great-granddaughter. 'Adam, dear boy. And where's Jackie?'

Adam could see that his grandfather was ill at ease, he could also see that he was pretending ignorance. Jackie would never leave without telling him. 'Majorca, for the spring holidays,' he replied, disturbed by how small and frail Joe looked.

'And you're left holding the baby,' Joe went on with forced joviality. 'Fortunately, however, Meera has offered to take over for an hour or two. I thought we could go to the pub.'

It was not in any way an easy talk Adam and Joe had at the pub, but a long wrangling near-quarrel as they rehashed old arguments, keeping to their old stands.

'None of you would even listen to me,' Adam complained. 'Everything I ever did or wanted to do was tied up with Mumtaz somehow. From our first days at college on. She was my past and my future. And that doesn't mean I'd have stopped being a Jew or she a Muslim.' Adam gave a weary sigh. 'Anyway, it's all one now. It doesn't matter.'

'So what next?' Joe asked, trying not to show how moved he felt.

'I'll ask you that. Jackie says you're thinking of selling. Would it make any difference if I came back into the business?' And, as Joe hesitated, he added, 'I've another shock for you. I'm going to synagogue these days.'

'You're not?' Joe responded, with disbelief and delight.

'I'm afraid it's Reform,' Adam added with a twinkle of mischief, happy to see the statement take effect.

'Those heretics. Like mother, like son.'

'So do you want me in the business or don't you?'

Joe struggled for a moment, overcome with remorse and gratitude. 'My dear boy, of course I do.'

Adam's first piece of business was to get rid of the foreman. The second was to negotiate a truce with Sattar's. He tried hard not to think of Mumtaz as he drove to her mother's factory, knowing regrets could only lead him back into despair. His life was finally beginning to take shape and meaning again. He had his entire family back. He had taken Fina to see his parents the day after Joe had come to see him. All channels were cleared with, thankfully, no references made to the past, and Adam knew how hard that had been for Sarah who liked everything put into words. He had a job again too, and that was to save Astler's. Its problems might be rooted in the past, as his own were, but the solutions lay in the present.

Looking fit and dapper in a grey business suit, Adam knocked on Sattar's office door and walked in, only to stop in his tracks as he saw Mumtaz at the filing cabinet. He simply wasn't prepared for the sight of her, and he felt himself grow pale.

'Sorry to barge in,' he said, turning finally to Shehnaaz who sat at the desk watching him. 'I should have rung to make an appointment.'

'I'll leave.' Mumtaz, too, addressed Shehnaaz. She had seen the expression on Adam's face, and was afraid of what her own might show.

Adam watched her leave, fancying that the room really seemed darker once she was gone.

'Yes?' Shehnaaz said. 'What can I do for you?'

Adam recollected himself. 'Astler's is not folding. We're in a mess, though. I can't make out which are our clients that you pinched, and which are yours that we nabbed.' His tone was friendly, but Shehnaaz gave him no encouragement, either by word or look.

'The foreman's gone,' Adam continued, stating the main point of his visit. He knew this was once what Shehnaaz had most wanted. 'And Mr Astler sends his regards.'

'Why doesn't he come himself?' Shehnaaz asked, reminding him of Mumtaz, the proud way she tilted her chin.

'It's not him you're dealing with now. I'd like to suggest a civilized discussion, so we both can tidy up loose ends.'

Shehnaaz gave him an appraising glance. 'Possibly. I'll be in touch.'

Mumtaz was sitting outside on the metal staircase staring at the bustle in the street below and didn't hear Adam leave the office. Something in her expression, a certain wistfulness, reminded him of when she'd first come to college.

'Look,' he said, making a last attempt to save the one friendship that had always meant the most to him. 'We're having a small party at the flat. The old college gang mostly, but with a few new friends. We hoped you and Said might come.'

'When?' Mumtaz asked, trying to keep the tremor out of her voice. He had startled her, or she'd have simply refused. She couldn't really imagine enjoying herself with her old friends – her real friends – when Said was there. Which was puzzling since Said was a genuinely kind and warm person.

'In a fortnight,' Adam was saying.

'I don't know.' She wished she felt free to say yes. 'We'll let you know.'

'Sure.' Adam was nonchalant. 'Just come if you can.'

Mumtaz watched him dash down the steps with a mixture of pain and pleasure. Pain that he was gone from her life, but pleasure at his obvious recovery.

She didn't tell Said about seeing Adam right away. She mulled over the meeting, as she did over her mother's account of Adam's business talk. The sight of him – tall, fit, and casually handsome – had reminded her of the first time she had seen him at sixth-form college. But then it was merely an untried exterior. He'd gone through many different highs and lows to acquire his present composure, and she'd been involved in them all. And now that he was finally getting his life together, it seemed so unfair that she wasn't able to have a part in it.

It took time for the emotional churning that had started up at the sight of Adam to subside. Gradually, the pressures of her final term, and her increasing involvement in Said's work, enabled Mumtaz to focus again on the present.

'Shouldn't you be revising?' Said asked, as they sat eating a take-away supper at the law centre.

'Mr Patel's submissions are overdue. He'll be deported before we've finished.' She pushed the carton of curry towards Said.

'That's yours,' he said. 'I can't. Mother overfeeds me.'

Mumtaz sighed. 'I wish we were married, and living at your home.' What had been the point of waiting? She couldn't remember now. It just seemed like another delay in which to waver. How much better if the whole business were settled. It was ridiculous, really, to think that she and Said were legally man and wife and still hadn't made love.

'Wait till you hear my mother screaming,' Said said, laughing.

'I won't mind.'

'Darling, you're not a nice traditional little girl any more.' Said spoke seriously and just a trifle sadly. 'Don't sell yourself short.'

'It's what your parents expect.'

'I'm working on them. We'll get a flat of our own.'

'Good,' Mumtaz said absently.

'What's wrong?' Said asked, his dark eyes regarding her more closely.

'Nothing. I saw Adam a while back. I don't know why I didn't mention it then. He invited us to a party.'

Said slowly put aside the file he'd been reading.

'Would you like to go?' he asked, willing but noncommittal. He wouldn't make this decision for her.

'No,' Mumtaz smiled, taking his hand.

As the time for her exams drew nearer, Mumtaz found herself unable to sleep. Night after night she would give up the fight against insomnia and, gathering her books together, go to the kitchen to study. But even then she had to cook rice, or eat left-overs or sweetmeats before she could settle down to work. What was really worrying her, she began to realize, was not the finals but the marriage ceremony to follow them. She tried to tell herself she was simply being a jittery Muslim bride. But she couldn't explain away the thoughts of Adam that continued to come unbidden.

'Mumtaz?' Sadiq, half-asleep, came stumbling into the

kitchen. 'I thought I heard somebody down here. What are you doing?'

'Revision,' she replied, stirring the rice.

Her father stared at the midnight banquet in preparation. 'Are you all right?'

'Fine. I didn't have much dinner.'

'Is it Said?' Sadiq asked. 'Is he still spending so much time at his conferences?'

'It is important. It is his work.'

'Work isn't everything,' Sadiq murmured. 'It is also important that you see one another.'

'Yes. And by the way, I suppose you know Hafiz is seeing Meera again!' Mumtaz was appalled at the irrelevant and bitter remark that had escaped her; appalled to find that she had been harbouring so deep, and surprising, a resentment.

Sadiq was staring at her. 'What is that to do with you?'

'Nothing,' she replied, admitting the relevancy to herself. If she couldn't have Adam, it was hard to see Hafiz and Meera together again.

'Sort yourself out, young lady. And don't bring stories to me.'

Deeply ashamed of her betrayal, Mumtaz woke Hafiz as soon as her father had gone back to bed. She didn't know what had got into her, what viper had taken hold of her tongue. But Hafiz was untroubled, even a bit amused.

'Don't worry. I have told him I see her. Meera and I are friends, that's all.'

'But you're always going round there,' Mumtaz said, revealing the fact that she had been keeping a close eye on what was happening at the flat.

'I like Meera. And Adam and Candy, too. We had a party the other night. Adam's a great cook.'

Mumtaz felt a sharp, unmistakable pang of jealousy. She should have been there.

'That's nice.'

'Since you have brought it up, I might as well tell you,' Hafiz began, giving her a confidential smile. 'I'm getting married in the autumn.'

Mumtaz sat bolt upright in shock. 'You just said you and Meera were only friends.'

'It is another girl. I met her on a business trip up north.' He gave a dreamy smile. 'Her name is Yasmin.'

'And father's agreed?'

'It took a while,' Hafiz confessed. 'They're Bengali. But at least this time she's a Muslim.'

They both laughed, somewhat uneasily.

'Well done.' Mumtaz kissed her brother goodnight and went back to her room, but only to lie awake wondering if Hafiz was simply choosing to be a good son, or if he really loved this Yasmin as he had once loved Meera.

Mumtaz had no time to think of happiness and marriage in the week before exams. Law took up every moment of her day. Suddenly fearful of failure, she realized that being awarded a certificate to practise as a lawyer was the one thing she had always been certain she wanted. She began studying more intensely, going at it so hard that she overslept on the morning of the first exam.

'What do you think? Do we invite your cousin Hassan to the wedding?' Shehnaaz asked as Mumtaz came downstairs, brushing her hair and making a grab for her coat. 'He won't come, but do we include his name?'

'Please, Mum. I'm late as it is. Just let me get through the exams, okay?'

'The guest list should have been finished long ago.'

'Who knows?' Mumtaz said airily. 'If I fail, Said might call the whole thing off.'

'That's not funny,' Shehnaaz admonished, hurrying into the hall for a final word.

But Mumtaz was already outside, racing down the road to catch the bus. She swung aboard, breathless, and collapsed in one of the front seats. She wished her mother would stop going on about the wedding; it was all she ever talked about.

'Taz? It is you, isn't it?'

Mumtaz looked up to see Candy standing in the aisle. Her face was thinner, her expression more thoughtful, but she still wore a red track-suit and corn-rowed her hair.

'Candy! Sit here, beside me.'

'Funny, I was thinking of you today. How I used to tease you. Adam was reminding me.'

'Oh, how is he?' Mumtaz never imagined she'd be begging news of Adam from her, but this older Candy seemed softer, more compassionate somehow.

'He's a pain,' she replied affectionately. 'I could break his neck. He wouldn't give me a lift.' And at Mumtaz's puzzled look. 'You don't know, I suppose. Got my legs battered in an accident and Adam appointed himself my therapist. Makes me walk and face the challenges of life,' she mocked.

'Oh, Candy. I'm sorry,' Mumtaz said, trying to fit Adam into this new role; feeling oddly bereft of this new unknown man.

'Want to have a coffee?'

'I'd love to, but I can't. I've got my first exam.'

'Oh, yeah. Adam just finished.'

'Is he happy?' Mumtaz asked suddenly. If he could be, then so could she. 'How's his daughter, and Jackie?'

'They're good. Kid's really bright. But Adam and Jackie, that finished a long time ago.'

'Are you his new –' Mumtaz didn't know how to finish the question, but Candy was howling with laughter.

'You randy sod. Certainly not!'


Mumtaz's new role in life began two days after her last exam, when she played hostess at a luncheon for Said's colleagues. She dressed carefully for the part in a fine, jade green *shalwar* and kept to her station, helping her irascible mother-in-law in the kitchen, along with the other female relatives.

'Hurry, girl!' Mrs Farrukh said, giving her a tray of sweetmeats. 'They'll be cold by the time the men get them.'

'Sorry, I must have been dreaming.'

'No more exams. No more work. It's over. So go along,' Mrs Farrukh said, giving her a gentle push in the direction of the living-room.

'Ah, the graduate,' Said's father said in proud greeting and Mumtaz was relieved that he had not called her the bride.

'It sounds as though you've done well in your exams. Ah, here comes your husband to claim you,' he went on, as Said approached.

'There are some people I would like to introduce you to.'

'Please, Said, can we speak for a moment?' Mumtaz asked, putting down her tray and going into the hallway.

'What is it?' he said, following her. 'You look beautiful today. I hear so from everyone.'

But Mumtaz felt only a sudden inexplicable fear. Everything was happening too fast.

'Can we go away together, on our own? To an hotel?'

'When?'

'Today, after this is over.' Maybe never, she thought.

'I have several meetings. Important ones.'

'Please,' Mumtaz insisted. 'Cancel them. This is more important.'

If she had thought a night of love-making would cure her uncertainty, she realized that she had made another mistake as soon as they were alone in their expensive hotel suite.

'It was odd registering, wasn't it? Mr and Mrs Farrukh,' she repeated, thinking that the name didn't apply to her, only to Said's mother.

'But we are legally Mr and Mrs Farrukh,' Said reminded her with a solicitous look that made her heart ache. Nobody could have been kinder, more gentle. No, it wasn't his love she questioned, but what was in her own heart.

'Can you hold me, please?' she asked, hoping that would make things better, if only for a moment. Said came to her, and she kissed him. It was a farewell embrace full of apology.

'I don't know how I've got you into this,' she began. 'I am so sorry. There's no way to tell you how sorry.'

'You're tired. Give yourself a break. You haven't stopped working for weeks. It's been a strain for you.'

Mumtaz shook her head. 'It's not that. Everything seems to be saying that I'm doing the wrong thing.'

'Have you seen him again?' Said asked, giving her a penetrating look. They didn't need to use a name where Adam was concerned.

'No.' It was the truth, yet she couldn't have felt guiltier if she had been seeing Adam.

'But you miss him?'

Mumtaz thought for a moment before replying. 'I'm frightened that I might miss him one day. I'd never want to be unfaithful to you in my heart.'

'If coming here has made you nervous, it's no problem. I will continue to wait until you are ready.'

'I have put this off too long already. I have been so unfair to you. And perhaps to myself. There's too much I've been denying. It seems as though everything's changed except me. I'm scared of waking up, but I must. It was you who taught me that!'

'But you don't love me?'

'I do love you. Very much,' Mumtaz told him and meant it. 'Right man. Wrong time. I want you to have all of me but I can't do it. I just need to be alone. I expect I always will be.'

Said insisted on taking Mumtaz home, and speaking to her parents, though she knew his presence would do nothing to ease the blow.

They found Sadiq and Shehnaaz spending a quiet evening in the sitting-room and Said gently announced their decision to call off the wedding. It was a mutual agreement, he said, though it was obvious neither of the Sattars believed him.

'It will mean a civil divorce,' Said concluded. 'But that won't be complicated.'

'And your career?' Sadiq asked, his face creased with concern.

'Oh, I will survive. So will Mumtaz. When she qualifies she will still have the law centre job with me.' He waited, but Sadiq said nothing more and Shehnaaz simply sat staring fixedly at the floor.

'Really, it will be all right. It is better that we have made our decision now than later,' Said told them again as he took his leave.

After seeing Said to the door, Mumtaz returned to the sitting-room to speak to her parents, but Sadiq sat with his head in his hands and Shehnaaz appeared to be speechless with rage.

'Do you know what you have done?' she finally said. 'You have thrown away your life, ruined your chances. And mine,' she added bitterly. 'Who do you think will pay back Tariq's loan now?'

Mumtaz was relieved that it would not be Mr Farrukh, but she dared not tell her mother that. Nor did she dare follow her impulse, her need to embrace Shehnaaz.

'Forgive me. I am sorry. I am truly sorry for all the shame I have brought on our house. I'll leave now,' she said, and rushed into the hall, startled to find Rashid lurking there, eavesdropping.

'You cow!' he screamed. 'You have ruined everything!'

Choking back sobs, Mumtaz ran away from the house, wondering if she would ever be welcome within its doors again. She headed towards the university and wandered around the deserted campus, too frightened by what she had just done to think of her safety in the city's night. All other emotions, guilt and humiliation, were overtaken by panic. Where would she go? How would she live? What would become of her faith without her family? There was only one person she could go to, she finally realized, and that was Jackie.

'I know how late it is, and I'm sorry,' Mumtaz said, when Jackie came to the door. She had started off speaking calmly, and now she suddenly burst into tears. 'I need somewhere to stay.'

Jackie didn't need to ask why. 'I'll take you over to the flat,' she said, reaching for her coat on the rack behind her.

'No!' Mumtaz protested. She couldn't see Adam now; not when she was like this.

'Adam's not there.' Jackie was, as always, brief and to the point. 'He's with his family. Only Meera and Candy are there.'

'I just need –' Mumtaz began again, and ended weeping in Jackie's outstretched arms.

'I know,' Jackie said, holding her tight. 'Remember? I know.'

The other girls were just as warm and welcoming, and just as casual, as though there had been no interruption to their friendship. Candy went off to put the kettle on while Meera fetched a nightgown, and Mumtaz, although still frightened and dazed, felt herself already a little buoyed up by the support of her old friends.

'My family won't forgive me,' she told them, summing up the events of the day. 'No reason why they should,' she finished sadly. 'I don't really know why I've done it.'

'Yes, you do.' Candy gave her a shrewd look.

'And if you don't know why now, you'll find out,' Meera said.

'I feel so strange,' Mumtaz confided, relieved to be able to finally share her thoughts. 'I believe in all the same things. I got what I always said I wanted, and then I couldn't go through with it.'

'There's room here,' Meera said. 'Adam is planning to move out.'

'Go for it, Taz.' Candy squeezed her hand. 'Join our special casualty list.'

'It gets better,' Jackie said, putting an arm round her. 'If you never leave, you can never go back again. They'll understand that sooner or later.'

Mumtaz wasn't altogether sure she understood it now. But she did know that she felt as though she'd come home, to a place of her own. Here she could have her same beliefs, but she would be practising them as Mumtaz Sattar; a person, not a daughter nor a wife.

It was a very warm day for September. Mumtaz had opened the windows to let in the balmy autumn breeze, and sat propped up in bed, dressed in faded jeans and a t-shirt, as she caught up on her casework. This was usually how she spent her day off; along with doing the laundry and tidying up the flat. But she didn't mind. She was content with her work and the quiet life she had made for herself since leaving home. She knew this was not the end of the changes in store, but for the present life was fine.

There had been some very rocky moments with her family. But Hafiz had always stayed close, and things had generally improved since his marriage. Mumtaz now saw Sadiq regularly at the community centre. Instead of his listening to her prayers, the two of them discussed the different verses they were presently studying in the Koran. Shehnaaz and Rashid were still very cool to her, but all she could do was hope that eventually they'd come round. She missed them, but she no longer doubted her decision. She was more comfortable now than she'd ever been. And she was breaking no rules, simply following her own path.

Mumtaz heard the downstairs door bang, and footsteps running up the stairs. 'Hello,' she called out, assuming it was either Candy or Meera, returning early from work. Meera was now in charge of her travel agency, and Candy gave piano lessons at a children's hospital.

But it was Adam who came into the bedroom.

'Taz! You're here,' he said, clearly as shocked as she was. They hadn't seen each other since last spring at Sattar's factory.

'It's okay. Come in,' Mumtaz said, as Adam stood there hesitating. He looked older, or perhaps it was just the conservative navy-blue suit. His hair was a little too long, the way he liked it, curling over his collar, and his clear blue eyes were wide with surprise.

'I'm interrupting you,' he said.

Mumtaz had wondered when she first moved in the flat, if Adam would come by. When he hadn't, she told herself she was better off alone.

'No, it's okay.'

'I won't be a minute,' Adam said. He had thought about Mumtaz incessantly. He had often been on the verge of going to the flat, but, afraid of a rebuff, he'd change his mind. Wouldn't she have got in touch with him if she wanted to see him? he'd tell himself.

'Just came for some things I left behind,' he said. 'I've been so busy these last months I never had a chance. But I think I'll be needing warm clothes soon.' He paused. 'I thought you'd be at the law centre.'

'It's my day off. Am I in the way?'

'No, no, of course not.' Adam went to the desk and picked up several books and some photographs.

'I took that one of you,' Mumtaz said, coming up beside him to look at the picture he was holding.

'I know.' Adam remembered everything about that day. She had been so shy with him. 'And I snapped this one of you,' he murmured.

'Thanks for everything you've done for Sattar's,' she suddenly said. She knew he had arranged the visit from Joe that had finally put an end to the Sattar–Astler war. Not only had they come to agreeable terms over the jeans and knitwear but Joe had paid back Tariq's loan.

'Oh, that was just good business.' Adam picked up a picture of Mumtaz standing in front of the college, looking absurdly young. He held it up for her to see and they exchanged a warm nostalgic smile.

'Did you know Hafiz got married?' Again Mumtaz attempted to bridge the distance between them. 'I went to the wedding.'

'I expect it was hard, with your family and all,' he said sympathetically.

'A bit chilly. At least we're all speaking. Just,' she added, thinking of her mother and Rashid.

'And what about your work?'

'Well, as you can see.' She gestured towards the bed where

she had left her files. There was a banner leaflet at the top of the heap that read: FIGHTING BACK AGAINST RACIAL IN-EQUALITY.

'Said got his seat, I hear.'

'He's a very gifted man,' was all Mumtaz said.

They were both silent for a moment and the room was charged with a current of uncertainty.

'I suppose I'd better go.'

'How are things with you?' Mumtaz asked. She couldn't let him go like that.

'Busy, busy,' Adam replied, grateful for a chance to prolong their conversation, however faltering it was. 'We've got Astler's back on the road at long last.'

'Been doing much painting? I can't imagine the business is going to hold your interest for ever,' Mumtaz said, and it began to seem more like the old days when they used to talk about his art.

'Actually, I'm looking around for a studio.'

'I'm thinking of getting a place too.'

'Not in another city?' Adam asked anxiously.

'No, Leicester for now. Maybe London later. I've a few contacts there.'

'Will you let me know?'

'Of course,' Mumtaz replied, wondering if this meant they wouldn't meet again until she was moving away.

'Well,' Adam started for the door, and then gave in to his impulse. 'You wouldn't fancy a meal, would you?'

'When?' she asked.

'Now. If you're free?'

Mumtaz looked at her files, her watch, then laughed quietly to herself. It was as if a great door had been flung open, and, unused to the blue sky and the sudden space, she hadn't recognized it. She and Adam might have had to find their freedom separately, but there was nothing to stop them from enjoying it together.

'Yes, I'm free,' she said.

# EMMA BLAIR

## WHEN DREAMS COME TRUE

Norma McKenzie's bubbly, irrepressible Glaswegian spirit ensured that she would never remain downtrodden. When her family are forced to move into a Glasgow tenement, it is not long before she meets popular, handsome, blue-eyed Midge Henderson. Captivated by each other, their lives seem blissfully entwined. Then suddenly, out of the blue, Norma's life is shattered by bitter betrayal . . .

It is many years before love re-enters Norma's life – a daring aristocratic Scots officer rekindles the flames of passion amidst the devastation of war. But returning to Glasgow as man and wife in 1945 imposes new strains on their relationship. And when Midge reappears, Norma feels her love for him returning and she is faced with the most agonising choice of her life . . .

0 7474 0024 5   GENERAL FICTION   £3.50

Also by Emma Blair in Sphere Books:

STREET SONG
THE PRINCESS OF POOR STREET

*A MAGNIFICENT AND MOVING*
*SAGA . . .*

# The
# LUSHAI GIRL

## ROBERTA FORREST

When Lieutenant Gerald Petrie, heir to a baronetcy
and a wealthy tea empire, falls deeply in love with the
exquisite Lushai tribal girl, a bitter scandal ensues.
For Gerald's aristocratic parents will never forgive
him for consorting with a common India servant. But
Mary is a remarkable and courageous woman, and her
marriage to Gerald transcends and defies all
convention . . .

In an extraordinary life of incident and drama, Mary
will finally be accepted as a woman in her own right
and will become the high-powered first-ever
chairwoman of the Petrie India company. But never
will she forget the heart-ache of leaving her Indian
homeland or her husband who gave her strength and
the first sweet taste of love . . .

0 7221 3589 0    GENERAL FICTION    £3.50

# FiNE THiNGS

## DANIELLE STEEL

### Bestselling author of WANDERLUST

Living on the crest of a highly successful career, he was moving too fast to realise that he had everything – except what he wanted most . . .

Sent to San Francisco to open the smartest department store in California, Bernie Fine becomes aware of the hollowness of his personal life. Despite his success he grows increasingly disenchanted with his existence – until five-year-old Jane O'Reilly gets lost in the store.

Through Jane, Bernie meets her mother Liz, who finally offers him the possibility of love. But the rare happiness they find together is disrupted by tragedy and Bernie must face the terrible price we sometimes have to pay for loving . . .

0 7221 8308 9     GENERAL FICTION     £3.50

A magnificent saga of the men and women who pioneered
the great age of railways . . .

# TUNNEL TIGERS

# ALEXANDER
# CORDELL

Brunel, Stephenson, Locke and Vignoles – these were the
magic names! And under them 10,000 laboured in a fierce
and muscular comradeship, blasting, shovelling and
digging, changing the contours of Britain for a new age of
railways. Men and women whose lives and loves, hopes and
dreams were fired with a passion as large as their hearts.

Among them is Nick Wortley, whose love for the daughter
of the local mill owner is cruelly thwarted. Taking flight, he
is drawn by the irresistible clamour of the great Sheffield to
Manchester, a railway which was preparing to drive a path
of steel under the Pennines. Stephenson said it was
impossible; Nick and his burly, brute-strong companions
prove him wrong, but at a terrible price . . .

*'A passionate tale'* DAILY MAIL

0 7221 2572 0    GENERAL FICTION    £3.50

A selection of bestsellers from SPHERE

**FICTION**

| | | |
|---|---|---|
| JUBILEE: THE POPPY CHRONICLES 1 | Claire Rayner | £3.50 ☐ |
| DAUGHTERS | Suzanne Goodwin | £3.50 ☐ |
| REDCOAT | Bernard Cornwell | £3.50 ☐ |
| WHEN DREAMS COME TRUE | Emma Blair | £3.50 ☐ |
| THE LEGACY OF HEOROT | Niven/Pournelle/Barnes | £3.50 ☐ |

**FILM AND TV TIE-IN**

| | | |
|---|---|---|
| BUSTER | Colin Shindler | £2.99 ☐ |
| COMING TOGETHER | Alexandra Hine | £2.99 ☐ |
| RUN FOR YOUR LIFE | Stuart Collins | £2.99 ☐ |
| BLACK FOREST CLINIC | Peter Heim | £2.99 ☐ |
| INTIMATE CONTACT | Jacqueline Osborne | £2.50 ☐ |

**NON-FICTION**

| | | |
|---|---|---|
| BARE-FACED MESSIAH | Russell Miller | £3.99 ☐ |
| THE COCHIN CONNECTION | Alison and Brian Milgate | £3.50 ☐ |
| HOWARD & MASCHLER ON FOOD | Elizabeth Jane Howard and Fay Maschler | £3.99 ☐ |
| FISH | Robyn Wilson | £2.50 ☐ |
| THE SACRED VIRGIN AND THE HOLY WHORE | Anthony Harris | £3.50 ☐ |

*All Sphere books are available at your local bookshop or newsagent, or can be ordered direct from the publisher. Just tick the titles you want and fill in the form below.*

Name _____

Address _____

_____

Write to Sphere Books, Cash Sales Department, P.O. Box 11, Falmouth, Cornwall TR10 9EN

Please enclose a cheque or postal order to the value of the cover price plus:

UK: 60p for the first book, 25p for the second book and 15p for each additional book ordered to a maximum charge of £1.90.

OVERSEAS & EIRE: £1.25 for the first book, 75p for the second book and 28p for each subsequent title ordered.

BFPO: 60p for the first book, 25p for the second book plus 15p per copy for the next 7 books, thereafter 9p per book.

*Sphere Books reserve the right to show new retail prices on covers which may differ from those previously advertised in the text elsewhere, and to increase postal rates in accordance with the P.O.*